THE VOICE OF EXPERIENCE

Georgina's half-sister Cressie was years younger than Georgina in age—but centuries older in worldly wisdom.

One visit to Georgina was enough to let her see how dissatisfied Georgina was with her married lot—and to tell Georgina how openly Georgina's husband sought satisfaction with the leading light ladies of London.

Cressie herself had no such problems. Love was not part of *her* marriage bargain. Instead it was pleasure she eagerly sought and easily found in the arms of ardent lovers—behind the back of her passion-besotted spouse.

Georgina knew she should have been shocked by Cressie's revelations—and outraged by Cressie's advice for her to do the same.

But instead Georgina found herself wondering: *Why not . . . ?*

THE MARRIAGE MART

D X

The Marriage Mart

Norma Lee Clark

A SIGNET BOOK

SIGNET
Published by the Penguin Group
Penguin Books USA Inc., 375 Hudson Street,
New York, New York 10014, U.S.A.
Penguin Books Ltd, 27 Wrights Lane,
London W8 5TZ, England
Penguin Books Australia Ltd, Ringwood,
Victoria, Australia
Penguin Books Canada Ltd, 2801 John Street,
Markham, Ontario, Canada L3R 1B4
Penguin Books (N.Z.) Ltd, 182–190 Wairau Road,
Auckland 10, New Zealand

Penguin Books Ltd, Registered Offices:
Harmondsworth, Middlesex, England

First Printing, March, 1984
11   10   9   8   7   6   5   4   3

Printed in the United States of America

*This book is dedicated
with great happiness
to*
Paolo Andres Carvajal

CHAPTER

1

The Honourable Georgina Sophia Blanche Fitzhardinge sat in the window seat of her bedroom, watching the approach of an elegant dark-grey travelling chariot up the carefully raked gravel of the drive. The carriage swept around the curve in front of the house and drew up precisely before the steps. Two footmen, who sat, arms folded and stiffly upright in their blue-and-grey liveries, on the box behind the coach, leaped down. One opened the carriage door, the other let down the steps, and a gentleman in a many-caped driving coat and beaver hat was handed out. The matched greys, as glossy as the carriage they drew, blew out twin streams of vapor as the gentleman proceeded up the steps and out of Georgina's view. A stableboy ran up from the other side of the house to show the way, the footmen resumed their positions, and the carriage rolled away at a stately pace to the stables at the back. All that was left to prove its existence were the tracks of the wheels left in the light mantle of rapidly melting late-April snow.

"So unsettling to have snow after spring has begun," complained Miss Hapgood, Georgina's governess, inaptly called Happy by all her charges, since Miss Hapgood's lugubrious expression matched her nature and put one instantly in mind of a basset hound. She was, however, an excellent governess and managed to instill a rudimentary amount of knowledge in even the most recalcitrant young female mind.

"Yes, Happy," replied Georgina, perfectly politely as she had been taught but with noticeable absentmindedness.

Miss Hapgood was on the point of reminding her that to display one's lack of interest was as discourteous as no reply at all, but changed her mind. After all, such a lapse must be forgiven on such a day. Miss Hapgood's old heart quivered, and she caught her breath. At this moment, downstairs in Lord Fitzhardinge's library, requesting Georgina's hand in marriage, was Myles Allured Boothby Barrowes, Earl of Trowbridge, Viscount Boston, Baron Trowbridge of Trowbridge. Miss Hapgood silently intoned his titles and honours with great relish, and as she pictured him a faint colour tinged her cheeks, for her dolorous temperament did not exclude a bent towards romanticism, and Lord Trowbridge was to her a beau ideal. That he also displayed a certain arrogance was, in Miss Hapgood's opinion, all to the good. Men were naturally so, she thought, and why not? So they should be, with their God-given superiority and advantages over women. She could not have respected a man who was not arrogant. The little thrill of fear she had experienced at her first meeting with Lord Trowbridge had been a sign to her that here was a man one could look up to, rely upon, admire as worthy of dear Georgina. Add to this a strong, jutting nose and chin, cool grey eyes (Miss Hapgood was convinced that grey eyes were a visible sign of honesty), and a firm, well-shaped mouth, and surely he became a man to engage the affection of any young girl. She brushed aside the difference in their ages as a triviality not worth considering. Georgina was, after all, an unusually mature eighteen-year-old, who did not seem to need, much less seek, the raptures of "falling head over ears in love," as most young girls did. She had been out one Season and had never looked twice at any of the younger men who showed an interest in her. Though Lord Trowbridge was not so slim and lithe as these young men, nevertheless he exuded an aura of authority and strength and an indefinable magnetism that had evidently appealed to Georgina more than the callow handsomeness of the younger men.

Miss Hapgood glanced up at Georgina, made shy by her thoughts, hoping to see reflected in the girl's face some signs of the agitation she surely must be experiencing. Georgina's face, however, expressed as little as it ever did. It was an unrevealing mask, as clear-cut in profile as a cameo; the thick, mat, creamy complexion, also cameo-like, was set off by the dark-auburn hair, glinting sparks of bronze and deep red in the pale sunlight, and her amber-coloured, black-lashed eyes.

Miss Hapgood sighed. How was it possible for a young girl

with an extremely eligible *parti* offering for her hand at that very moment to sit calmly staring at the landscape as though nothing at all out of the way was transpiring? Not that Miss Hapgood would have approved of tears or giggles or any other unseemly behavior . . . still . . .

"Lord Trowbridge keeps a very fine carriage, does he not, Miss Georgina?" she ventured.

"Very fine," agreed Georgina.

"I daresay he will allow you to choose any colour you like for your own. I have always been partial to a carriage lined with red squabs, but I daresay with your colouring you will prefer blue or green." She waited a moment, but when no response was forthcoming, continued undaunted, "No doubt he will make you a prodigious allowance. He will be used to it, for it is said, you know, that his mama was dreadfully extravagant, particularly about jewels. I suppose those will come to you, since she had no daughters. That is, aside from the family heirlooms, of course. There are the Trowbridge pearls—*quite* famous, and the tiara with the emerald—the size of a hen's egg, so I have been told—though it is terribly old-fashioned . . . the tiara, that is. It is too bad it could not be reset—but there, an heirloom, after all, and in the family since the Conqueror. It will do for a Queen's Drawing Room, however, and perhaps my lord will give you something new and more suitable when—"

"You are rather rushing ahead, Happy," Georgina interjected mildly.

"It cannot hurt to discuss—" Miss Hapgood stopped abruptly, her eyes widening in dismay. "You—you cannot mean to refuse him, child?"

Georgina turned at this and studied Miss Hapgood's face for a long moment before she relented and said, "No, Happy, I shan't refuse him."

Miss Hapgood's heart, which seemed to have stopped for a moment, thudded in painful relief inside her bony chest, but before she could speak, the sound of loudly raised voices could be heard from the schoolroom next door. Miss Hapgood rose at once, muttering as she left the room that she might have known she couldn't leave those three girls alone all this time without their commencing to squabble, though they had promised her to be on their best behavior, and no doubt they could be heard all over the house and Lord Trowbridge was at this moment wondering what sort of madhouse he had wandered into. Georgina turned back to her contemplation of the scenery.

In spite of her outward demeanour, Georgina was experiencing something, though not in the area of her heart, since that organ was not affected by the present situation. She felt slightly nauseated, and her hands were cold and damp. This was only nerves, she knew, and she never allowed herself to exhibit nervousness, nor for that matter any other emotion, except very rarely. Not that she did not have emotions, but she had long ago schooled herself to suppress any show of feeling.

She leaned her forehead against the cold windowpane and swallowed convulsively. I will not be sick, she decided. After all, this is not an earth-shaking experience, not a matter of life or death. All over England at this very moment offers of marriage are being made and accepted or refused.

It calmed her to think of herself as part of a group, however unknown and nameless, all sharing an experience.

She was puzzled by this bout of nerves. It was not as though she had not been expecting Lord Trowbridge to speak to her father. She had known he would and had already made up her mind that she would have him. The development of their acquaintance had been unhurried, almost deliberate, though it had taken place in the course of a few short months. The result had been, though unspoken, communicated in some way between them almost from the first meeting. He had been invited to her come-out in London and had stood up with her twice. The next morning he had called, and she had received him. She had ridden with him in the Park, gone for chaperoned carriage drives, and danced with him nearly every night at various balls and parties. The greatest impression he had made upon her then derived from the difference in age between him and her other dancing partners. She had learned that he was eight and thirty, which though seeming an advanced age to one of eighteen, had not made him seem old to her. It had only set him apart. She had thought the young men she met insipid and gauche, their conversation limited to horseflesh or waistcoats or gossip, their compliments awkward or overblown to insincerity. At least Trowbridge had ideas on literature, politics, and travel and expressed them with precision and polish, and his compliments were delivered with a graceful simplicity that did not make her blush. He allowed her to become aware of his admiration without making it a burden. Apart from that, the solidity of his well-muscled, almost stockily compact body and the warmth and vitality he exuded had attracted and comforted her in the midst of the whirl of her first Season.

Lady Fitzhardinge, in a positive dither of excitement at his obvious partiality for her stepdaughter, talked of him continuously. Soon Georgina knew all there was to know of his wealth, his titles, his property, his family. She also learned of his elusiveness for at least twenty years, during which enterprising mamas with marriageable daughters pursued him unmercifully, and determined debutantes threw out every possible lure, which he eluded with every courtesy. Oh, he was charming, that everyone agreed upon. He made an appearance at most of the balls and come-outs of each Season, was introduced to the belle of the evening, requested the honour of a dance, and, duty done, left.

"But now, my dear, there is every reason to believe—well, actually, one is much more than encouraged to be sure—that he intends to make an offer. It is very gratifying, and of course you have behaved just as you ought. Your papa is most pleased with you, I assure you. I only hope Cressy will do as well."

The interest of such a gentleman could not but flatter, and Georgina, despite outward appearances, was not immune to it. She had not fallen in love with him, but he interested her, he was not physically repulsive—and one must marry.

Papa had summoned her to his library before they had even left for the London Season to make this point quite clear. "This entire business will cost me a pretty packet, what with having to open the house in town and entertain, not to speak of the gowns and gee-gaws you must have, so I will expect you to be sensible. There will be no sighing and fancy flights over handsome second sons or romantic young lieutenants, nor tears and tantrums over any perfectly acceptable offers received and approved by me. You may trust me to be sure the man is of good family and substantial income with entrée into the best drawing rooms. Naturally I will satisfy myself that the man is not given over to any reprehensible vices, so you may be assured you will not be receiving the attentions of someone you should not encourage. I expect you to approach this matter

seriously, for I am not a wealthy man and have three more
daughters to provide for in the next few years. When you are
married, you will be in a position to help me in this."

"Naturally my first consideration," she murmured.

"What is that?" he barked, his cold eyes narrowing at her
suspiciously.

"I only said perhaps I would not take," she answered.

"I do not care for street cant on the lips of young girls,
Georgina. You will please not use such a vulgar expression
again."

"I beg your pardon, sir. I meant to say, perhaps no one
will make me an offer."

"Nonsense. I wish you will not be ridiculous. You have
only to exert yourself to be a bit more pleasant and forthcoming.
You are of good blood, you will have an adequate dowry,
and you are a well-enough-looking young female."

"All my teeth, not spavined or short in the wind," remarked Georgina absently, staring into the fire.

"I cannot approve this frivolity, miss! I had not thought to
see it in you or I should not have attempted a serious discussion of this nature with you," Lord Fitzhardinge said icily.

"Again I beg your pardon, sir," she replied stiffly. "I
shall of course do my best to please you and to be of
assistance to my sisters. I hope, however, I am not so blind to
my own shortcomings as not to feel that my desire to do my
duty by my family may not be all that will be required in this
matter. Also, there is one blot on the family escutcheon that
we have not discussed that may—"

"We need not speak of that," he interrupted her. "It was
many years ago and mostly forgotten by now. You will
certainly not be held responsible for the actions of—"

"My mother," she interrupted in her turn.

"I said we will not discuss it," he said with flat finality
and dismissed her.

Remembering the discussion now, she nursed her hot cheek
against the cold pane and wondered if he was pleased with
her at last, for she had done better than even he could have
hoped for, whether he would condescend to acknowledge it
or not.

The door flew open, and Georgina's stepmother entered in
a flutter of draperies. She was a vapidly pretty woman,
clearly half her husband's age. "What *are* you doing, dream-

ing away there, Georgina? You must make yourself ready. Your papa is sure to be sending for you at any moment now!''

"I *am* ready, Mama.''

"Stand up, dear, so that I can see you properly. Oh, yes, charming. But I wonder, should it have been the pale-orange muslin? Perhaps it—but no! No, no, no! I was right about the white. So sweetly pretty, so virginal. I am never wrong in these things, if I do say it myself. Now, the hair.'' She cocked her head to one side and narrowed her eyes. "No. Definitely no. Too severe altogether. Carstairs should know better.'' Carstairs was Lady Fitzhardinge's dresser and had been sent by her mistress to dress Georgina and arrange her hair for this momentous occasion. Lady Fitzhardinge was no less eager than her husband for this match. Though her reasoning took a different route, her object was the same: to make way for her own three daughters. There was Cressy, for instance, already clamoring to put up her hair and let down her skirts, flirting with every male who came her way. A real hoyden, that girl, and the sooner brought out and safely married off the better. "Sit down, my dear," she said warmly, "I know just what is needed.''

"I told Carstairs to do it so,'' Georgina confessed, sitting down before her dressing table. Lady Fitzhardinge set to work, humming quietly to herself as she teased short tendrils out of their slicked-back confinement and brushed them into a soft frame of curls about Georgina's face. Then she pulled the pins from the smooth, thick knot at the crown, brushed the long mane of hair into loose ringlets, and tied a white ribband where the knot had been.

"There, now,'' she said, standing back, "that is much better, is it not?'' This was obviously a rhetorical question, for she didn't pause for an answer. "Young, but not juvenile. How I envy you your hair, my dear.''

Lady Fitzhardinge sighed, for her own pale-blond head owed its deceptive ringlets to the art of Carstairs and the curling tongs. Unfortunately all three of her daughters had inherited her thin flaxen locks. Georgina, she decided, must have got her hair from her mother, for the lord knew she couldn't have had it from Fitzhardinge, whose few remaining strands were mouse-brown.

The thought of her husband caused her to pull her wandering thoughts together and address herself to the task that he had imposed on her many days ago and that she had postposed to this last possible moment out of a certain shyness she had always felt with her cool, self-possessed stepdaughter. How could she ever approach the subject of maidenly behavior with such a girl? Of course, she knew perfectly well what her husband wanted of her; it was just difficult to put into words something most young women practiced without any tutoring at all: to meet a gentleman's admiration or compliment or proposal with a modest lowering of the eyes and some maidenly confusion, rather than a frank, considering, even slightly derisory stare. So off-putting for a man—for a woman too, for that matter, thought Lady Fitzhardinge, who was sure Georgina would give her just such a look no matter how delicately she approached the subject.

"My dear, your father thinks—that is, of course we both feel . . ." she was beginning tentatively, when Carstairs came in to announce that my lord requested Miss Georgina and my lady to present themselves in the library at once. Lady Fitzhardinge could not prevent a guilty sigh of relief at being thus saved from an impossible task and bent to the glass to make sure her lace cap was straight. She never ordinarily wore a cap, feeling that at six and thirty she was much too young. Striving, however, for a dignity she knew was not hers had caused her to put it on for this meeting; besides, it was enormously flattering—all that soft lace ruffling about the face and the blond curls just peeking out. Fitzhardinge, of course, would not notice, but Lord Trowbridge had a certain reputation for appreciating good looks. She herself had seen three mistresses of his, all ravishing beauties. Lord, but he was an attractive man. Not just in the ordinary way, not truly handsome, but—powerful. She shivered slightly at the thought. Of course she would never dream—but still, just to experience again that indescribable moment when eyes met and there was that knowing, that awareness between a man and a woman—and with such a man!

Her eyes were vacant and her breath coming shallowly, her hand had halted halfway to her cap, when Georgina said, "Mama?"

Lady Fitzhardinge whipped around guiltily, colour flooding into her face, and met Georgina's quizzically amused eyes. As though she knows exactly what I was thinking, Lady

Fitzhardinge thought, much flustered. She hustled across the room and out the door, trying to regain her composure.

Three blond heads appeared instantly from the schoolroom doorway. These were Cressida, sixteen, Harriet, fourteen, and Lydia, thirteen, Georgina's stepsisters.

"Georgie, are you nervous?" hissed Lydia.

"A little," Georgina admitted. Lydia, pert, coltish, and always in hot water, was the only one in Georgina's family that she truly cared for. She admired Lydia's spirit and courage and above all her honesty, and always treated Lydia as an equal.

"Why are you dawdling about like this?" scolded their mother. "Where is Miss Hapgood?"

"She went to her room to find Harry a pink ribband to keep her quiet, the crybaby! She says I took her ribband. As if I would ever wear pink!" retorted Lydia, rolling her eyes in eloquent disgust.

"So you did take it. Mama, you should *do* something," Harriet whined, her pale-blue eyes pink-rimmed from recent tears.

"Shush, all of you, before your papa—"

"Really, Mama, I cannot think why I must be kept penned up in the schoolroom with these children," Cressida interrupted loftily. "They are giving me the headache with their squabbles. I want to go for a ride. I am sure I have no interest in being introduced to Lord Trowbridge. Ugh! Practically doddering! How you *can*, Georgie!"

"She means she wants to go down to the stables and ogle the new groom," confided Lydia irrepressibly.

"Miss Lydia! All of you! Go back inside at once. Not another word!" Miss Hapgood rushed past a harrassed-looking Lady Fitzhardinge, shooed the girls before her into the room, and closed the door behind herself with a snap.

Lady Fitzhardinge sighed with relief and turned to the stairs. "Come along, Georgina. I am sure to have a scold from Fitz for dawdling as it is. Now, I know you are feeling shy and blushful," she said, thoughts of her husband scolding her inspiring her at the last moment, "but that is only what is expected, even hoped for, by a gentleman making a proposal. He would not want to see the young woman he hoped to make his wife completely self-possessed in such a situation. He would not think her delicate to be so."

There, she thought with satisfaction, nothing could be clearer, if she will only heed my words.

She was not, however, reassured by Georgina's cool little smile in response, or her measured, unhurried tread as she proceeded down the stairs, or by the fact that her hand on the railing did not betray the least tremble to indicate her awareness of the importance of the moment.

Really, thought Lady Fitzhardinge crossly, she will be bound to give Trowbridge a great disgust of her if she goes on like this.

CHAPTER

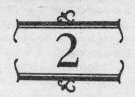

Lord Trowbridge, having made his formal request for the hand of Lord Fitzhardinge's daughter in marriage and been assured by Lord Fitzhardinge of his approval of the match, sat back in his chair as the old gentleman crossed to pull the bell to summon a servant and felt muscles relaxing that he had not realized were tensed.

The worst was over, thank God. Of course, the settlements and allowances had not yet been discussed, neither man caring to introduce so mercenary a subject at this juncture. Nor was it in the least necessary. Lord Fitzhardinge knows to a penny how much I am worth, Lord Trowbridge thought with some amusement, as well as how many seats I have and how many acres are attached to each, and certainly Georgina's dowry means very little to me. Trowbridge knew that this must all be gone into, of course, and naturally the proposal in form to Georgina herself was still ahead, but that, he felt, was a mere formality. If there had been any doubt in his mind about her acceptance, he would not have offered for her in the first place. He had made his intentions clear to her from the outset, and had the girl any objections she would have made *those* clear also. She was not the sort of girl to encourage a suit she had no taste for.

The moment he had met her he had felt he knew exactly what sort of girl she was. Her startling beauty and colouring might have captured his immediate attention, as they had every man in the room, but it was her cool regard and proud lift of chin, disdaining all missish displays, that had riveted him.

He was aware that his family and friends had given up all hope that he would marry, but he had not. He was not in the least disinclined to marry, but had until now never met a woman who interested him enough to bother. Georgina Fitzhardinge could not be dismissed so lightly. Here at last was a suitable Countess of Trowbridge, a worthy mother for his heir, with unblemished bloodlines and impeccable family.

It was only after he had been introduced to Lady Fitzhardinge that he remembered she was Georgina's stepmother and was reminded that there had been some scandal about the first Lady Fitzhardinge years ago, though he could not call it to mind at the moment. The details came to him in the middle of the night and they were unsavoury enough to give him pause. Before the night was over, however, the problem came to seem minor and easily surmountable. After all, whatever the woman had done, her family had been titled far back into the mists of antiquity, when his own had still been tilling fields, and the daughter should surely not be held accountable for the mother's sins, in any case.

Further acquaintance with Georgina only made his resolve to marry her more firm and his need to possess her more urgent. He had never been attracted by easy conquests, and her withdrawn, distancing air was a direct challenge to his manhood. He longed to see her eyes melting with warmth at his touch, to see her creamy skin flushed with passion. He was convinced her cold demeanour was only a thin disguise for a fiery temperament. No one with such colouring could be other than warm-spirited, any more than they could completely suppress their true nature for long—not once the fire was lit. Picturing that igniting caused him more than one sleepless night.

The only doubt he had was in regard to himself. Was he too old for her? Did she think of him as elderly? Was she secretly repelled by the thought of of marrying a man twenty years older than herself? Was she only marrying him for his money, his title, in obedience to her father's wishes? Had he been able to convince himself that any of these reasons was the true one, his pride and vanity would have caused him to abandon his suit. But these very qualities had finally sustained him in his belief that she was choosing him freely. After all, he assured himself, he was not exactly ready to turn up his toes yet and was considered to be a well-enough-looking man with not a gray hair or wrinkle to disgust the most fastidious. He was besides in excellent, even vigorous, health, and his mistresses had never complained of his abilities in the arts of love. As for the breeding of sons, he had proof of his virility in that quarter already, one that he acknowledged as a certainty, being the result of a youthful liaison with his sister's governess who had indisputably been a virgin. He had set her up with a house and a respectable settlement and finally been instrumental in finding her a suitable husband. He even visited her from time to time to check on the welfare of the boy, now a fine-looking youth of nearly twenty years. There were others he was not so certain of, though he had treated their mothers' claims with generosity, if without any real interest.

Gradually he had stilled his faint misgivings about Georgina's motives and pursued his suit, never receiving from her the least sign that she found him repulsive nor detecting the least interest on her part in any of the hopeful young sprigs who came nosing around. He became convinced at last that though she might not show any of the usual signs of a young girl in love, his declaration would be welcomed. He was not aware that had she shown any such signs, his own ardour would have cooled considerably. He only admired her the more for her unreach-ability.

He was prepared, therefore, and not the least dismayed, when the door open and she stood before him, regarding him dispassionately. Her stepmother nudged her slightly, and he thought he detected a slight twinkle of laughter lighting her amber eyes before she lowered them to her shoe-tops. A further nudge of Lady Fitzhardinge's elbow propelled Georgina forward, and she came to a halt before him and dropped a schoolgirlish curtsey, murmuring, "Good day, my lord," with a patently false pretense of being unable to overcome her shyness long enough to meet his eyes.

The minx, he thought exultantly, I was right about her!

But then she did look up, and he was not so sure. Her eyes held no secret message, her manner was as disengaged as always. Lady Fitzhardinge moved forward, her hand extended, to greet him. He bent to kiss it, as he was clearly expected to do, and when he straightened up, Georgina was seated decorously upright in a satin-upholstered straight chair before the fire, staring into the flames.

"Georgina, Lord Trowbridge has something to say to you, with my permission, of course," said Lord Fitzhardinge abruptly. He took his wife's arm and led her to the door. "My dear, perhaps you will order some refreshments to be brought in." The door closed behind them, and the couple were left alone.

Trowbridge crossed to stand before the fire. "You know why I am here, Georgina." It was a statement, not a question.

She drew her eyes away from the flames slowly, almost reluctantly, and looked up. "Do I, my lord?"

"Yes, I am sure you do. Nevertheless, I am aware there is a certain ritual expected on these occasions, and I am quite willing to follow it if it will please you." He stepped closer to her, and taking her hands, drew her gently to her feet. "I am sure you cannot be unaware of my feelings for you, and I have been encouraged to hope that you are not entirely indifferent to me. I would be honoured if you would accept my hand in marriage. Will you, Georgina?"

She looked at him for a long moment then replied, "Yes, my lord, I will." She disengaged her hand and resumed her seat with complete composure.

He felt a flick of annoyance. "Well, I admire your poise, my dear. You might have been agreeing to take a glass of lemonade at a ball."

She drew her brows together in mock dismay. "Ah, I did not follow the ritual expected on these occasions. I beg your pardon. I should have said, 'My lord, I am most sensible of the great honour you do me and I accept with all humility.' Or would you prefer that I make a pretense of refusal the first time? I believe that is the acceptable mode of behavior in these situations now. You, of course, will understand that it is only maidenly diffidence and will return in a few days to repeat your offer, confident that the proprieties having been observed and the first refusal out of the way, you will be successful."

He stared at her silently for a moment, disconcerted by her attitude. "You are very young to be so cynical," he said finally.

"Is cynicism then the exclusive prerogative of the old?" she returned without heat.

He flinched. He knew she was not insinuating anything about his age, for she was too well bred to display such bad manners. Still, the very question seemed to set them apart, to define the years between them. "Cynicism is the result of disillusion,'' he replied, managing to sound tolerant and amused, ''and you, surely, cannot have experienced much of that in the few months you have been out in the world.''

''I do not think disillusionment is limited only to the time one has been out in the world. Nearly all we know of life from birth is illusion, is it not? Growing up is, in fact, a slow process of disillusionment.''

He eyed her in dismay. There was no self-pity in her words, yet he could not remember ever hearing expressed a more depressing thought—or a more irrefutable one. ''My dear, this is a sad discussion to be having at such a moment—'' he began.

''Oh, I beg your pardon—how stupid you must think me. Please do not—''

Now she was blushing and exhibiting all the maidenly confusion her stepmother could have wished, the first he had seen in her, and he was perversely happy to see it. He immediately felt a restoration of his usual aplomb and in charge of the situation once more. He bent over, and tipping her chin up, kissed her firmly on the mouth.

''I have proposed and have, I believe, been accepted, so it is my privilege to kiss my betrothed,'' he said, smiling down at her, resisting the temptation to take further advantage of his privilege.

The creamy cheeks did not flush with passion at his kiss. On the contrary, they lost the blush they had just shown, and she seemed to turn paler than ever.

Good God, he thought in dismay, is it revulsion? Can I have so mistaken her?

Before he could come to any conclusions, however, there was the sound of Lady Fitzhardinge's voice, raised no doubt in warning to the lovers within, and the next moment the door opened.

''Forgive me, my lord, for being away so long,'' Lady Fitzhardinge apologized speciously, ''my younger children demanded my attention. I hope you are not quite parched with thirst.''

''Not at all,'' he replied courteously, ''I have the happiness to inform you, dear lady, that your daughter has done me the honour of accepting my proposal of marriage.''

Lady Fitzhardinge immediately erupted into a gush of exclamations of surprise and joy, embracing Georgina at great length and even managing a few tears. She then rushed to the door to call for her husband to come at once before turning to embrace her future son-in-law and bestow upon him a somewhat more than motherly kiss. She drew away, flushed, to skip across to the door again and take her husband's arm as he entered. "My dear, it is all so thrilling, so romantic! I cannot begin to express my happiness . . . our darling Georgina . . . such a surprise . . ." she babbled, while her husband disengaged his arm, solemnly shook hands with Trowbridge, and then bent to plant an austere kiss on Georgina's forehead.

The butler entered at this point with wine and glasses on a tray. A toast was drunk to the engaged couple, the younger daughters were summoned to make their curtsies to Lord Trowbridge, and at last he had nothing more to do but take his leave, without any further opportunity of being alone with his betrothed.

Before Georgina could quite believe it, she found herself being sent upstairs to lie down on her bed, "For I feel sure, my dear, you must be fagged to death after so much excitement and will want to rest before dinner," Lady Fitzhardinge exclaimed.

Not being in the least fagged, and being quite sure that simply going to bed would be much too anticlimactic after what had transpired, she turned instead into the schoolroom. Miss Hapgood came rushing to embrace her warmly, and the three girls began to bombard her with questions.

"Did you kiss, Georgie?" Lydia wanted to know.

"Lydie! You are disgusting. I shall tell Mama," Harriet began primly.

"That would not surprise me in the least," Lydia declared contemptuously, "for a bigger telltale than you does not exist. Did you, Georgie?"

"Well, yes," Georgina admitted.

"Ugh! How revolting! Like kissing one's papa," shuddered Cressida fastidiously.

"Why, no, Cressy, not really. Papa has never kissed me on the mouth," Georgina said.

"I cannot think, young ladies, that this is quite nice as a topic of discussion," protested Miss Hapgood ineffectually.

"How did it feel, Georgie?" persisted Lydia.

"Happy, I really think this disgusting child should be sent to bed," Harriet pronounced loftily.

"Harry, this is a scientific discussion. I wish you will not keep interrupting with your stupidly missish objections."

"A little more missishness from you would be a very good thing, if you ask me. You are altogether too forward in your ways," snapped Harriet.

"Some day, Sister, *if you are very lucky*," Lydia replied, emphasizing her words meaningfully, "you may be glad of this discussion. How are women to know anything if we do not tell one another?"

"You learn these things from experience, Lydia, not from discussion, Cressida declared.

"*You* do, no doubt," retorted Lydia, "if what I saw in the tack room yesterday was anything to go by, but—"

"Why, you little sneaksby!" shouted Cressy, turning fiery red and delivering a sharp box to her little sister's ear.

Lydia stared at her stonily, refusing to cry, while Miss Hapgood raised her voice at such an unseemly display, and Cressy protested her innocence at any wrongdoing at the top of her voice to be heard over Harriet, who was informing them that Lydia was a hoyden and Cressy a bully and her nerves could not tolerate these scenes. Georgina reached out for Lydia's hand and held it tightly without speaking.

When order was finally restored, Lydia, undeterred, returned to her scientific investigation. "Did you like it, Georgie?"

"It was . . . not unpleasant. It was only for a brief instant, you see. One can hardly form an opinion in so short a time."

"Do you feel different?"

"Different?"

"You know—changed, a new person, your spirit released by the touch of his lips—"

"Have you been reading those silly romances again?" interjected Harriet. "You know very well Mama does not—"

"Do be quiet. Do you, Georgie?"

"No, not really, dear."

But she did, though she could not have said quite how. A door had opened, revealing just a crack far away down a tunnel of bleakness, and light shone there. Not a thing she could have described to Lydia, who didn't seem to know about bleakness.

Georgina had learned about it as early as two, when she remembered asking for her mama and being told by someone—her nurse?—that Mama had gone away. She had begun to scream and cry and would not stop, and the woman had finally fetched Papa, who had taken her hand, led her into a dark room, and shut the door on her, telling her she must stay there until she learned to behave properly. She had not understood what he meant. She only knew that she wanted her mama and she was frightened and cold and hungry and—after a time—soiled. She had huddled down miserably where she stood in the middle of the floor. After a time the dark space around her had seemed to expand, while she felt herself to be growing smaller and smaller until she felt only a dot in a void that stretched into infinity. She screamed and screamed in terror, but no one came.

This became a nightmare that recurred again and again in times of stress, but she learned not to scream. That brought only further punishment from her papa. She also learned not to ask for her mother, nor was her mother ever mentioned by anyone in the household. She disappeared from Georgina's life as though she had never been, and after a year a different woman came into her life, who she was told to call Mama, though it was many years before she could bring herself to do so. Not that the new Lady Fitzhardinge was ever consciously unkind to her, but she was very soon pregnant with Cressida and most unwell, besides being too young and foolish really to understand her stepdaughter, who seemed to her a strange, unmanageable, and unloving child.

When Georgina was twelve, she began asking Miss Hapgood how her mother had died. Miss Hapgood tried to evade the questions, but finally was forced to tell her that her mother was not dead, only gone away. The realization that she had been abandoned as an infant by her own mother and left behind with a man with whom she herself could obviously not stay had done nothing at all to give Georgina the self-assurance she needed to melt the chill of isolation she had erected around her feelings.

It was only when she began to go about in Society that Miss Hapgood, instructed by Lord Fitzhardinge, had told her the details about her mother's disappearance. No doubt her papa feared she would hear gossip in London in any case and wanted her to be prepared. Her mama, it seemed, had eloped with a young lieutenant and sailed to India with him. Lord Fitzhardinge had been granted a divorce.

"She was but sixteen when she was forced to marry your papa," explained Miss Hapgood, attempting to soften the blow, "only a child really. And I am sure she felt she was doing the right thing by not subjecting such an infant as you were then to the rigours of the voyage half around the world."

Georgina was not particularly upset by the story, as she might have been had she heard it earlier. In some way she had come to admire her mother for having the courage to leave. It must have been Papa's fault, she thought.

Though cold and unbending, Lord Fitzhardinge was not a cruel man, but his shame and rage had blinded him to his infant daughter's needs, and by the time a new wife and some years had somewhat softened his attitude, it was too late. A wall had grown between him and Georgina, and there was nothing left but impatience and guilt on his part and a subdued, cold obedience on hers. She never touched her father voluntarily after the night he had taken her hand and led her into the dark room.

She thought now about that crack of light she had experienced rather than actually seen while with Trowbridge. Was it truly a sign of light and warmth ahead or was it a false promise? Would she dare to trust it? Was she to repeat her mother's pattern by marrying an older man and repenting it? Of course, her mother had been but sixteen—Cressy's age, she thought in amazement, trying to imagine Cressy as a married woman—and had no doubt been singularly unprepared for the responsibilities of a household and a child and the crankiness of a man set in the habits of a forty-two-year-old bachelor.

I, on the other hand, am quite used to living with such a man, she thought, and Trowbridge does not seem at all cross and mean, like Papa. Of course, he would not show himself in that light to me now, even if he were so. Why has he never married before this? I wonder. And why has he decided to do so now? He cannot love me; he barely knows me. The most he knows of me is that I am cynical, she thought, remembering her confusion when she realized what she had revealed to him and her fear that he would be disgusted with her for such an attitude. What if he had changed his mind and withdrawn his proposal?

She had known at that moment that she did not want him to do so, that she wanted to marry this man. But of course, he could not have honorably withdrawn at that point, poor man.

Perhaps he does not care about what I think. Perhaps he only wants to marry to get an heir. She shuddered suddenly at this thought, a cold apprehension spreading outward through her body. What did that entail exactly? Lydia is right, we know nothing, and there is no one I can ask.

She remembered the feeling of his mouth on hers, her surprise at the soft warmth of it and the corresponding flash of heat she had felt within herself, which had so terrified her she had thought she might faint. What in God's name had caused that? And what must she do to prevent it happening again?

CHAPTER

3

Georgina stood patiently in her bedroom while Prentiss, her new abigail, hooked up the back of her new gown of jonquil sarsenet. She knew the shade suited her perfectly, setting off the glossy auburn curls and bringing out the faint tinge of colour in her cheeks. The neckline was cut just low enough to reveal the first swelling of her breasts without being in any way immodest by the standards of the day, which allowed women to reveal a great deal more of themselves. Lady Fitzhardinge had calculated the demarcation to the exact milli-meter she thought proper for a young, unmarried, but betrothed, girl, as well as the degree of fullness in the tiny puffed sleeves and the drape of the gored skirt, which ended in three van-dyked flounces just above the white kid slippers.

This was the only new gown Georgina was to have for the period between her bethrothal and her wedding at the end of June, for Lord Fitzhardinge had baulked at providing more, having outfitted her for her come-out and presentation at Court only a few months previously and now being forced to lay out even larger sums for a trousseau. Lady Fitzhardinge, in her element with modistes and lingerie-makers and silk warehouses, had soothed him by declaring it was absolutely unnecessary for Georgina to have more than one new gown.

"After all, my dear, she can make do with all she has from her Season, though people will be bound to remark on it, of course. But naturally you will not want her to appear at Lady Cunliff's dinner party in an old gown, with all Trowbridge's relatives there to be presented for the first time to his bride."

Lord Fitzhardinge retired from the battle, with the uneasy suspicion that though she allowed it to seem that he won these small engagements, she would prove in the long run to

27

have won the war. For instance, she had insisted that with so many parties in honour of the betrothal, apart from those of the regular Season, to which she would be required to chaperone Georgina, she could not spare the services of Carstairs. Therefore Georgina must have her own maid to dress her. When he had dug in his heels at such an outrageous outlay, she had coaxed him around by reminding him it would be a matter of only two months' wages, after which it would become Trowbridge's responsibility.

"And after all, Fitz dear, I have not complained once about the carriage, which is sadly shabby and should be painted and relined, nor the drawing room curtains, which I have a positive dread will fall to pieces while I am entertaining and cause me the most horrid embarrassment. As for the servants' liveries . . ."

Lord Fitzhardinge retreated in full rout, and Lady Fitzhardinge sat down at once to write to an agency stating her requirements for an abigail who should present herself at the Fitzhardinge house in London in one week. When the party arrived in London from the country, Prentiss was waiting, and both Lady Fitzhardinge and Georgina had liked her at once. She was young and outspoken with Georgina, though never in Lady Fitzhardinge's presence.

Finished now with the hooks of Georgina's gown, Prentiss crossed to the dressing table and picked up the hairbrush. Georgina obediently seated herself before the glass. She almost caught her breath in shock at her image in the mirror. Only this morning, at Prentiss's and Lady Fitzhardinge's urging, Mme. de Tournay, the famous hairdresser, had been summoned. She had weighed Georgina's long chestnut mane in her hand for a long moment before murmuring "*Quand même*" and setting to work with her scissors. In a very short time Georgina's hair was cropped into a cap of ringlets à la Titus, while she sat frozen with horror.

She had refused to look at herself all day, but now could not help herself, and the sight was shattering. She watched dumbly as Prentiss wound a gold ribband through the artfully careless curls and attached a small white plume on one side with an oval diamond brooch from Lady Fitzhardinge's jewel box. Next she clasped a double strand of pearls, also lent by her stepmother, about Georgina's throat and stood back admiringly.

"There now! You'll knock spots off all of 'em, Miss Georgina. All the crack, that haircut. The other ladies will be gnashing their teeth in envy."

Or hiding their smiles of ridicule behind their fans, thought Georgina, fighting down the tears she could feel preparing to rise. Why did I let myself be persuaded to this ruinous cut? I have never wanted to be a glass of fashion. I cannot go. I cannot! Enough to be paraded before a roomful of relatives like a prize mare, but like this? Her face stared back at her as impassively as always, not revealing, even to herself, the panic that was roiling her insides.

She forced her stiff mouth into a smile and said, "Thank you, Prentiss. Hand me my gloves, will you please?"

Lord, will you look at her, thought Prentiss as she fetched the long white kid gloves from the bureau, as calm as you please. With them looks she could've held out for a duke at least.

Myles thought very much the same thing when his butler announced them and she appeared in the drawing room doorway beside her stepmother with her father behind them. The party already assembled stopped talking and swung around to the door as Myles hurried forward.

He had seen little of her since their betrothal. The past week had been filled with business affairs in connection with the forthcoming marriage, which had kept him tied up in London, and since the Fitzhardinges' arrival in town three days ago he had managed to be alone with her only for a few moments after a dinner given by the Fitzhardinges for my lord's few, and all ancient, remaining relatives. She had been then as remote as always, with very little to say for herself. He had felt awkward and stupid as he struggled to carry on a one-sided conversation and he had experienced a cold dismay for the first time, wondering if he had made a terrible mistake by offering for this ice princess. Perhaps the proud face concealed a lack of intelligence, and the warm colour of hair and eye a heart as resistant as marble. Since it was far too late to cry off, he had reassured himself that her little speech on disillusionment could not have come from a want-wit, and her warmth or lack of it was not, after all, an insuperable obstacle for a successful marriage. If she proved unresponsive, he could console himself elsewhere, so long as she provided an heir. His infatuation with her would not grow into love, perhaps, but they would manage to go along well enough together. Most of the marriages he knew were like that, after all.

Just the same, seeing her now in her shimmering yellow gown, with her bronze ringlets glinting with sparks of fire and her chin lifted proudly, caused his heart to swell with pride and his pulses to race with excitement. He hurried to her side, kissed her fingers warmly, and smiled down into her amber eyes. "You are enchanting, my dear. You have done something to your hair that is highly becoming to you."

Her eyes lit up with pleasure, and she smiled at his words. Good lord! Was it possible she was in need of reassurance? She had not seemed the sort of girl to be put out of countenance by any situation, but perhaps this was somewhat out of the ordinary for her to be meeting her future relatives for the first time. He pressed her hand and pulled it through his arm before turning to greet Lord and Lady Fitzhardinge. As he led them into the room, a path seemed to open of itself before them, a path leading straight up to a thin elderly lady seated before the fire, back straight as a ramrod, disdaining the comfort offered by the upholstered back and cushions of her chair, one hand holding a *face à main*, the other a crystal goblet of wine. She wore grey satin over hoops in the style that had long since gone out of fashion and a grey tulle turban featuring an aigrette pinned with a large ruby brooch.

She raised the *face à main* and surveyed Georgina intimidatingly as Myles presented his bride. Georgina curtsied respectfully and straightened up, gazing calmly back at the old lady, hands clasped loosely before her.

Suddenly Lady Cunliffe gave a sharp bark of laughter. "Myles, fetch her a chair, I want to talk to her. And get me more wine." She drained what remained in her glass and thrust it at him. He murmured something as he bent to take it, and she said ungraciously, "Oh, very well."

Myles turned to the Fitzhardinges and presented them to her. She nodded brusquely in acknowledgement and then turned to Georgina, who was just seating herself in a chair placed by a footman. Myles suggested that perhaps he should take Georgina around the room first to meet the others.

"That rabble? Ain't worth bothering her with," retorted Lady Cunliffe, not troubling to lower her voice, waving a contemptuous hand at the rabble, who were evidently inured to her opinion of them, for none looked affronted by her words. "Introduce her relatives to 'em. Here, you, bring us both wine," she ordered the footman, who scurried away immediately.

Myles led Lord and Lady Fitzhardinge away, but not quickly enough for them to escape Lady Cunliffe's tart assessment. "I never could abide those po-faced blonds, though she looks to have your papa in leading strings."

Georgina fought down an almost hysterical giggle. In her wildest imaginings she could never have conjured up such a creature as this.

"Well, well," said Lady Cunliffe, "here's your wine. Drink it up, girl. Good for you. People always telling me I drink too much of it, but I cannot think why. Don't have gout, don't have apoplexy. Also don't have much other trouble to get into at my age, so why should I give up the only pleasure left to an old woman? Well, speak up girl. What do you have to say for yourself, eh? Is that the latest crack in hair styles?"

"Slap up to the echo," replied Georgina solemnly.

The old lady cackled. "No flies on you, eh, gel? Suits you, that hair, though it won't many. Not that that will stop 'em. Silly geese, most women. Never could abide 'em. Always liked men better. What about you?"

"I—cannot really say. I have known so few men besides my father."

"Cross-grained man—see that at a glance. Won't have given you a good opinion of the sex. Pity. I have always been partial to 'em. Well, well, now you have Myles. Fine figure of a man, eh? Should be able to satisfy even a young girl like you, and a good-hearted creature to boot. Not like that scapegrace brother of his. Want to start breeding at once, do you, gel?"

Georgina would have been shocked had she not realized this was exactly the reaction the old woman was hoping to induce. So she looked Lady Cunliffe straight in the eye and said, "Why, as to that, what would be your advice?"

The old lady cackled happily. "If there is a choice, I would say wait. It's little enough fun you will have once you start. I like you, gel. You may call me Aunt Selina. Not like those simpering granddaughters of mine, all blushes and giggles. Hen-witted, the lot of them, just like their mothers. Not one of my daughters but had more hair than wit."

"Now who have you got your needle into, Auntie?" drawled a masculine voice behind them. Lady Cunliffe started and turned. The elegant young man came around her chair, bent to kiss her cheek, and then stared admiringly at Georgina. "Well, well," he said softly.

"None of your tricks now, you rapscallion. This is Myles's fiancée. M'nephew, Georgina, Dominick Barrowes."

Georgina could see a definite resemblance to Myles, though Dominick Barrowes was taller than his brother, and while Myles was stockier and more compact, this young man was slim and lithe. He was also arrestingly handsome, with a long fringe of lashes around his glowing dark eyes that any woman would envy. He bent to take Georgina's hand and pressed a lingering kiss onto her fingers.

"Well, Dominick, you have condescended to arrive at last," said Myles, appearing suddenly at Georgina's side.

"As you see, Brother," Dominick replied lazily.

"You might have contrived to be on time for once in your life."

"And so I should have been, had I the least idea . . ." Dominick's eyes turned back to Georgina and strayed insinuatingly over her. Georgina saw that Myles only smiled indulgently at his brother's rudeness, but she felt suddenly defensive about her husband-to-be, as though he had been attacked unfairly. She stared coolly back at Dominick, refusing to blush, and held out her wine goblet.

"Will you mind setting my glass on that table, sir? Thank you. Now, my lord," she said, rising and taking Myles's arm, "I think it is time for me to make the acquaintance of the rest of your relatives." She smiled down at Lady Cunliffe, who grinned and winked at her, nodded to Dominick, and turned away.

"As nice a set-down as I've seen in years," crowed Lady Cunliffe, "and well deserved too."

"Hope Myles means to keep a firm hand on the reins there. She wants taming, if you ask me."

"Well, you needn't be sharpening *your* spurs, Sir Wicked. Now sit down and tell me what you've been up to."

Georgina's ears burned as she was led away and she wondered if Myles had heard his aunt. She flicked a glance up to find him smiling down at her. "You must not mind them.

They are both reprobates and go out of their way to discompose everyone they meet.''

"I like your aunt very much.''

"And it is clear she returns the feeling. It is not easy to win her approval, I can tell you. She despises most of her relatives, including her daughters, poor things. She browbeat them unmercifully and then called them ninnies because they would not stand up to her.''

"Well, she told me she was not partial to women. She seems very fond of you and your brother.''

"Oh, I am in her good graces at the present for having become betrothed, and now she has met you, I believe my credit has gone up considerably. As for Dominick, she has always had a soft spot for a rake.''

"Is he so?''

"Not really, though I think he likes to be thought of in that light. Now, come along. After those two the rest will be easy. They are all panting to meet you and prepared to approve.''

She met Lady Cunliffe's daughters, all plump, dark-haired women who spoke most kindly to her, though they left little immediate impression, any more than the others. They were all welcoming and friendly. She supposed they had none of them entertained serious hopes of coming into any of Lord Trowbridge's money or titles with Dominick very much in the picture as his brother's presumptive heir should he not marry and produce his own. This thought caused her to speculate for the first time about Dominick's feelings in this matter. Had he hoped for quite a few years now that he would eventually inherit? Had the announcement of Trowbridge's betrothal put Dominick's nose out of joint enough for him to feel resentful of her?

Whenever she happened to glance in Dominick's direction as the evening progressed, he seemed to be watching her, and though his eyes seemed to smoulder, she did not think it was with resentment. When they sat down to dinner, she found herself on Myles's right with Dominick next to her, and was made acutely uncomfortable by his proximity. He conversed with her politely, but it seemed to her he always seemed to be implying something else beneath his words, as though they shared a secret intimacy. She knew he must be an adept as conducting a 'flirt' in this way under the watchful eyes of a whole roomful of people, but she was not and as a consequence found the dinner very trying.

She was glad to escape when the women withdrew and breathed a sigh of relief as the dining room doors closed behind them. Lady Cunliffe gave her a shrewd glance. She had not missed any of the byplay, though she had been all the way down at the other end of the table and seemingly engaged in dominating her conversation with Lord Fitzhardinge.

She seated herself squarely before the drawing room fire and raised her skirt to expose her skinny, silk-clad legs to the warmth, waving Georgina into the chair beside her. "Saw Dominick up to his tricks in there. Don't let it turn your head, gel."

"I hope I shall know how to conduct myself with my future brother-in-law," replied Georgina with a lift of her chin.

"Now don't come all stiff-rumped at me, child. I have seen him spin older heads than yours. Devilish handsome, that boy, and no heart to speak of at all. Had it all his own way with women since he was in short-petticoats."

"He surely cannot be so lost to all sense of propriety as to try such things with his own brother's—"

"Oh, *wouldn't* he?" retorted Lady Cunliffe sardonically.

"You make him sound a monster, yet I made sure you are very fond of him."

"He can always get around me, but I am not so blind I cannot see his faults, like some."

"Trowbridge says his brother is not so bad as he would like to pretend."

"He is worse, though Trowbridge won't see it, so you be careful, my girl," snapped Lady Cunliffe.

CHAPTER

4

Myles, his head bent attentively to the breathless wheezes of old Lady Venables, was at the same time watching his bride covertly as she conversed with the vicar, Sir John Venables, and Mr. Eldred Knyvet, the local squire. Despite the past unsettling month since their marriage, he was proud of Georgina. She had dreaded this evening, but was managing to carry it off with so much style and graciousness that only he was aware of the tension in her smile and the set of her shoulders.

That she could face without a blink, the brilliant wits of the Paris salons and a London drawing room filled with the *ton*, as he had seen her do, and still be nervous at entertaining his country neighbors was only one of the mysteries of his wife's nature that he was continuously attempting to solve. It had gradually become clear to him that with her peers or with the lower orders she was completely at ease, but the petty gentry, that fell between these categories, agitated her. When he had questioned her about it, she had told him she always feared she would strike the wrong note, offend them by an unconscious condescension of tone or manner.

This had been so incomprehensible to him that he had not known how to answer her. It was, however, only one in a long list of incomprehensions, for she remained bafflingly out of his grasp, in spite of the intimacies of the marriage bed, although their experiences in that area had not resulted in any great intimacy either, if he were to be honest with himself.

Their wedding night had been spent in separate bedrooms at his London residence, Trowbridge House. She had been a breathtaking bride in blond lace over white satin, poised and regal through the long ceremony and even longer reception and dinner to follow. The effort to maintain her stance had all too obviously exhausted her, however, and one look at her drained, white face when they were finally alone, had caused him to kiss her brow gently and say good night. She had studied his face for a long moment, then given him a weary little smile and disappeared into her bedroom.

He had read gratitude into her smile, and his disappointment had evaporated in a righteous glow of self-sacrifice. Later, however, as he tossed restlessly in his empty bed, the glow shredded as he began to wonder if she had not been expressing something else. Disdain, perhaps, that he lacked the vigour to come to her after such a tiring day? Or, worse, was the smile hiding her own disappointment?

He had wrestled with the problem sleeplessly, his pride unable to accept that she might be feeling either of those things about him. Should he?—but no, he could hardly force himself on her at this hour. She would doubtless be asleep by now, whatever she may have felt when he said goodnight to her. At last he rose and sat before his fire, drinking brandy, until he was able to soothe his agitation. Only a monster would demand anything further from his bride after such a day. She was little more than a child, really, for all her poise, and a delicately nurtured child at that, who must be handled with great understanding. Of course, he wanted her and looked forward to the consummation of their marriage, but he was not so desperate he must needs ruin every chance of that wedded intimacy he had begun looking forward to. He could afford to wait for the propitious moment when she would indicate to him that she was ready to receive him.

That moment had not come. They had set off the next morning in his elaborately fitted travelling coach for Dover and the crossing to France; Prentiss and his valet, Giddens, followed in another carriage piled high with luggage. The winds being propitious, they had been hustled immediately aboard, where Georgina had succumbed almost at once to *mal de mer*. Two days at an inn in Calais had been required for her recovery after landing, during which she was seen only by Prentiss. Then came two days on the road to Paris.

After three days in Paris she seemed to have recovered her spirits and health entirely, but while the smile she bestowed on him each night as they parted was no longer weary, neither was it expressive of anything else. She seemed contented that things should continue as they had begun. During the day she shopped, visited modistes, rode with him in the Bois, paid calls with him, and went sightseeing with evident pleasure, and revelled in the parties, theatre, opera, and ballet that filled their evenings. But never by word or gesture did she attempt to encourage anything more between them.

At last it came to him that she must be waiting for him to initiate things. She was not a flirt or a tease, and had never to his knowledge been involved with any other man. It was clear she had no idea of what was expected of her. He quailed at the thought of her entire ignorance, but pushed the thought firmly aside. The situation was becoming intolerable, farcical, and the longer it went on, the more difficult it would become.

One evening in Paris when they returned from a dinner party, he had let her go up to bed before him, telling her that he wanted to dash off a note to his agent in England and would come up later. She faltered for a moment, and he saw her brows draw together fractionally, but she only nodded and turned away to the stairs.

He had taken a leisurely glass of brandy before going up himself to let Giddens assist him out of his evening clothes and into a dark-red silk dressing robe. When he judged she had had enough time for all the little rituals women go through before sleep, he walked across the hall and tapped on her door. Prentiss opened it after a moment. She looked flustered, glanced back into the room, then dropped him a curtsey and stepped back to admit him.

Georgina was still at her dressing table, her back to the door. "I will not need you further, Prentiss. Good night," she said.

"Good night, m'lady," whispered Prentiss, bobbing again to both of them and scuttling out the door. Myles closed it behind her and advanced into the room. Georgina did not turn around, but met his eyes squarely in the glass. She was in a dressing robe of pale-blue silk trimmed at throat and hem with swansdown, her hair sending off red sparks in the candlelight. He came up behind her and laid his hands gently on her shoulders. He felt a slight tremor go through her.

"You are very beautiful, Lady Trowbridge." He smiled into her eyes in the glass. "This colour becomes you. You must have a gown made up in it, a ball gown, perhaps," he added lightly, caressing her shoulders, savouring their round softness through the silk. She sat mutely, unmoving, her eyes wide and unwavering. Like a mesmerized rabbit, he thought with a flick of irritation. Enough of this! He stepped around and pulled her from the chair into his arms with more force than he had intended to use and crushed his lips against hers, forcing her lips apart roughly. She winced away, but he was beyond noticing now. The feel of her slim body, her breasts pressed against him, had roused all the passion so carefully and considerately held at bay. One arm clamping her close, he pulled the blue silk down, then the sheer lawn of her bed gown yielded one bare shoulder and high, rounded breast. He grasped it, and his mouth left hers to fasten on the rosy nipple.

She drew a long gasping breath, but did not move. Suddenly he straightened, pulled gown and robe down to fall around her feet, and lifting her in his arms, carried her to the bed. Through what followed she lay without speaking or moving, though not opposing him in any way.

Indeed, in the nights to follow she cooperated by removing her bed gown herself before he came to her, but she remained mute and unresponsive.

Myles, whose only experience had been with the muslin company and mistresses he kept, was at first puzzled by this lack of response. He could not believe she could remain so unmoved by the experience. What he did not realize was that the women he had bedded before were professionals with a stake in pleasing him. They had made love to *him*, rousing his passion and, if not roused themselves, clever at simulating desire to give him the further pleasure of feeling he was irresistible. He had come to think himself as an adept in the art of lovemaking, a virile giver of pleasure, and felt rather smug about his prowess. He had never been with a woman whom he had to rouse, so he had no knowledge of how to set about awakening a young, inexperienced girl to the joys of making love and the pleasure to be found in her own body.

He began to feel brutish and guilty, as though he were taking advantage of her, and the guilt led inevitably to resentment. However, he still became weak with desire for her at the thought of her resiliently pliant body with its tiny waist and rounded hips that led down in such a beautiful line to the long, full thighs, and boneless-looking dimpled knees and up to the delicious, high-standing breasts and the flawlessly molded shoulders. He continued to go to her bed often, but the hoped-for intimacy never developed. They never dallied in bed after their lovemaking, talking of their love, exchanging confidences about the day and the people they had been with and how they felt about this and that. Nor did they by a shared glance or a touch of hands during the day make promises of more to come when they could again be alone.

During their public hours he continued to be proud of her graceful carriage, her taste, and the admiring glances her beauty attracted, and charmed by her enthusiasm and child-like delight with Paris.

They had returned to England after a month and come straight down to Falconley, the principal seat of the earls of Trowbridge, the summer being too far advanced by this time to make London a pleasant place in which to linger, especially as the Season was now over and the town empty of friends. His servants both indoors and out had adored her on sight and treated her with a mixture of awed deference and an almost parental pride. His tenants on the estate came running to greet her every appearance, beaming their pleasure at the opportunity to pay their respects to her ladyship. She was at her very best with all these people, Myles thought, never cold or tense with them, her amber eyes warm with kindness and consideration, while never losing a jot of the dignity she knew they wanted in her.

However, when he had informed her that she must send cards to the local minor gentry for a dinner, her eyes had taken on a hunted expression that had mystified him. It was then that she had explained to him her fears of offending them. She had nevertheless requested a list from him and sent out cards.

The menu she planned was elaborate enough to honour them while not so ostentatious as to intimidate even the vicar's wife, a tiny woman of mouselike aspect who spoke in whispers. Georgina wore one of her new Paris gowns of sapphire-blue silk with the long double strand of Trowbridge pearls and Myles's gift of pearl and diamond earrings. The company was openly gratified by this resplendence, so obviously she had been right when she had insisted that if she did not dress grand enough they would take it that she did not consider them worth the effort and be affronted.

So far, all the care and thought she had put into the evening had resulted in a group of neighbors who had known each other for years and saw each other frequently enough to be rather bored with one another being elevated by good food and wine and elegant atmosphere into a relaxed vivacity, exerting themselves to be interesting and to be amused by their neighbors' best stories, though they had heard them before.

Old Lady Venables, her fat face dangerously empurpled and shining with enthusiasm, her several chins wobbling, leaned forward with a massive creaking of stays to lay a plump hand on Myles's arm. "My dear Trowbridge, how very wise you have been in your choice of a bride. A more suitable countess could not have been found, had you gone on searching another twenty years. We had all quite despaired of you, you know, but you have succeeded in restoring all our fondest hopes for you. We none of us could rejoice at the thought of Dominick inheriting Falconley. Of course, you have dashed the hopes of some of our young ladies, one in particular." She nudged him in the ribs with a massive elbow and rolled her eyes toward Hester Knyvet. "Not but what certain persons who shall remain nameless were not casting their eyes far beyond any sane expectations. As I said to Venables, I am sure Trowbridge has broken hearts with far more right to hope than—"

"My dear Lady Venables," Myles interrupted desperately, "you must allow Georgina to come by one day and see your gardens. I have told her of your great success with roses, and nothing will satisfy her but to have some cuttings and try her own hand."

Lady Venables protested that nothing could give her greater pleasure and the dear child should have all she wanted, and launched into her favourite subject. Myles sighed with relief, for if there was one topic that embarrassed him more than any other it was Hester Knyvet's unfortunate obsession with himself. He had known the girl all her life, but had spent very little time in her company, since he was away from Falconley for a good part of the year. Even when he was there, their paths crossed but rarely. Still, she had been hinting at her infatuation to the entire neighborhood since she was a schoolgirl and did not seem to mind that they laughed at her behind their hands for cherishing hopes that he might some day turn to her.

"The girl's a moonling," declared Lady Venables whenever the topic came up. "Trowbridge, indeed! Her mother should do something, is what I say, to drepress such pretensions!"

To her credit, Mrs. Knyvet had timidly, from time to time, attempted to point out to Hester the unlikelihood of such hopes ever coming to fruition, but even her mother was unaware of the forcefulness of Hester's determination. A lifetime of overindulgence by her doting parents had encouraged her to believe that the world revolved about her own person and succeeded in persuading her that if she wanted something—even Myles, Lord Trowbridge—there was no reason she should not have it. She had become infatuated with Myles at twelve and had never wavered in her belief that she would some day marry him. Hester was a vivacious blond, who, though not a raving beauty, was certainly accounted the prettiest girl in Trowbridge. She never wanted for partners when there was dancing, and had several local swains ready to throw themselves at her feet. She was of medium stature and possessed a pretty, high-bosomed figure. She was at the very peak of her looks at twenty-four. Her overly sharp nose and chin would not age gracefully, nor would the slightly too thin lips, but only those who made a study of such things would have known it. She had been educated at the most exclusive boarding schools and was always more expensively gowned than any other young woman in the neighbourhood. She felt that her assets were so numerous that there could be little room for doubt that they would one day be added up by the elusive Lord Trowbridge and he would waste no time in proposing.

It was therefore a double shock to her when the news of his betrothal reached Trowbridge village. She subjected her parents to a temper tantrum, followed by two days of hysterical weeping. His actual marriage brought on a state of murderous brooding even more difficult for her poor beset parents to cope with, and at times they quite feared for her sanity.

For days after Lord Trowbridge brought his new bride to Falconley, the Knyvets eyed their daughter nervously, wondering if she had heard the news and dreading her reaction. When the invitation to meet the new Lady Trowbridge arrived, they were at first too terrified to tell her of it. She surprised them when they finally did so by snapping abruptly out of her dismals and ordering a devastating new evening gown of peach-bloom gauze.

Myles, though aware of her feelings for himself, did not think about them at all except when actually in her presence. He was very fond of the girl's father and thought Miss Knyvet a handsome enough girl, but the thought of marriage to her had never occurred to him, any more than it would have occurred to him that she could entertain such a notion.

He had not thought to warn Georgina of the situation, but it had not taken Lady Venables' heavy-handed hints to remind him that perhaps he should have done so. Hester herself made matters quite clear to him, when he had come forward to greet her and her parents, by pressing his hand significantly and staring into his eyes with unnerving urgency. During dinner she managed to catch his eye several times and each time bestowed upon him a small, secret, knowing sort of smile, as though indulgently forgiving him for his small transgression.

He willed himself not to allow it to disconcert him, but now he could not suppress his irritation as he watched Georgina walk up to her smilingly and speak. Hester fanned herself languidly, disdaining to return the smile, and when Georgina had finished her speech, Hester gave a cold little bow and walked away to sit beside her mother on a sofa and commence a sparkling flirtation with the curate, who had been conversing politely to Mrs. Knyvet. Georgina, unable to account for such a high-handed snub in her own drawing room, stood looking after her in bewilderment.

Myles excused himself to Lady Venables and crossed to his wife at once. Pulling her arm through his own, he smiled reassuringly into her eyes. "Well, my love, what a very successful business you have made of your first dinner party."

"Well, I had thought so, but now I cannot be quite so content. Miss Knyvet seems—"

"Ah, you must not mind her, my dearest. She is used to being the prettiest girl in the room, and you have quite put her nose out of joint."

"Now you will embarrass me, and I shall blush before all your friends," she protested laughingly.

Lady Venables sailed up, booming out her praises for the dinner, and then, lowering her voice to a confidential whisper, she said, "Pay no attention to that silly little chit, Lady

Trowbridge. For all her education and accomplishments, she has not learned how to conduct herself properly. Most unstable.''

"What are her accomplishments, Lady Venables?" asked Georgina.

"She is a tolerable performer at the pianoforte and is quite a pretty watercolourist. Were it not for the ridiculous bee she has in her bonnet about . . ." she swivelled her eyes significantly towards Myles, and suddenly Georgina understood all. Her lips curved up, and her eyes sparkled mischievously at Myles, who flushed and looked distinctly uncomfortable. He turned with relief to Mr. Knyvet and the vicar, who strolled up to join them at that moment.

The conversation turned to crops and cattle, and after a few moments Georgina left the gentlemen and Lady Venables and crossed determinedly to Mrs. Knyvet and Hester. Mrs. Knyvet turned to her hostess eagerly, but Hester continued to speak with the curate as though unaware of Georgina's presence. The curate flushed uncomfortably, longing to turn to this beautiful woman but unable to be rude to Hester, who would not release him.

Georgina, though listening with grave attention to Mrs. Knyvet's compliments on the evening, was aware of the curate's predicament. She heard Hester ask him a question, and before he could reply, broke into their conversation.

"Forgive me, Mr. Peasley, but I have come to beg a favour of Miss Knyvet. Lady Venables tells me''—Georgina turned to Hester—"that you are an accomplished performer on the pianoforte, Miss Knyvet. Will you not honour us with some music?''

Now Hester was truly torn, for she was very proud of her accomplishment and indeed she was a fine pianist, cold but technically precise. In the space of one second many conflicting emotions rose and were dealt with almost simultaneously in her mind. If she insulted Georgina by refusing, as she dearly longed to do, she might never be invited back, thus cutting herself off from one possibility of seeing Myles. If she refused to play, she also lost the opportunity of showing herself to him in the best possible light, for she thought she made a most romantic and appealing picture seated at the pianoforte. So though her scorn and rage with the woman who in her mind had stolen Myles from her rose as bitter as bile in her throat, she swallowed it down and with a condescending little nod, fearful to speak lest some venom escape in spite of herself, she rose and crossed to the instrument.

Georgina looked across the room to her husband and raised one eyebrow infinitesimally. He pantomimed applause and winked at her, causing her lips to twitch irrepressibly. It was the most intimate moment they had shared so far.

CHAPTER

5

Cressy flounced out of Georgina's bedroom, slamming the door behind her, and Georgina flinched and reached for her eau de cologne. She sprinkled it on her handkerchief and touched it to her throbbing temples, wondering yet again how she had allowed her stepmother to leave London without taking her eldest daughter with her.

Cressy's visit had been proposed several times before, but lately with increasing pressure. When Georgina continued to demur, Lady Fitzhardinge had brought Cressy to London and more or less deposited her on Georgina's doorstep. Georgina had received letters from Lydia explaining why her mother was so insistent in the matter. Cressy, it seemed, had been "carrying on" with a stableman. Though Lydia was not yet informed enough to tell Georgina exactly what was entailed beyond a rough embrace which she herself had witnessed, she did know it had gone far enough to cause Papa to lock Cressy in her room for a week while Mama took to her bed. Lydia also hinted darkly that she found it difficult to believe Georgina could so far neglect her sisterly duty as to have failed to explain to her in detail exactly what was the involvement between men and women in the married state, purely as a matter of scientific interest.

When she answered these letters Georgina ignored her sister's hints, for in truth she could not imagine herself putting into words either verbally or on paper a description which defied belief. The pleasures of the marriage bed had so far eluded her.

It was pleasant, of course, to be one's own mistress at last and order one's own household as one wanted it, to be in command of a sufficient allowance and not be forced to apply to Papa for every penny. It was also not unpleasant to have for a husband an attractive man who never failed to notice and compliment one on a new gown or coiffure and who was unfailingly kind and courteous and never scolded or grumbled about bills. All these assets of the married state, however, would be old news to Lydia, who could have figured them out for herself or whose mama would have pointed them out. What her mama would not tell her was the rest. Lady Fitzhardinge undoubtedly felt it was not necessary to tell Lydia anything until her actual wedding night loomed. Then she would give her the same lecture she had given Georgina, which involved a woman's duty to yield to her husband, a duty that she would not necessarily enjoy, but on the other hand nice women were not supposed to enjoy it, and a great deal more on those lines, which circumambulated any solid information.

Georgina often speculated on this state of affairs as it affected Lady Fitzhardinge. Was it possible she enjoyed her husband's attentions? Did any woman? On the other hand she never pondered about her father or other married men. It was perfectly clear that it was not only pleasureful but also necessary for men. She could not help feeling there was something inherently unfair in the way God had arranged these matters so that women must not only suffer the indignity of what was mystifyingly called lovemaking but also receive no pleasure from it and then had to endure the pain of childbearing as well. Lady Fitzhardinge had not spared herself on these details, telling her stepdaughter the dire details of the birth of each of her children.

One became inured to the first after a time, of course, and she could only suppose the joys of motherhood compensated for the rest. That she had so far been denied even this compensation was a source of great unhappiness to her as well as of guilt, for she felt she was failing in her duty. As for Lydia, she supposed she could assure her that it was the beginning that was bad: the initial fear of what was to happen, the disbelief that it could actually be *this*, and a certain amount of pain the first time.

She looked back now to those early days of marriage with awe at her own innocence—or stupidity. She had been too exhausted and ill to think much about it the first week and had been grateful for Myles's sympathetic understanding and care for her every comfort. After she had recovered, in Paris, she had even more cause for gratitude, for he seemed determined to give her everything, take her everywhere, introduce her proudly. But she had become aware of a difference in the way he kissed her, of a mounting urgency in his embrace when he bade her good night. She guarded herself carefully from the frightening response she had experienced the first time he kissed her, however, and found she could smother all those feelings at will. When finally he had come to her room, she had known instinctively that now she was to learn the rest of the mystery. What had transpired had been so shocking and painful that there had been no need to guard her feelings other than to prevent herself from crying. That she would not allow herself to do. Mercifully it had been over quite quickly.

He was never brutal to her purposefully, and she had come to accept that this was her wife's role and even managed to forget about it during the day. She enjoyed going about with him and entertaining his friends and was unaware there could be any more expected of her but to give him an heir.

She had never been a confiding sort of girl, and in any case there had never been anyone in her life to whom she would or could unburden herself about her problems. She trusted Myles, but it would never have occurred to her to talk to him about her feelings or hopes or even her expectations. She was too much in the habit of defending them from everyone to break the habit voluntarily. To cry, to feel, to want were all things that brought the dreaded loneliness nightmare, and she had spent years building up barriers against any possible recurrence of it.

During the past year they had lived at Falconley and gone to London for the Season, visited her family, and returned again to Falconley. Sometimes they visited briefly one or another of his many seats, but not often. Now it was June, and they were back in London, this time for a special grand fete at Carlton House to celebrate the Prince of Wales's inauguration as Regent. Lord and Lady Trowbridge were among some two thousand guests to receive invitations.

Cressy had not stopped teasing Georgina since she had heard of it, "For surely among so many one more guest will never be noticed, Georgie."

"It is simply not possible, Cressy. Please stop teasing when you know I cannot take you. If every guest felt free to bring his own guests, why, there would be thousands more than invited. Then it would not be the Regent's party anymore, with those he wants to entertain.''

"Oh, pray do not lecture, Georgie. As if everyone would bring guests! You speak as though if you do so, everyone will, whereas you know most people would not even think of it.''

"Nor will I.''

"But I am sure if the Regent knew me he would invite me.''

"You are ridiculous! Whyever should he do so?—a girl just out of the schoolroom who has not even been presented yet or made her come-out.''

"Oh, he would,'' replied Cressy with a confident toss of her head, "I know how to make gentlemen do what I want.''

"Oh, yes, no doubt your wiles have been well rehearsed, though I doubt any gentlemen were involved.''

"I suppose you have had letters from that pea-goose of a Lydia. I shall have to attend to her when I get home. Just the same, Georgie, I think you are being monstrously unfair. You don't even care about going to the party and you get to go, while I . . .''

On and on went Cressy. This conversation or variations on it had been repeated interminably for the past week. Georgina, who had been feeling vaguely unwell, was relieved when Cressy at last slammed out of the room. She set aside her cup of morning chocolate, which had succeeded in calming her uneasy stomach, and snuggled gratefully down into her bed.

Cressy, undaunted by her failure, never having had any real expectation of succeeding in any case, rang for Prentiss to help her dress. An hour later she emerged resplendent in the new riding dress she had wheedled out of her mother before her departure, a bright leaf-green, embroidered with dashing black braid down the front and on the cuffs, *à la militaire*. Her small hat was of black beaver with gold cordon and tassels, with a long green ostrich feather in front. Her half-boots were black fringed with green, her gloves York tan, her mouth curved up in a smile of great complacency.

She had not confided to Georgina that she had arranged the previous evening at dinner to ride this morning with Dominick, for she knew very well Georgina would not have allowed her to go. For some reason Georgina did not trust her brother-in-law and had warned Cressy several times that he was considered a dangerous flirt and she must watch her step with him. Cressy, however, liked flirts, the more dangerous the better, and thought Dominick the most attractive man she had ever met. She shivered with excitement just to remember the way his knowing dark eyes had raked lazily over her figure, seeming to leave trails of heat on her skin, and the warmth of his voice with its suggestiveness of an intimacy between them that set them apart from everyone else in the room. They had seemed to know each other from the first meeting of their eyes, and there was no question in her mind that she would taste those carved lips with her own. The only question was how and when this would be achieved. She ached for it, but also enjoyed the waiting, the anticipation.

Her experiences until now had all been with the scarlet-faced, tongue-tied scions of the local gentry at home and with the eager fumblings of various of Lord Fitzhardinge's staff, all easy to manipulate and control. Until the last, of course, but he had been a man: hard-eyed, well-muscled, and sun-browned. The first day she had seen him in her papa's stables she had been determined to evoke some response from that unsmiling countenance. He remained polite and unbending, seeming not even to see her long, bold stares or the little smiles she directed at him. She was not dismayed, did not even believe in his lack of interest. All men were interested, but some knew how to play the game better than others. Benton, a handsome gypsy-dark man, had obviously had a great deal of experience both with horses and with women.

One day she had sauntered into the stableyard to be told her mare was lame and that Benton was with her. She had not hesitated a moment. Sun-blinded, she had stood in the cool, dim interior of the barn for a moment, excited by the scent of hay and horse dung and sweat. She went to the mare's stall, and there was Benton, bending to run his fingers over the quivering fetlock, soothing the mare in a low murmur. She walked up behind him and bent over his shoulder, deliberately pressing her breast against him.

"Oh, what has happened to the poor darling," she breathed, almost into his ear.

He remained perfectly still without answering for a long moment before he straightened and turned to face her, only inches away.

"A sore spot. Not a sprain. She'll need to rest it for a few days," he said without inflexion or any sign of discomfiture.

"I see. Will *you* attend to her?"

"Certainly, m'lady."

"Then I will come back later to see how she goes on," she said somewhat breathlessly.

"Will I saddle up the other mare for you, m'lady?"

"Yes, please."

She watched him intently as he did so, but was unable to detect the least sign in him of any response to her overtures. When the mare was ready, he held his hands for her to step into, tossed her up, and turned away without a word. She rode reluctantly out of the stableyard with a quick glance over her shoulder to check if he were watching her. He had disappeared entirely. Angry colour rose in her cheeks, and she silently apostrophized him as a bumptious gape-seed and determined to give him a sharp set-down when she returned from her ride to show him with whom he was dealing. Her imagined conversation with him slowly turned from icy sarcasm to an imagined apology, which in turn led to more satisfying scenes. She cut her ride short.

As she approached the stableyard, she saw no one around and dawdled along slowly until she saw Benton emerge from the stables. Then she trotted into the yard.

"Help me down, Benton," she ordered.

He came forward slowly, hands on his hips, and stared hard at her, eyes flinty and unreadable. She smiled and put her hands on his shoulders, and at last he reached up to her waist and lifted her down. She left her hands on his shoulders a moment longer than necessary. He dropped his hands at once and stepped around her to take the mare's reins and lead her into the stable.

"I could not enjoy my ride," she confided, following him into the dim interior. "I was too concerned for my mare. How is she?"

"Too soon for change," he replied. He led the mare into her stall and began unsaddling her, while Cressy stood in the entrance, watching the play of muscle in his broad back. He took a cloth and began rubbing the mare down, and she moved forward.

"Shall I help?"

"No need, m'lady."

"You handle her very well," she said, moving closer.

He turned at last and studied her without speaking, his black eyes roving insolently from her eyes to her mouth and down to her heaving bosom. Nothing in her experience had ever excited her more than this. The blood seemed to sizzle through her veins, and her breath came in gasps.

Suddenly his arm shot out and clamped her against him, and his mouth came down bruisingly on hers, grinding her lips apart, his tongue filling her mouth. Then she was standing alone, and he was again rubbing down the mare. "Run along now," he ordered, "I'm busy."

She turned and dazedly made her way out of the stable, not even seeing Lydia standing just inside the doorway. Cressy spent the rest of the day trying to recapture the brief moment and forcibly restraining herself from going back to the stables again.

The next morning she dressed in her habit and hurried down to the stables. When Benton saw her, he turned to fetch a horse for her, and she followed him.

"Show me my mare," she demanded. "Is her leg better?"

He led the way to the mare's stall, and she made a pretense of examining her before turning to him. This time she was prepared, and her arms went up as he reached for her. Except that she was more actively involved, caressing his back and shoulders, arching her body urgently against him, the experience was the same as the previous day, again over much too soon, leaving her tingling and speechless. This applied to the following morning also, but then her need overcame her discretion, and she decided worry for her mare gave her every reason to return to the stables in the afternoon. She dressed in a diaphanous sprig muslin, cut much too low for her years, but showing to advantage a generous portion of her bosom.

When Benton saw her coming, his lips curled into a sardonic smile before he turned into the stables. She flushed, but followed him. At the mare's stall there were no specious inquiries on her part or any pretense of examination on his. He pulled her roughly into his arms and began to kiss her, his hand coming between them to slide into the front of her gown to knead her breast almost painfully. The exquisite pleasure she experienced at this was rudely interupted by an outraged roar of "*Cressida*!"

They sprang apart instantly, and Cressy shrieked as she

saw her father standing there, red-faced and eyes popping with fury. Cressy fled past him and straight up to her room. She never knew what happened to Benton, for she never saw him again. She endured a bellowed lecture from her papa, a tediously weepy one from her mother, and a week locked in her room. She was then rewarded with a trip to London to visit Georgie, which could not have been more agreeable to her.

Not that she forgot Benton. Indeed, he occupied a great many of her waking moments, causing her a form of frustrating, painful pleasure as she remembered the feel of his rough, calloused palm on her breast.

Dominick Barrowes was as different from Benton as it was possible to imagine, being a witty conversationalist and a smoothly accomplished, well-dressed gentleman, but Cressy saw a great similarity in their hard, ruthless dark eyes and knew Dominick would not hesitate to take what he wanted any more than Benton.

Her ride with Dominick was as pleasureful as she had anticipated. They flirted outrageously, every word freighted with unspoken meaning, every meeting of the eyes explicit with promise. Dominick was at great pains, however, to make his position clear to her.

"I shall never marry, my dear," he declared airily in response to a teasing question from her. "I have no desire to have my life disrupted, nor the least itch for home fires and a nursery full of brats. I leave all that to Myles."

"Oh, but surely—" she began to protest.

"No, Cressy," he interrupted her firmly, giving her a hard stare that she could not pretend to misunderstand. She mentally shrugged. She was quite sure in any case that she would not want him for a husband. She needed a husband much more controllable than Dominick.

A young man hailed them at that moment and edged his horse towards them through the crowds of riders and carriages. He was stout and nearly strangled by an intricately tied neckcloth and high shirt points. He doffed his hat to reveal a tumble of artfully arranged red curls, his slightly protrubent pale-blue eyes ogling Cressy appreciatively as Dominick introduced them.

"Mis Fitzhardinge, allow me to present Mr. Wyndham Hughes-Jones to you."

Cressy dimpled demurely and then proceeded to treat Dominick to a display of her technique in dazzling young gentlemen. When Mr. Hughes-Jones left them at last, after extracting permission to pay her a morning call on the following day, she burst into giggles at Dominick's cynically lifted eyebrow.

"Most edifying, my dear. I cannot think where a schoolroom chit learned such tricks."

"I am seventeen and shall be making my come-out soon," she retorted, tossing her head.

"If you do not marry first. That young man could be snapped up tomorrow evidently. You could do worse. Rich as Golden Ball and the very model of a complaisant husband, if ever I saw one. And if I know anything of the matter, you will do well to provide yourself with a complaisant husband."

"Why should you think any such thing?" she said, bridling archly.

"Because I can see clear through to your shallow little heart, minx, and I know perfectly well what you want."

"I suppose I want what every girl wants."

"Not you," he retorted with a grin.

"What do I want, then?"

What I shall give you by and by, he thought to himself. He knew very well that by any code of conduct what he knew would happen between them would be unacceptable. To debauch a seventeen-year-old girl of good family, sister to his own brother's wife, was not the conduct of an English gentleman. But Dominick had no morals at all and behaved in a gentlemanly way only when it suited him to do so. Besides, he knew very well this was not an innocent young girl. She knew what she was up to and was obviously able to take care of herself. She was asking for it, and he was more than happy to oblige her by relieving her of the virginity that was so clearly a burden to her. Someone was going to do so in the very near future, if she had her way in the matter, and he thought it might as well be himself.

CHAPTER

6

25 June, 1811

My very dear Lydia,

I have received yours of the 2 June, and you will, I hope, forgive my late reply. The past four weeks have been taken up with preparations for Prinny's celebration of his Regency, which took place after several postponements on 19 June. I was teased constantly by Cressy to be allowed to accompany us to the Gala, but that, of course, was not possible. I shall be very happy when she returns home, for I cannot like the responsibility for her conduct. More of that later, for I know you will be bursting for news of the celebration. It was truly beyond anything for a gorgeous Spectacle, and though attended by at least two thousand people, was perfectly organized. The Regent greeted his guests in the uniform of a Field Marshal, quite resplendent, though it did not disguise his enormous girth or the fact that he was heavily corseted! However, he was perfectly charming to everyone.

There were mountains of food, oceans, all served on silver. It all began at nine in the evening, though we did not arrive before twelve. Then at half past two we and two hundred of the Regent's most honoured guests sat down to supper. In front of his place was a miniature fountain from which a silver-bedded stream flowed down each side of the table through mossy, flowering banks and under the arches of tiny bridges spanning the water here and there. Most amazing of all, there were swimming along in the stream minute silver and gold fish! Alas, some were dead and floated along the top, white bellies turned up most pitifully. It quite put me off the most delicious food, but then I have had little appetite of late.

I wore white silvered lamé on gauze and the Trowbridge tiara with the emerald. Please tell Happy that the stone is indeed as big as a hen's egg, though not as vulgar-looking as that would seem to be, nor is the tiara old-fashioned, though it became heavy after some hours of wearing. Everyone was most splendidly dressed, but I will wait to describe some of the gowns until we can be together, for I would be writing forever if I attempted to put it all down on paper.

The Regent's mama was not there. No doubt she felt it unsuitable to celebrate while the poor, mad King lies so ill. Nor was his daughter, which I can only guess was because he could not bear to have the attention focussed on anyone but himself on this long-awaited day, and Princess Charlotte does command a great deal of attention when she appears. Of course, that poor, wretched wife of his was not there either. His guest of honour was the Duchesse d'Angoulême, who sat on his right. On his left was his brother York's wife. Others were the ducs d'Angoulême, de Bourbon, and de Berri, the comtes de Lisle and d'Artois, and the Prince de Condé.

Oh, dear, how tiring it is to write of, but I will try to remember further details for our next meeting. As for Cressy, she has collected an assortment of young men who clutter up the drawing room nearly every morning. I cannot think where she had met them all, for I have not had the time to take her about. None of them are in the least suitable as a serious *parti* to my mind, and I am sure Papa would not approve, though one, a man named Hughes-Jones, is very, very rich, I have been told. I shall have to write to Mama that she had much better keep Cressy in the country until her come-out.

Georgina dropped her pen and rose to pace restlessly to the windows. She wondered nervously where at this moment Cressy might be. When the morning callers had left, Georgina had retired to the library to write her letter to Lydia, and Cressy had gone upstairs. Some time later Georgina had heard the sound of the street door closing softly and had gone

to see who had left the house. The hall was empty until
Honeyman, the butler, came from the servants' quarters on
the same errand.

"Oh, Honeyman, I thought I heard someone close the front
door."

"Yes, m'lady," he said noncommittally.

"We were both wrong, apparently. Well, please send Prentiss
to me in the library."

"Yes, m'lady."

When Prentiss arrived, Georgina sent her up to inquire if
Miss Cressida would like to go out for a drive. Prentiss
returned to report, as Georgina had suspected, that the young
miss was not in her room. On several occasions Georgina had
suspected Cressy was slipping out of the house without informing anyone, and now her worst fears were confirmed.
The servants must all be aware of it, for Honeyman would
admit Cressy when she returned each time and would speak
of it to the others. Naturally he would not feel it right to
speak of such a thing to his mistress, for that would imply he
was daring to make a judgement on the behaviour of his betters.

Papa would never be done scolding if he came to hear of it,
and if Cressy got into any sort of trouble or caused a scandal,
Lord Fitzhardinge would hold Georgina directly responsible,
though how he could expect her to spend her every waking
moment standing guard over the girl she could not imagine.

It was all most unsettling, and not the least of her worries
was that Dominick played some part in the busines. She had
seen the flirting between them, the exchange of meaningful
glances, and mentioned it to Myles, who had only laughed at
her and said her sister and his brother were two of a kind and
understood each other very well, so she was not to bother her
head with that. Well, she would have to speak to Myles
again. Even though Dominick might be awake on all suits,
she doubted Cressy was, though she was the slyest thing in
nature.

Honeyman came in to announce, "Lady Cunliffe, m'lady,"
and Georgina forgot everything to hurry across the room to
embrace the old lady.

"Dearest Aunt Selina, how could you know I was dying
for distraction? Come, sit down, and we will have a lovely
coze. Honeyman, bring some wine and biscuits."

"Well, well, my dear, let me look at you. No, you have

not changed as a result of the great honour of sitting down to supper with the Regent,'' she said sardonically.

Georgina laughed. ''I think I lost several pounds from exhaustion. You are looking remarkably well, I must say. Ah, here is the wine.'' She poured them each a glass and sat down. They sipped their wine and spoke of the Regent's party and various acquaintances before Georgina rose and began to pace about, straightening a picture, moving a vase of flowers, fluffing a pillow.

''You give me the fidgets, girl! What ever is wrong with you today?''

''Oh, I'm sorry.'' Georgina returned to her chair. ''It is Cressy, I suppose. She is—well—bothersome.''

''Hmm. That fool of a mother of hers should never have brought her here. The girl has no morals at all. Worse than Dominick.''

''Oh, lord, what *shall* I do, Aunt Selina?''

''Send her home. Not your responsibility.''

Georgina sighed, overcome with lassitude at all the unpleasantness such a course of action would arouse. ''Yes, I suppose you are right, though she will be bound to raise a fuss, and they obviously cannot cope with her at home either. I must ask Myles what to do.''

Lady Cunliffe eyed her sharply for a moment. ''All this round of gaiety becoming too much for you?''

Georgina sat up straighter and forced a bright, artificial smile. ''Not in the least. I enjoy it very much.''

''Nonetheless you look a bit peaky to me.''

''Nonsense.''

They sat in companionable silence, gazing into the flames of the small fire. At least Georgina did so, while Lady Cunliffe gazed at her. After some moments she shattered the silence abruptly.

''Breeding, aren't you, m'dear?''

Georgina dropped her wine glass, and the dark-red wine sank into the carpet. ''I—I—I—no—that is—at least—my goodness . . .''

''Thought so the moment I came in. Always shows. The skin takes on a sort of transparency. Take my word for it, I am always right in these things.'' Lady Cunliffe took a large gulp of her wine in satisfaction. Georgina picked up her glass and dabbed uselessly at the spilled wine with a napkin, her mind in complete disarray. Was it possible? She tried to count back, but could not order her thoughts well enough for it. She had not been feeling well, and her appetite had become strangely capricious.

"I—I cannot think—naturally I would be very happy if—it has been a year now. I had begun to think something was wrong with me."

"Trowbridge will be very pleased."

"Oh, yes, of course." Georgina's response was mechanical, her mind still whirling, turned in on itself. "I am sure he had begun to despair."

"Pooh! Myles is not given to such flights as that."

"No, of course he is not. How foolish of me to speak so of him."

"He has never said anything to give you such an idea, has he?"

"Oh, goodness no. He is much too kind to dream of doing such a thing."

"Kind." Lady Cunliffe tasted the word, then made a slight moue, as though it did not agree with her. "A strange word to use of one's husband. An elderly word, somehow, that I associate with vicars."

"For me it is a very important quality. I should not care for a husband who was not so."

"In the first year of marriage, when one is still in love with one's husband, one should prefer him to be hot-blooded, demanding, even unkind at times. All those delicious little making-ups. I know I should prefer it."

"We never quarrel," Georgina replied smugly.

"Good Lord! How very dull. No wonder you describe him as kind. You are clearly not in love with him."

Georgina fired up defensively. "I love him very much! I have never cared for anyone more."

"Very commendable, but hardly the same thing," replied Lady Cunliffe drily. "Since you do not know the difference, you can never have been in love."

"I do not understand you. Surely it is better to love one's husband truly than to profess some schoolgirlish infatuation."

"Schoolgirlish? No, no, not at all. In spite of my years I have not forgotten the last time I fell in love. I was fifty-three at the time, and it was as rapturous as the first time, when I was fifteen. The same dazed feeling, as though the rest of the world was seen through a mist and only my lover appeared to me in sharp focus, the same heating of the blood in the veins, the same exquisite torment of trying not to touch in public. Ah, even now the remembrance gives me pleasure.''

Her usual terse way of speaking had disappeared, her voice had become soft, and the words came slowly and dreamily. Georgina tried not to look shocked, though she found it profoundly so. An old woman speaking of such things! Georgina was too young and ignorant not to be prudish and condemning, and much too terrified of exposing her own heart to the possibility of pain to find falling in love a desirable state to be in. It all sounded too much out of one's control to appeal to her, and in her own mind she was satisfied that Myles would not have approved of such wild behaviour on her part. Certainly he did not act toward her in such a way. He was good and kind and loved her just the way she loved him.

Lady Cunliffe saw that Georgina disapproved and sighed for her. Poor child, she thought, so beautiful and so much backbone, even humour, and still so pitiful somehow. It must be Myles's fault. Had he set about things properly, she would be in love with him by now, though she was not when he married her. I would take my oath there is banked-down fire there, a passionate nature untouched. She is the spit of her own mama, and lord knows there was plenty of volatility there!

Strangely enough, Georgina was also thinking of her own mother, but along quite different lines. She thought that falling in love had been her mother's downfall. She had ruined her life, caused the first divorce in her own and the Fitzhardinge family, created a great deal of unhappiness for her husband—and abandoned her own child. Georgina unconsciously put both hands over her stomach, as though to protect the newly discovered life there.

I shall never leave my child, she thought fiercely.

The silence between the two women stretched out lengthily as each pursued her own thoughts, until Lady Cunliffe said, as though there had been no pause, "It is a pleasure, Georgina, a joy like no other on earth. I hope you will some day know it." Then abruptly, "Don't enjoy the physical part of marriage, do you?"

Georgina started, flushed, opened her mouth and closed it, then shrugged slightly. "Did you?"

"Good God!" exclaimed Lady Cunliffe in disbelief.

"It is not the most important part of marriage," Georgina cried mulishly, not liking the implied criticism in the old lady's voice, which seemed to say that she, Georgina, was lacking in something.

"Don't know where you come by such ideas. In my day girls had more sap to 'em. No doubt that po-faced stepmother of yours taught you these things. Never could abide those pale blond sorts of women. No spine at all and too prudish to admit to normal appetites like the rest of us. Pah! Makes me sick! You listen to me, my girl. If you want to hang on to your husband, rid your mind of all that duty rubbish." Georgina looked up, startled. "Oh, yes, I know all about that lecture on wifely duty. Never gave it to my girls. Told 'em what's what, I did. All hair-brained, my girls, but not so stupid they couldn't appreciate it. I told 'em straight out what—"

The door opened to admit Myles, who smiled and crossed the room to kiss his aunt, then Georgina. "Now, what are you ladies hatching up?"

"We were speaking of love, my boy, conjugal love," snapped his aunt aggressively, "and in my opinion—"

"Pour Aunt Selina another glass of wine, Myles," Georgina interrupted hastily, throwing Lady Cunliffe such a pleading look that the old lady took pity and desisted.

"No. I won't take any more. I must go now if I'm to have my nap before dinner. Give me your hand up, Myles."

He helped her out of the chair, and she bade Georgina good-bye and stumped across the room, still filled with all the things she would have liked to say to her nephew regarding his failings. However, if the dear girl did not want her to, she would not. Myles raised an eyebrow at Georgina and followed her out to help her into her carriage.

As she passed the cross street, Lady Cunliffe saw that a carriage had pulled up some way along, and stepping from it was Cressida Fitzhardinge, who tripped toward her, then round the corner to Trowbridge House. The carriage turned in the middle of the street and drove back the way it had come, but not before Lady Cunliffe had identified it.

That's Dominick's rig, she thought, I would know those

blacks anywhere. Now what is he up to with that cat-faced little chit? Nothing good, I'll be bound, she decided grimly.

Myles returned to the library and his wife. "Why are you in here, my dear, rather than the drawing room?"

"Oh, I like this room. It is more comfortable, and I came to write a letter to Lydia." Georgina, full of her secret, felt shy and uncomfortable with her husband. She should tell him, she knew, but simply could not think of how to do so. To avoid it a little longer she said, "Myles, I am worried about Cressy. She went out today, and I suspect many other times, unchaperoned and without telling anyone. What must I do?"

"Send her back to her mother. I cannot think why—" he broke off at the sound of the door knocker. "Now who can that be at such an hour, just when one is about to change for dinner?"

"Maybe Cressy . . ."

Myles crossed swiftly to the door and looked out just in time to see Honeyman admitting Cressy. "Come in here, if you please, Cressida," he commanded.

She came at once. "Myles! How you startled me. Hello, Georgie, darling."

Her blue eyes were wide with pretended innocence, and her cheeks flushed becomingly. She had, as Lady Cunliffe so aptly noted, a cat-faced look, her eyes wide-spaced, her face narrowing to a small, pointed chin, and just now a smug look of having lapped up a bowl of cream.

"Cressy, where have you been?" demanded Georgina.

"Only out for a walk. I became so restless, you see."

"You know perfectly well you must not go about the streets unaccompanied. If you had told me you wanted to go out, I would have taken you out in the carriage."

"Oh, well, then, next time I shall," Cressy said carelessly, having no intention of doing so. She had for nearly a month now carried on an affair with Dominick with great success. Today was the first time anyone but Honeyman had ever known she had gone out. She slipped out at least twice a week. Dominick picked her up around the corner in a closed carriage and drove her to his house on Jermyn Street. His servants were always discreetly out of sight and they went straight to his bedroom. If his lovemaking contained little of love, it was expert and ravishing nonetheless, and they en-

joyed each other thoroughly. The only problem for Cressy
was that it was of necessity curtailed to an hour, for even she
dared not be out longer. It was never enough, and now could
be even less. However, Georgina surely could not know any
of this and probably was not even aware that she had been out
before today. Cressy knew her sister would never question
the servants and allow them to suspect anything was wrong,
so if she just remained quite calm and matter-of-fact about
today, it would all blow over with no harm done. Myles dealt
this hope a deathblow.

"Cressida, I have decided to take Georgina to visit her
parents before going to Falconley for the rest of the summer.
We shall be leaving in the next few days, whenever Georgina
likes," Myles announced very firmly. He did not like the
idea of Georgina being worried by the responsibility of her
sister. It seemed to him she was not looking quite the thing,
so a stay in the country might be beneficial to her in any case.

"You mean you shall take me home?" Cressy asked in
disbelief.

"Well, we can hardly leave you here alone."

"But I do not want to go!"

"Naturally, I am sorry to be disobliging," he said politely.

"Oh, I think you are mean! You only want to be rid of
me."

"Cressy! How dare you speak to Trowbridge in that
manner?" demanded Georgina furiously.

"But what have I done that is so terrible?" stormed Cressy.

"Only you can know that, Cressida," Myles reminded her
quietly, "but if in order to do it you must slip out of the
house without informing anyone, we cannot be blamed for
putting a less than sanguine construction on your behaviour."

"Oh, I hate you! You are both cruel!" Cressy cried and
ran out of the room, sobbing noisily. She rushed to her room
to pen a hasty note to Dominick to tell him of her predicament.

Myles turned to Georgina helplessly. "I suppose I did not
handle that very well."

"Of course you did. You must not mind her. She is always
behaving tiresomely. Storms and tears and tantrums all to get
her own way."

"You will not mind going to Falconley so early?"

"Oh, no. I shall like it above all things!" Her eyes shone
with happiness at the thought, and the fire behind her haloed

her hair with gold. She was achingly beautiful, and he pulled her into his arms. She stiffened immediately, but did not pull away. He carressed her back, and they stood quietly, each enjoying the moment, though in very different ways. Myles loved to touch her still, though he rarely did so, since she did not seem to like him to, so the moment was precious to him. Georgina, though resisting automatically at first, realized almost at the same instant that she wanted him to hold her. Now, more than at any time in their married life so far, she felt the need of his protection and love. Now, she thought, now I can tell him.

CHAPTER

7

They made only a very brief stay with the Fitzhardinges, during which they were treated to Cressy's sulks, Lady Fitzhardinge's despondent sighs at having her difficult daughter on her hands again, and Lord Fitzhardinge's cold displeasure when he learned from Myles the reason for Cressy's return.

The only joy for Georgina was the time spent with Lydia and dear old Happy, who burst into tears when she learned Georgina was pregnant and sniffled happily for the length of their stay. Lydia, still in pursuit of science, dragged Georgina off for a walk down a country road and demanded to have the entire process explained to her. Georgina forced herself to tell everything to her sister, for she knew Lady Fitzhardinge would never do so, nor anyone else for that matter, and anything was better than the ignorance with which she herself had faced her wedding night. While it might revolt Lydia to hear now, she would by the time of her own marriage have grown so used to the facts that she would be inured to the whole business.

Lydia greeted the knowledge with a long, profound silence, during which Georgina feared she had after all done the wrong thing by exposing her young and innocent mind to such horrific truths. However, Lydia surprised her. "Well, given the fact that God equipped us so, it seems a reasonable arrangement," she said finally, with so much solemn practicality that Georgina could not help laughing.

She wished very much that she could take Lydia off to Falconley for a visit, but she knew Cressy would be outraged and Harriet would nag that it was surely her turn before Lydia's. The prospect of several weeks in Harriet's company caused Georgina to hold her peace, and after three days she and Myles proceeded on their way alone.

Cressy made life very difficult for her family after they had departed, bickering continually with her sisters, saucing her parents, sulking, weeping, and raging in turn at the least provocation. She watched the post anxiously for some word from Dominick, but no letter came, as she had known in her heart it would not. She had managed but one brief meeting with him before she was dragged away from London, and he had seemed more amused than distraught by their sudden parting and said casually that if he were in that part of the country, he would, of course come to call. She had longed to box his ear. She still longed to do so every time she remembered the look on his face.

Then one morning after she had been home two weeks she woke feeling uncommonly nauseous. This happened on several mornings before she realized what had befallen her. She sat down at once to write Dominick since she could not think of anything else to do. She got her father to frank her letter by telling him it was only a request to Trowbridge's brother to send her several books she wanted.

Naturally she did not receive any response to this letter, but within a week she was summoned to the drawing room, where she found her parents entertaining Mr. Hughes-Jones. He rose eagerly as she entered, his smile nearly cracking his face in two. He advanced upon her and kissed her hand fervently.

"Miss Fitzhardinge, how delightful this is. I hope you will forgive my arriving in this way without notice of my visit, but as I have just explained to your dear parents, I had business in this direction and could not deny myself the pleasure of paying my respects, especially after Barrowes mentioned your inquiring after me with such particularity. I had no idea that you—that is to say, of course since the moment we first met I—" He seemed to recollect his audience and ended lamely, "So of course I came at once." He pulled out a very large handkerchief and mopped his perspiring brow.

His thinning red hair stood up in a quiff over his round, red face, his pale-blue eyes were starting from their sockets, his fat chin was wobbling with his earnestness on its supporting neckcloth and high shirt points. Altogether he was a most unprepossessing figure, indeed, but to Cressy at that moment he was splendid. If ever she saw rescue at hand, this was it.

She dropped her eyes shyly and made him a small curtsey. "How very good of you, sir, to come. You are most welcome." She spoke with such heartfelt sincerity as to cause both her parents, who had received Mr. Hughes-Jones with rather haughty disapproval, to sit up and stare at her suspiciously.

"You are too kind. I was devastated when Barrowes told me you had returned home, I assure you, dear Miss Fitzhardinge. I—" He stopped to turn politely to her parents. "Oh, I do beg your pardon for blathering away in this fashion."

"Please sit down, sir," Cressy invited and sat down herself. "Mama, Mr. Hughes-Jones is a dear friend of Trowbridge's brother, Dominick Barrowes. Is it not kind of him to remember us and call?"

"Oh, yes, indeed." Lady Fitzhardinge looked flustered and somewhat bewildered by her daughter's enthusiasm. She could not imagine any woman's eyes lighting up at sight of so homely a man as Mr. Hughes-Jones.

"He called frequently at Trowbridge House to visit Georgie, so we became great friends," Cressy continued, varnishing the truth ever so slightly and giving the much smitten Mr. Hughes-Jones such a blinding smile that he was struck dumb and could only gaze at her bemusedly.

Lord Fitzhardinge cleared his throat disapprovingly. "Do you make a long stay in Kent, sir?"

"Oh, well, I—that is to say, several days."

"Do you visit friends, Mr.—ah—" asked Lady Fitzhardinge dutifully.

"Er—no. I am at the Bull and Crown in Eastly. They do you very well there, and only two miles away."

"Well, perhaps we may see you again before you return to London," said Lord Fitzhardinge, rising to his feet. "I must leave you now. Business, you know." He had clearly seen all he needed to see of this guest to convince him that he need not waste any more time on courtesies.

"Oh, but you must stay and take dinner with us, must he not, Mama?" declared Cressy.

Lady Fitzhardinge cast a nervous glance at her husband, but could do nothing but endorse her daughter's invitation.

"No, no," Mr. Hughes-Jones protested, turning brick-red

with embarrassment and gratification, "I would not dream of imposing myself on you in such a way."

"Please do not deny us, sir. We have so little company here we shall consider you are doing us a favour," replied Cressy gaily, ignoring her Papa's grim expression. "Now to pass the time I shall show you the gardens. They are quite lovely now. Just talk to Mama for a few moments while I fetch a bonnet, and we will go out."

She tripped happily away, her brain ticking over rapidly with plans for taking advantage of this unexpected windfall of luck. It was clear Dominick had sent this ridiculous man here and equally clear why: He was showing her his solution to her difficulty. The only problem now was Papa, who would be bound to forbid her marrying a man with so little address as Hughes-Jones, and at seventeen she would need her father's consent. No matter what her straits, she would never make herself the laughingstock of London by eloping with such a person. No, it must be a grand wedding and a prolonged wedding trip, and the wedding must take place as soon as possible.

She never paused to consider that she had not as yet received a proposal, for that, she knew full well, would present no problem. She could bring him up to scratch this very afternoon if she cared to, she thought with a giggle. In fact, she would do so! There was no time to waste, after all.

She returned to the drawing room, put her hand confidingly on his arm, and with a demure smile allowed herself to be led away to view the gardens. Fifteen minutes of shy glances up at him through her lashes, teasing little smiles, and soft sighs brought him to a strangled, inarticulate declaration of his feelings. Ten further minutes brought on an impassioned proposal. When she bashfully agreed to become his wife, he pressed her ardently to his stout chest and kissed her clumsily. She did not mind. She was much too elated with having proved herself right. Now for the difficult part.

"You will have to speak to my papa, of course, and I am not sure . . ." She pretended to falter as though overset with embarrassment. "My portion will be small, I fear . . ."

"My dearest girl, what could I possibly want with your portion? I have more than we could possibly spend in several lifetimes," he assured her eagerly.

She knew this very well, but she wanted to make sure he

made the fact very clear to her papa. It was his only trump card, and she had great faith in the persuasive power of money on her father's thinking. She encouraged her new fiancé to tackle the problem at once and escorted him into the house and up to the library door, where she allowed him to kiss her again for courage before she ran up the stairs to find her mama.

Lady Fitzhardinge, happily unaware of the blow fate had in store for her, sat before the glass in her dressing room, trying on several bonnets she had ordered from London. She turned from side to side to view the delicious Venetian bonnet trimmed with wreaths of straw and flowers, which she thought most becoming to her, and smiled as she saw Cressy entering the room.

"Is not this the most divine bonnet, Cressy? I vow I have not had one this age that suited me half so well. What have you done with Mr. Crewes-Smith?"

"Hughes-Jones," Cressy corrected her automatically. "He is speaking with Papa."

"Oh, you should not have allowed that, dearest, for it was clear as clear your papa took him in great dislike at first sight, though I was sure you would not be able to bear his company alone until dinner. Such an infinitely boring young man, with so little address. It was really too bad of you, Cressy, to fob him off on your papa after inviting him to stay to dinner in that forward way." Lady Fitzhardinge leaned forward to pull a curl over her ear and inspect the result. "There, that looks even better, do not you agree? Whatever made you do such a thing anyway?"

"He is asking Papa for my hand," Cressy said bluntly.

"Wh-a-a-t!" shrieked Lady Fitzhardinge.

"I said he is asking Papa for my hand," Cressy repeated, much enjoying the sensation she had created.

"My vinaigrette—where?" Lady Fitzhardinge scrabbled about amongst the scent bottles and pots of rouge on her dressing table, found what she sought, and waved it below her nose. "You cannot be serious, Cressy dear. You are only saying that to tease me, are you not?" she begged faintly.

"No."

"But why would you allow him to do such a thing? It will only make your papa cross."

"Well, if I am to marry him, he must ask Papa for permission, of course."

"Marry him?" Lady Fitzhardinge again had recourse to her vinaigrette. "You are cruel to tease me so," she whimpered. "Do leave off and go away."

"Mama, I am going to marry him."

"You cannot. Why, you are not even out yet. To throw away all your chances on that jumped-up mushroom—"

"He is no such thing. He is from a very good family and has masses of money."

"Ah! In trade, of course. No, no, dear child, it will not do. Why, he is not even good-looking. One might understand an infatuation with an attractive—"

"Oh, for heaven's sake, Mama," Cressy exclaimed in exasperation, wearying of the game, "I have accepted his proposal and we are to marry and that is that."

"Never! I will never consent to it, nor will your papa, if I know anything," declared Lady Fitzhardinge stoutly.

"Well, you will, and so will he," cried Cressy furiously, her eyes flashing.

"Go to your room at once, Cressida. I do not care to discuss this further," ordered her mother loftily.

"Mama—I—*must*—marry." Cressy spaced the words out carefully, pointedly. Lady Fitzhardinge, about to order her away again, turned to her, eyes wide and searching. As Cressy's meaning slowly penetrated her understanding, her look changed to one of horror. "Oh, Cressy, darling—please, no—"

"Yes, Mama," Cressy said inexorably.

"Not—not his?"

"Of course not." Cressy looked her contempt at such a silly question.

"Who—?"

"Oh, what difference does that make? *He* will not marry me. Nor would I want him. Hughes-Jones will do me very well. He's rich as Croesus and has entrée everywhere, despite his looks."

A maid tapped at the door and entered looking somewhat frightened. "M'lady, m'lord wants you and Miss in the drawing room. *At once*, he says."

"There! I knew it would be so. In a great taking, I make no doubt?" The maid nodded. "You see, Cressy!"

"Come along, Mama. Take off the bonnet. That will do," Cressy said, turning to the maid, and waited for her to leave the room before continuing. "Now, you must convince Papa that this is a good match and that you approve. Remember how rich he is, and I will help with Harriet and Lydia's dowries," she added with rash inspiration.

She pulled her wavering mama from her seat and led her downstairs to the drawing room, where her father waited, his expression one of affront and outrage.

"Oh, Fitz," faltered Lady Fitzhardinge, seeing his face.

"One moment, madam, if you please. Cressida, that dreadful young man has had the unprecedented effrontery to come to me with a request for your hand in marriage."

"Yes, yes, Fitz, is it not wonderful? He—"

"You will oblige me by remaining silent while I am speaking, madam! Now, Cressida, he further tells me that he has made you an offer and has been accepted. Explain this to me, if you please."

"He has proposed, and I have accepted. We hope we may have your blessing, Papa."

"My *blessing*?" Lord Fitzhardinge thundered. "Can you seriously suppose I would give my blessing to such a match for you? Have you lost your senses entirely? I will lock you in your room for a year first!"

Cressy gave her mother a meaningful look, and Lady Fitzhardinge, realizing the disastrous result of any such course of action, sprang to her daughter's defense. "Really, Fitz, how will that answer to anything? I cannot think why you have taken so against Mr. Drews-Forbes. I find him a perfectly unexceptionable *parti* for Cressy."

"You must be mad," whispered Lord Fitzhardinge, staring at his wife as though he had never seen her before.

"And simply enormously wealthy, Fitz, with entrée everywhere. Why, you heard yourself he is received at Trowbridge House. He is *very* rich, Fitz."

"But he is ridiculous! You will make yourself a laughing stock. He has no breeding at all, an absolute want of conduct! I could never bear such a son-in-law. I cannot—How rich?"

"Millions of pounds," Cressy answered promptly.

"And they will help with Harriet and Lydia, Cressy says, Fitz," added Lady Fitzhardinge triumphantly.

"You are only seventeen, Cressida. You have not had

any opportunity to meet other young men,'' Lord Fitzhardinge persisted, unwilling to give in easily.

"Now, Fitz, you must not stand in the way of young love. Besides, no matter how much she looked about, she would never find a man with more m— Well, to my mind it is a very good thing. You know how volatile Cressy is,'' she added significantly.

Lord Fitzhardinge threw up his hands in defeat. He knew very well how volatile his daughter was, though he would have called it something else. Well, well, the man was very wealthy, and the Lord knew he needed help with the other girls' dowries. At least he would not any longer fear to find her in the arms of a stableman. That would now be Hughes-Jones's responsibility.

CHAPTER

8

Myles smiled around at Georgina as he expertly maneuvered the curricle around a sharp curve, and she, aware of his look, smiled back almost shyly. Their pleasure in each other's company had grown each day since their return to Falconley. Her news that they might expect a child by next January had filled him with an elation he had never known, and with it a surge of tenderness and renewed passion for his girl-bride. He had during the past year slowly begun to accept that she would never be able to give him the sort of love he had hoped for in a wife. Oh, he knew very well that she loved him. She had told him so shyly but with such obvious sincerity that he could not doubt her. She did not, however, enjoy him making love to her. She never rejected him, of course, but neither did she try to pretend it was other than a duty to which she resigned herself. He pitied her, but could only suppose it was so with most young, delicately bred girls, who were not allowed, as were young men, to develop that side of their nature. Some young women, of course, regardless of their station, seemed to have the knowledge and urge anyway, like Cressy. Not that he would want a girl like Cressy for a wife. He shuddered at the thought and wondered yet again at her choice of Hughes-Jones for a husband. She could have married him only for his money, or perhaps it had been necessary for her to make such a precipitate marriage. She had been caught slipping out of the house only the one time, but no doubt she had managed to do so many other times. He remembered Georgina's suggestion regarding Dominick, but he brushed it aside again. Dominick would never behave so, in spite of his reputation. He had written Myles a sardonic but hilarious description of the wedding, which he had attended in the role of best man.

Georgina had been inclined to feel she must post back to London for the event, but Myles had put his foot down adamantly, and she had been feeling too unwell to oppose him.

For the past several days, however, she had been much improved. The dark smudges had disappeared from beneath her eyes, which seemed now to sparkle with good health. She was more beautiful than ever, he thought, and also softer and more yielding somehow. She had liked him to hold her when she had felt ill, and now she was better, she still seemed to find it pleasant. His hopes were high.

He reached out impulsively to press her gloved hands, clasped together in her lap. She cast her eyes up in a brief smile and then looked away hastily from the warmth in his eyes, as they were just passing through the village and were being observed with great interest by Mrs. Hatchby, the vicar's wife, and Hester Knyvet.

Hester smiled meaningfully at Myles, ignoring Georgina's bow, and turned to comment with acid satisfaction that she thought Georgina was looking somewhat dragged.

"Well, I must say, if you will forgive me disagreeing with you, dear Miss Knyvet, that I thought she looked exceptionally well. Of course"—Mrs. Hatchby tittered and blushed at her daring—"if she did look dragged to you, there is reason enough, I think."

"Reason?"

"Well, she is—ah—increasing. Did you not hear, Miss Knyvet?"

Hester seemed to sway, and her eyes rolled up so far in her head that Mrs. Hatchby screamed and looked about wildly for help. Hester recovered, however, turned without a word of farewell, and marched stiffly away, a white line of rage visible about her grimly compressed mouth.

Blessedly unaware of all this, Myles and Georgina bowled on through the village and arrived home again. He helped her down from the carriage and up the steps with such exaggerated care that she could not help laughing.

"I am not made of glass, sir," she teased.

"No, something far more precious and beautiful than that, my love," he said ardently. She laughed up at him, her amber eyes glowing with happiness, and abruptly he pulled her into his arms and kissed her. She was taken off guard, her defenses forgotten after the joy of the afternoon they had shared, and the touch of his mouth sent a sweetness sweeping through her like a brush fire. She melted against him, her mouth softening, seeking, her head swirling, her senses clamouring—out of control—then suddenly she was pushing him away, her eyes wide with shock. She turned abruptly and flew up the stairs, unaware of the satisfied grin on her husband's face as he watched her go.

She closed the door of her room and stood gasping, her hands pressed to her hot cheeks as though to push back the colour. Good God! What had come over her to behave so? She felt as though she had been teetering precariously at the edge of an abyss. One more moment—one second!—and she would have plunged into chaos. All her carefully built-up control of her feelings lost in one unguarded moment.

No, no it would never do. Those abandoned, wanton feelings had no doubt led her own mother to her downfall, but they must never be allowed to hold sway over herself. It did not occur to her that her mother had not behaved with her own husband as she herself had done. If it had occurred to her, no doubt she would instantly have found an argument against it just the same, for she had invested too many years in protecting her emotions to be able to give way so easily.

Within a week Myles found it necessary to return to London to confer with his man of business. The hopes raised by Georgina's moment of surrender had been regretfully relinquished. Perhaps it had been foolish of him to have expected more. Perhaps no girl whom a gentleman would be willing to marry was capable of passion, which would explain why nearly every married man of his acquaintance kept a mistress.

He thought of Angelique, tiny and dark and deliciously curved, who had cried when he had said good-bye to her on his marriage. She had been set up a month later by Lord Heatherton and was still with him. He sighed regretfully, then shrugged. There were, after all, many others.

Georgina, waiting for Lydia's arrival, strolled slowly up and down the length of the picture gallery at Falconley, which was lined on one side with enormous muddy paintings of long-dead Barrowes ancestors and on the other with long French windows overlooking the flagged terrace and shallow steps leading down to the flower gardens, shrubbery walk, maze, lake, and at the end the greenhouse that provided fresh fruit and flowers the year round to the house.

On pleasant days the windows were thrown open, so one could walk out onto the terrace, but today a storm lashed the trees into frenzies and threw the rain against the glass, so that it sounded like a giant throwing pebbles. Georgina had ordered fires to be made up in the two large fireplaces, and they crackled cheerfully, dispelling the damp chill and giving the room a confortable glow, despite its enormous length and rather echoing emptiness. The gallery was also the Falconley ballroom and contained little in the way of furnishings beyond the stiff little gilt chairs lining the walls beneath the pictures.

This was one of Georgina's favourite places when the weather made outdoor activity impossible, as it did today. Not that she was capable of a great deal of activity anymore, she thought, looking down at her burgeoning figure. She clasped her hands across her stomach protectively and strolled on, wrapped in a mindless contentment. All the nagging fears and doubts regarding her relationship with her husband had evaporated in these past months to be replaced by this placid euphoria. It was the first time in her life she could remember feeling that she owed nothing to anyone. She was so patently fulfilling her obligations that nothing more could possibly be expected of her. She could spend endless stretches of time staring into a fire or just into space, thinking of nothing at all in particular and probably, she thought, looking for all the world like a cow. No wonder Myles found so many reasons to be away. Not that she minded being alone, she rather enjoyed it, but she knew she *should* find it intolerable. But while she could acknowledge the fact, she could only shrug in response. She could not be bothered with guilt for her shortcomings when something so physically momentous was happening within her own body.

This blissful state had slowly overtaken and drowned the vague uneasiness she had experienced for several weeks after her last visit in London with Lady Cunliffe, whose talk of being in love and enjoying going to bed with one's husband had caused Georgina to feel less than her usual complacence about her marriage. She had been previously rather smug about it, feeling she and Myles got along very well together, always solicitous for each other's comfort and well-being, never indulging in little fits of pique or crossness that might set off a quarrel. It had all seemed very adult and reasonable and soothing. Such courteous kindness between them could never lead to the sort of scenes she had had to endure between her irrascible, cold father and her flighty but manipulative stepmother and surely never to the heartless self-indulgence of her own mother.

No, no, she was sure Myles liked her just the way she was, and if she had never experienced any of those ecstatic emotions described by Lady Cunliffe, neither had she exposed herself to the possibility of pain. It seemed to her a fair exchange. She enjoyed the even, measured pace of their lives, and cocooned in her pregnancy, accepted Myles's more and more frequent and prolonged absences with equanimity. After all, there was little reason for him to stay, for she knew she was a far from stimulating companion now, and the other thing had been tacitly finished between them since her fourth month, he having sensed her reluctance and with gentle tact refrained from coming to her bed. She did miss the contact of being held in his arms, the only part of lovemaking she enjoyed, when after the embarrassing assault on her body, he lay warm and solid against her, enveloping her as she drifted off to sleep, her head on his muscular shoulder, emcompassed in the security his presence gave her. At those times she came closest to what Aunt Selina described as being in love with him. It was incomprehensible to her that she could enjoy those moments so much when she shied away from caresses at other times. She could not realize that any submission to his caresses before the act might seem encouragement for him to come to her bed, but the lovemaking being an accomplished fact, she could relax her guard and enjoy his presence.

She shivered now, remembering the heat of his body with sudden yearning, and went to stand before the fire, hugging her shawl closer about her. He had written that he would be returning in a week or ten days and had meanwhile sent his own old nurse, Nanny Apple, to attend her, and that good woman was already ensconced in the nursery suite, knitting away contentedly while she awaited her new charge.

The door at the far end of the room crashed open suddenly and Lydia swooped down the room to embrace her. "Georgie, darling! Heavenly to be here at last! How glorious to see you, and how very much more of you there is to see!" She giggled happily and stood back to admire. "You are monumental!"

Georgina laughed. "You will make me self-conscious. Am I so large?"

"Well, certainly. How strange if you were not! Oh, Georgie, thank you for inviting me. Harriet was furious! Not that she really wanted to come. In fact she would be embarrassed to death even to see you like this, you know what a prude she is, but she felt done out of her rights, if you know what I mean. What a tiresome creature she is, to be sure, and now, with Cressy gone, one somehow *feels* Harry more. What a divine room!" She suddenly spun away and waltzed down the shining parquet floor, her arms spread wide.

Georgina felt all at once light-hearted and gay and longed to waltz herself. She laughed delightedly and held out her hands. "Come back, darling, and we will go into my sitting room and have some hot chocolate and a long coze. Oh, how glad I am that you came."

When they were settled before Georgina's sitting room fire with their chocolate and a plate of cakes between them, Lydia sighed happily and stretched her toes toward the warmth. "Oh, heaven to be away from home, though I shall miss my lessons."

Georgina looked up. "Lessons? But you no longer do lessons, do you?" Lydia was nearly fifteen now and must surely be out of the schoolroom.

"Oh, I thought I had written you about it. I decided I should learn some useful things, so I made Papa get someone to teach me a more advanced French than Happy's and some Spanish."

"Spanish? Good lord, of what use will Spanish be to you?"

"Well, you never know . . ." Lydia blushed and turned her face away. This was so unprecedented that it caused Georgina to study her closely. She said nothing, however, for she would never try to pry confidences out of anyone. Presently Lydia looked back at her rather shyly and continued, "Do you remember Tarquin Ladbrook, Georgie?"

"A revolting little boy with black curls and toads in his pockets," responded Georgina promptly. "Goodness, I have not thought of him for years. Papa and Sir Gareth Ladbrook were great friends, and they came to stay once years ago."

"Yes, that one. He is not at all revolting any more, though."

"Aha! You are smitten with the young man, I take it," Georgina teased.

Lydia blushed furiously but looked at her steadily. "Yes," she said with devastating seriousness.

"Why, my dear, forgive me for teasing you. I had no idea, of course. Tell me about him," Georgina requested contritely.

"Well, Papa met him in London and wrote to say he was bringing him down and hinted that he hoped Harry was looking her best, and Mama got all twittery and silly and had a new gown made up for Harry and had Carstairs do her hair with the curling iron. Harry went about for days before they arrived looking mysterious and fraught. You know how she does."

Georgina nodded. "Like a constipated goose."

Lydia giggled. "Exactly. Then they arrived, and oh, Georgie, you should see him! All those black curls and soft black eyes and so tall and self-confident."

"He was always that. I still remember him walking up to me without the least hesitation and dropping one of those horrid toads down the front of my gown." Georgina shuddered.

"I *remember* that. How you did shriek! Oh, he *was* wicked! But now he is in the Army—a lieutenant, on Wellington's staff."

"Oh? *Oh*—hence the French and Spanish. You plan to follow the drum?"

"Well, if we were still at war," replied Lydia with her usual practicality.

"But my darling girl, you are only fifteen, and Papa would never allow it."

"Yes, I know. We shall have to elope, though I am not *entirely* sure I can persuade Tarq to do it."

"I am happy to hear one of you is sensible. But you have left out a great deal, surely. I mean, if he was brought home for Harriet—"

"Oh, I am sure you can imagine. Scenes and tantrums and accusations that I had deliberately set out to steal him away from her out of spite. I pointed out that he was hardly hers to be stolen, if you take my meaning, and I could hardly help it if he preferred to talk with me about his war to following her about picking up her fan every five minutes, which she conceives to be a most flirtatious way to behave. Honestly, Georgie, if you could *see* her, all those awful curls bouncing around and looking coy and simpering at him. It would put any man off. And it isn't as though she really cared for him herself!'' Lydia concluded indignantly.

"No, I am sure she did not,'' soothed Georgina, "she does not really care for men at all.''

"But she is *possessed* to marry. I shudder with pity for the poor man she finally captures.''

Georgina hesitated for a moment before she said carefully, "Darling, you are still very young to be thinking of marriage.''

"Oh, yes, I know that. But I am prepared to wait, and he has told me that *he* will, so that is all right. I shall just go along with my lessons and develop patience. Tarq says soldiers must learn a great deal of patience, since between battles things can be very boring.''

Georgina's lips twitched at her seriousness, but she only said, "Who are you studying with?''

"The curate. Young, nice-looking, and just the *kindest* person imaginable. He knows all about Tarq and never teases or lectures me. He is even nice to Harry, though you can tell he does not like her, for she ogles him shamelessly. I shan't have him too long, I fear. He has a very important patron with several livings in his gift who has promised him the next vacancy.''

"Has anyone heard when Cressy will be returning from her wedding journey?'' Georgina was not terribly interested in impecunious curates, however kind.

"In a week or so, I believe. She is breeding, too, you know.''

"What? So soon?''

"Well, not so soon as all that, or do I mean quite a bit sooner than should have been expected of her?''

"I cannot quite untangle that. Please stop being mysterious and tell me what you mean.''

"Well, you know I told you about Hughes-Jones just appearing that day and becoming betrothed to Cressy before dinner? I just happened to be outside Mama's dressing room door that day.'' Georgina raised a sardonic eyebrow. "Yes, well, I happened to be there because I saw Cressy come in with him from the garden and take him to Papa's study and let him kiss her. Ugh! He was all fat and red and damp! Anyway, then she went running up to Mama, all sort of excited-looking, and I followed and—listened.''

Lydia repeated what she had overheard that day. "And

while I can never get anyone to tell me what is going on, I hope I am not such a pea-brain that I could not put the real meaning to that. She was pregnant, knew the man would not marry her, and wasted no time getting poor old Windy to come up to scratch. Really, Georgie, one has to admire her for looking out for the main chance. They were not in the garden quite half an hour, and I will swear she never gave him the time of day in London. I mean, you could not imagine *anyone* encouraging him unless they were desperate.''

"So that was what all the rush was about. I wanted to come to the wedding, but I was feeling so unwell myself just then that Myles would not hear of returning to London. It must have happened while she was visiting us there, and I suppose I must be held responsible for not watching her more carefully.''

"Believe me, no one could do so if she did not want them to. She is so sly! Like a cat, really, and always lands on her feet too!''

At that moment Cressy was a very sick cat, lying on her bed in the cabin as the ship wallowed through the waves of a rough Channel crossing. Her ungainly figure rolled from side to side, and she moaned miserably, feeling extremely sorry for herself.

She had sent her husband in search of hot water, thinking that if she could only wash her face, she would surely feel better. Windy had set off eagerly, happy to be of service. He had tried to take care of her when her abigail had succumbed to even worse *mal de mer* than her mistress, but he knew he was making a poor job of it. He was oppressed by guilt for having insisted that they must return to England for the birth of his child, for not suffering sea sickness, for causing his wife to be pregnant, and for the dreadful weather. Only the first was his responsibility, though he was not aware of this, naturally.

He found a steward and ordered the bowl of hot water, and when it was brought, took it from the man and carried it to his wife's bedside.

"Here we are, my dear, and a cloth and towel. I will just bathe your face and arms, and you will feel very much better in a trice, I promise you." He leaned lovingly over her, his red face perspiring from the closeness of the cabin. Cressy rolled her head on the pillow and groaned, too wretched to care what he did. She had already forgotten about the hot water. Her blond hair lay in limp strands over the pillow, her eyes were sunk back into darkened hollows, and her skin was pallid and doughy-looking. "Poor old girl, you do look a sight," he said commiseratingly.

"Arg-g-g." Cressy gurgled with rage and flung up a hand, tipping the bowl of hot water down the front of her husband's clothes.

"Oh! Now that was too bad of you, dearest," he said, trying not to be cross.

"Get out," she whispered weakly.

He set the empty bowl on the bedside table and tried to take her hand. "Now, my love, you know I would not leave you—"

"Get out," she repeated more forcefully.

He spluttered and muttered, but made his way to the door, where he turned back to say, "I know what will set you up, dear girl. You need something on your stomach, a nice basin of gruel. I shall go and—"

Before he could finish, she had, with the strength of righteous anger, picked up the empty bowl and hurled it across the cabin, where it missed his head by inches and shattered on the doorframe. His pale-blue eyes bulged in horror at her for a brief instant before he retreated hastily.

She lay back in exhaustion, tears of self-pity rolling down to soak her already damp pillow. How will I ever be able to bear the man? she thought. However, she knew this was only because she felt so wretched at the moment. Actually, he did very well for her. She had twenty-three trunks full of gowns and bonnets and furs and lingerie in the hold as well as her stuffed jewel box under the bed and as complaisant a husband as could be desired. He gave her everything she wanted, made very few demands of his own, and was more gullible than she would have dreamed possible. She had carried on two delectable affairs in Paris under his very nose, and he had known nothing of them at all. She had not wanted to return to England until after her child was born, not only because it would be much easier to subtract a month from its age that way and no one could really be sure, but also because Frenchmen seemed to find the fecund woman extremely desirable.

Here, however, she had found the one thing upon which Windy was adamant. His child must be born in the ancestral home, as he and a long line of first-born Hughes-Jones sons had been, and nothing could budge him from this stand. As a result she had been forced to return to England, and of course he must choose to sail on a day like this, when the rough seas guaranteed one would become ill. She moaned most piteously as the ship plunged down a wave and then climbed steeply up another.

CHAPTER

9

It was Lydia who first met Mrs. Conyers. With the ebullience and energy of her youth and the eager friendliness of her open nature, Lydia had rapidly made the acquaintance of every neighbour within riding or driving distance from Falconley. Though Georgina went out daily in good weather for a walk in the shrubberies or a sedate drive to take the air, she rarely went beyond the Park, and naturally did not ride any more at all, being now in her seventh month. Lydia, however, accompanied by a groom, rode every day, and besides driving Georgina about for her airing, was often driven into the village on errands or to make calls there or at nearby manors on her expanding list of friends. She had become a pet of old Lady Venables, who chaperoned her to evening parties considered suitable for a fifteen-year-old after Georgina began to feel her condition too obvious to allow her to appear at such functions. It was at one of these parties that Lydia was introduced to Mrs. Conyers and came home extolling her to Georgina.

"A perfectly delightful woman, Georgie, and so young-looking, for all her hair is snow-white, and so amusing, though there is something sort of mysterious and sad about her eyes at times."

"Good heavens, so many contradictions. Next you will tell me she is a rare beauty though an antidote and poor as a church mouse though wearing a king's ransom in jewels," teased Georgina.

"Just the opposite. She is wealthy as Croesus and wears no jewelry at all," riposted Lydia defensively.

"Now there *is* a contradiction, and so tiresome of her. How is one to know she is wealthy if she will not oblige us with some display of jewelry?'' complained Georgina with mock seriousness.

"Well, she has taken Cobhill Priory, which Lady Venables calls a vast pile like a castle, and it has been entirely restored and refurnished and is simply crawling with servants, and she keeps three carriages and a large stable," returned Lydia triumphantly, "so I think there can be no doubt she has money. Oh, Georgie, don't laugh at me, pray. You will see I am right about her when you meet her and you will love her at once, as I did. As everyone does. She is all the rage hereabouts, I do assure you, everyone falling all over themselves to entertain her."

Georgina, accustomed to Lydia's enthusiastic flights, only smiled indulgently and said, "No doubt you are right, darling, but as I do not go about at all, it is unlikely that I—"

"Well, actually, Georgie, I invited her to call. I hope you will not think I am too forward. It is your house, I know, but I cannot like you never going about or having anyone amusing to talk to."

"But I am perfectly content, Lydia."

"Well, you should not be. Trowbridge should be here more, taking you into company, entertaining here. It cannot be wholesome to be so turned in upon yourself."

"Oh, come now. Myles cannot be forever hanging over me, nor would I want him to be, and as for company, I have you and enjoy you very much, and you bring me news of the outside world."

"It is not good enough," Lydia maintained stubbornly, feeling there was something left out of the argument, but not sure enough of her ground to be able to state her feelings clearly. "Anyway, will you receive Mrs. Conyers if she calls?"

"I hope you do not think I would be rude to a friend of yours, Lydia," reproved Georgina gently, wishing nevertheless that Lydia had not invited the woman. For the past two months Georgina had paid no calls and had discouraged visitors, being more and more reluctant to have the cocoon she had woven about herself and the child she carried disturbed. She had accommodated Lydia within it and the occasional descents upon Falconley by Myles, but did not care for any other intrusions, content with the slow, uneventful cycle of the days as they unrolled toward the birth of her child.

In the event she received Lydia's new friend graciously and found Mrs. Conyers to be all that Lydia had claimed for her, though Georgina's initial reaction did not match her sister's enthusiasm, since she was not the sort of person open to immediate and warm response to new people. She gave her trust and regard only after enough time had passed to make certain a too hasty judgement would not end in distress for herself.

When Honeyman, the butler, announced Mrs. Conyers four mornings later, Georgina looked up from her embroidery to see an elderly white-haired woman in the doorway. As the lady advanced across the room, however, the most unnerving transformation seemed to occur, as though with each step she shed years, until she halted to extend her hand, and Georgina saw as she rose to greet her that the lady could not be more than forty years old, if indeed that. Her complexion was fresh and unlined, her eyes bright, her smile delightful.

Georgina was in a state of some confusion, for added to the other phenomenon was the conviction that she had met Mrs. Conyers before, and this so teased her mind for some moments that she was grateful for Lydia's entrance and eager greeting, which carried them through the first moments. When they were all again seated and wine had been ordered, Georgina resumed her embroidery and covertly studied her guest while she and Lydia exchanged neighbourhood news. Mrs. Conyers was girlishly slim and tall, with something regal in her carriage that was belied by the striking warmth and kindness of her manner. She was dressed entirely in black, a recent widow, Georgina surmised, though nothing had been said on the subject. She wore no jewelry at all, as Lydia had reported, not even a wedding ring, though the permanent-looking indentation at the base of her ring finger indicated one had long had residence there.

During a pause between the other two Georgina took up her duty as hostess. "Lydia tells me you have taken Cobhill Priory, Mrs. Conyers. It has remained uninhabited for so many years you must have found it in a sad state of disrepair."

"Not when I finally moved into it, Lady Trowbridge. My agent bought it for me and had all set to rights before I ventured into it."

"You bought it sight unseen?" Lydia exclaimed.

"Yes. I was—out of the country, you see, and wished to

move into it directly I arrived in England. I do not care for London.''

"How courageous of you," replied Lydia admiringly. "What if you had disliked the house or this part of the country?''

"Why, then I suppose I should have had to find another place," said Mrs. Conyers calmly.

"You are from this neighbourhood, Mrs. Conyers? Before you left the country, I mean.''

"No. It was recommended to me," said Mrs. Conyers. "Of course, the house is far too large for my needs, and a great many hands are required to keep it up, but I like it very well, and I suppose it provides employment for many people around here who might be forced otherwise to take service far from home.''

The visit ended after a correct half-hour, and though nothing of any importance was discussed, Georgina found Mrs. Conyers pleasant and somehow soothing. Her presence did not chafe by airs or fidgets or inquisitiveness, nor her conversation unsettle by speculation or innuendo or subtle malice against absent acquaintances. While not breathless with anticipation for her next visit, for it had been settled that she would call again, Georgina was still able to accept the idea with pleasure.

By the time Lydia's visit came to an end, Mrs. Conyers was well established as a regular friend of the household and without any discussion took over Lydia's few duties when she had gone.

There had been no snow at all as yet, though December was well advanced, and the weather remained mild, with enough warmth for Mrs. Conyers to drive Georgina about the Park nearly every day and take dinner with her several times a week. She did not try to force the friendship into intimacy, never confided her inmost feelings or details of her life, nor asked for those things from Georgina, seeming content to provide only pleasant conversation and companionship with no demands. She seemed to know intuitively that Georgina wanted only those things from her, and so slowly Mrs. Conyers was accepted into Georgina's cocoon in Lydia's place.

Whatever the older woman's thoughts regarding Lord Trowbridge's continued absence, she never expressed them. She gathered from occasional remarks made by Georgina that my lord was much occupied with the smooth running of his various estates and was often required in London to take his seat in the House and that Georgina was not discontented that this should be so.

Mrs. Conyers began to worry, however, when the carriage rides became more and more sporadic and finally ceased altogether as Georgina professed to a disinclination to move from her sofa before the fire. Mrs. Conyers's disquiet grew as Georgina became paler and her eyes seemed to sink deeper into the dark smudges that surrounded them. She gently questioned her about her health, but desisted when Georgina cried out that she could not bear to be nagged about how she was feeling. A moment later she apologized for her outburst and begged Mrs. Conyers to forgive her.

"Dearest Georgina, indeed I do understand perfectly and must ask your pardon, for I feel just as you do when I am not feeling my best and so should have known better. Let us not speak of it again. Have you heard from dear Lydia?"

"Oh, I meant to tell you at once. She wrote from London. The family have taken Harriet up for her second season, but Lydia says it is all a waste of time and money. She does not believe Harriet has much chance with all the London beauties to outshine her and thinks she would be better off at home, where she might tempt some gentleman looking to marry up."

Mrs. Conyers laughed at this typically caustic wisdom from Lydia. "Oh, the darling girl, how I do miss her!"

"And I. But of course it must be much duller for you, dear Mrs. Conyers. I am not very amusing company, and you must be sadly moped by me."

"Oh, I am content. I prefer a quiet life, you see."

"Still, I feel sure all your friends must be quite out of charity with me for taking up so much of your time."

"My dear, they have all been very kind to me, so newly come into their midst, but I cannot with the greatest good will in the world claim to crave the excitement of a morning visit from Mrs. Hatchby or a musical evening at the Knyvets," replied Mrs. Conyers drily. "At this moment I would far rather be where I am hearing of Lydia's doings in London. What else had she to relate?"

The moment passed without further comment, but before she left that evening, Mrs. Conyers suggested casually that the doctor had best be asked to come around and prescribe a tonic to bring the colour back into Georgina's cheeks before Lord Trowbridge arrived and became alarmed by her paleness. Georgina agreed to this, and Mrs. Conyers promised to speak to the man on the following morning.

The doctor's recommendations of beef tea and port wine did little to restore Georgina or even arrest what Mrs. Conyers considered a rapidly deterioratióng condition. She wished there were some member of Georgina's family she could apply to. Lady Fitzhardinge would have been the obvious choice, though what Mrs. Conyers had learned of her from Lydia did not incline her to turn to that lady for advice. She considered writing of her worry to Lord Trowbridge, but feared he as well as Georgina herself might consider it unwarrantable interference on her part, as though she, a comparative stranger, thought fit to tell my lord Trowbridge how he should go on. However, when Prentiss drew her aside one morning to whisper worriedly that my lady was surely in a bad way, "For did I not see it happen so with me own mam and her losin' blood in the same way before she lost her last two," Mrs. Conyers forgot all the petty niceties that had inhibited her until now and sent a message posthaste to Lord Trowbridge in London.

She then calmly but with great authority led a weakly protesting Georgina away from the breakfast table and upstairs to her room, where with Prentiss's help she put Georgina to bed and sent a tearful Nurse Apple off to order a groom be sent to fetch the doctor again.

The old doctor examined Georgina and declared there was little amiss that would not right itself by her staying in her bed for a few days. After again stressing the benefits of beef tea and port wine, he went away, a smile of amused tolerance expressing his feelings about women's tendency to take alarm over the least things.

Two days later Georgina went into violent though mercifully brief labour and delivered a tiny eighth-month girl in such a welter of blood that for many hours Mrs. Conyers and Prentiss, working grimly to stop the flow, feared her life must surely be draining away. The doctor, convinced his summons was again the result of hysteria, did not feel it necessary to respond with any undue haste, and so found the emergency over when he did arrive. Faced with a premature baby whose life expectancy was dim and a young mother unconscious and as white as the linen of her pillow, he could only cluck with distress and commend Mrs. Conyers on her skill in bringing the hemorrhage under control. The weary contempt in her eyes caused him to hurry away busily to the nursery. Nurse Apple had wrapped the baby warmly and put it in a crib before the blazing fireplace in a nest of hot bricks. The doctor shook his head and clucked again. When he had examined the tiny scrap of humanity and declared she could hardly be expected to survive many hours, Nurse Apple pursed her lips stubbornly and turned her back on him.

Though the bleeding had ceased, Georgina's temperature began to rise, and by nightfall she was delirious, calling out piteously for Myles, and once, in a strangely childish voice, for Mama. Mrs. Conyers continued wringing out cold cloths and laying them on the burning forehead, while the tears poured down her face unheeded.

Georgina became lucid at intervals and asked for her child. Finally Mrs. Conyers told her that they dared not move the baby from Nurse Apple's care at present.

"A . . . boy?" Georgina whispered weakly.

"A girl, my love. Do not talk any more now. You must rest."

Prentiss carried in fresh basins of cold water every few minutes as Mrs. Conyers continued bathing Georgina's burning body, and at last the fever broke. They then wrapped her in several blankets, carried her to the chaise longue, and changed the soaking sheets. This process was repeated three more times before the night was over, but when the first faint light of day began to show, Georgina's fever abated, and she sank into a normal sleep. The worst was over.

Prentiss brought Mrs. Conyers a cup of chocolate and forced her to sit down and drink it. Just as she leaned back wearily to take a sip, a maid came running with the news that Lord Trowbridge's carriage had just entered the drive. Mrs. Conyers set the cup aside, rose to smooth her hair, and went down the stairs to face yet another ordeal.

CHAPTER

10

When Honeyman had relieved him of his coat and hat, Myles strode quickly across the hall for the stairs, then halted in surprise as he saw the woman coming down. She seemed elderly and leaned heavily on the banister, her face white and drawn, dark circles of fatigue beneath her eyes.

"My Lord Trowbridge, do not—please—it is all over," Mrs. Conyers faltered uncharacteristically in her eagerness to allay the fear she could see in his eyes.

He stiffened, the colour draining out of his face. "What—?" he said harshly.

"It is a girl, my lord," she replied coldly, thinking that was the news he sought.

"No—my wife?"

"Oh, forgive me, I thought—She will be well now, though it was very difficult for her. She—"

His body slumped a bit, and a hand came up to cover his eyes for a moment, then he was bounding up the stairs past her. At the top he turned. "Oh—I beg your pardon for my rudeness. You are—?"

"Mrs. Conyers."

"Of course, Georgina's friend. How do you do? Is the child well? A girl, you said?"

"Yes, my lord, to both questions," she said, smiling.

"Fine."

He turned and hurried away to Georgina's room and let himself in. Prentiss was bustling silently about, tidying the room. He motioned her away with his head and turned to the still figure on the bed. He knelt beside Georgina and put a tentative hand on her shoulder. Her eyes fluttered open. "My dear, are you all right?"

"It is . . . not a boy, Myles," she whispered sadly.

"I know, my love. It is a lovely girl."

She turned her head away sharply to hide the tears that stung her eyes. Myles reached to turn her face back to him. "Why, Georgina, what is it? Why are you crying?"

"You wanted . . . wanted an heir, and I—did not . . ."

He felt love and compassion flood through him so forcefully that he nearly cried aloud. He pulled her into his arms and held her close. "I only want you to be well!" he whispered brokenly into her hair, realizing in that moment that nothing in his life was as important as this girl. The nightmare ride from London after Mrs. Conyers's urgent message, the mounting, unthinkable fear, the dreadful moment on the stairs when the woman had said it was all over and he had thought Georgina lost to him forever, and the ragged, clawing pain of desolation that had seemed to tear him asunder had all led to this moment of revelation when he acknowledged the true depth of his feelings for her. He knew now that all his brash thinking in the past regarding the married state had been mere whistling in the wind to convince himself he did not need a wife's love so long as she gave him heirs and he had a mistress to answer his needs. This was not true and had never been. He wanted only Georgina and he wanted her to love him. He wanted intimacy and loving companionship with this woman only and, by God, he would have it!

"Myles . . . I . . . I am very tired," Georgina said faintly.

He laid her tenderly back upon the pillows. "Forgive me, love. I have wearied you. Go to sleep now, and I will just sit here quite quietly and hold your hand."

She fell asleep almost instantly, and he sat unmoving for over an hour, her hand in his. Then Mrs. Conyers came in.

"Sir," she whispered, "you will forgive me for ordering your servants, I hope, but I made sure you would be wanting your dinner and asked that it be prepared. Will you not step down to the dining room? Prentiss will sit with Georgina."

He put Georgina's hand down carefully on the coverlet and rose with stiffly protesting muscles to follow her out of the room. In the hallway he said, "I will just go along now to see the child first and will join you when I have washed and changed." She nodded and turned away and he went along the hall to the nursery.

Nurse Apple curtsied and beamed and bustled over to the

crib before the blazing fire. "Come, Master Myles, and see your daughter," she ordered, in the same voice with which she used to bid him to wash his hands when she had charge of him as a small boy.

He bent over the small scrap of humanity, too tiny to seem real, and touched the tip of an infinitisimal nose. "She is very small," he murmured.

"And what would you expect and her a month before her time," demanded Mrs. Apple belligerantly. "She is very well for all that."

"Yes, of course she is," he replied soothingly. "May I pick her up?"

"No, you may not. The less she is handled at this stage, the better. You tend to your wife. She is a brave girl," commended Mrs. Apple decisively. Then she told him of Georgina's ordeal and all Mrs. Conyers had done.

When he entered the dining room later, he felt almost lightheaded with exultation, relief, exhaustion, and hunger. Mrs. Conyers joined him a moment later, and he noticed that she had changed into a dinner gown of black velvet, stark in its simplicity but exceedingly elegant. He realized with something of a shock that despite the white hair she was not the elderly lady he had first thought her to be. The dark circles were still there, but it was clear that the lady was a long way from elderly, was probably in fact a near-contemporary of his. He began to rise, but she waved him back.

"Please do not stand on ceremony with me tonight, Lord Trowbridge. I know you must have ridden hard to have arrived here so soon after my message and must be exhausted." She took the chair Honeyman held for her.

"Then you must not stand on ceremony with me, Mrs. Conyers, but must call me Myles," he returned with a tired smile.

"Very well, Myles, I will do so, thank you."

"Nurse Apple has told me how indebted I am to you. It is her opinion Georgina could not—have survived her ordeal without you." The wine glass he held trembled as he stumbled over the words, and he set it down abruptly.

She did not remark upon this, saying only, "Then I am glad I was here. Georgina has become very dear to me in the brief time of our acquaintance."

He looked at her appreciatively. What an admirably restful

woman this is, he thought. He liked her lack of mannerisms, the uncluttered directness of her replies, her serenity. "I think we are all fortunate in that. Georgina wrote me of all you have done for her since you came into the neighbourhood. Are you from these parts, Mrs. Conyers?"

"No, I came from Devon, but the neighbourhood was recommended to me by a friend after I returned from India."

They went on together very comfortably, speaking of the house she had taken and her experiences in India. She asked him of his plans now, and he told her he would remain at Falconley for some time, that nothing could induce him to leave while his wife was so ill.

"I only regret that I was not here when I was needed."

"You could hardly have foreseen that it would be necessary to return so soon."

"I should have returned long ago. I should never have left her—"

"You must not get into the way of thinking you could have prevented the course of events by your presence. You had after all your estates to attend to and your business in London."

He thought guiltily of his "business" in London, and decided that tomorrow he would write to his solicitor, instruct him to deliver a handsome sum to his latest mistress, and be done with her once for all. There would be no more mistresses for him.

For the next two weeks, while Georgina was confined to her room, he spent most of the time there with her. He sat quietly while she slept, fed her himself, read to her, brushed her hair, and carried news of the baby from nursery to mother. When Nurse Apple felt it was safe, he carried the baby herself and put her into Georgina's arms.

"What name have you chosen for her, my love," he asked.

"Selina, for your aunt," she said promptly.

"Well, well, my Lady Selina, how does that suit you?" he said, bending over to plant a hearty kiss on the little face.

"Oh, be careful, Myles! She is so—so delicate," cried Georgina anxiously.

"Pooh, she is only small," he assured her. "You must not worry so, my dear."

But Georgina did worry through every waking moment and was plagued by fearful dreams besides. Each time she heard the child crying she sent Prentiss or Myles running to inquire the reason, and her first waking thought each day was to wonder if the child had survived the night. When she was able to be on her feet again, she went herself each morning to assure herself on this point before she rang for Prentiss to bring her chocolate.

Despite these anxieties, however, she displayed little outward demonstration of love for the baby, rarely picking her up or cuddling her, seeming content to stand by and watch while Nurse tended her. She knew that Nurse Apple and Myles were puzzled by this, but could not explain her behaviour even to herself.

Only Mrs. Conyers understood that Georgina, always fearful of opening her heart before she was assured she would not suffer hurt, was still haunted by her fear that the child would not live and held her love at bay. It only expressed itself in her continuous anxiety. Mrs. Conyers said nothing, however, aware that this was not the kind of fear that could be allayed by the reassurances of others, which to Georgina would be only empty words. Only time and, God willing, Selina's continued good health would ease the problem.

Mrs. Conyers came to dine nearly every night, and when Georgina had recovered sufficiently, accompanied her first on walks about the grounds on good days and later for drives. Myles gradually relaxed his vigilance and spent more time on long-neglected estate affairs. When these required him to be away for part of a day, he was reassured by the presence of Mrs. Conyers. He never stayed away for more than a few hours and always returned for dinner. Afterwards Georgina liked to sit beside him on the sofa, holding his hand, or lying against his chest, his arm about her, if they were alone, while he read aloud to her.

So the cold, grey days of the new year wore away in quiet and healing, as Georgina regained her health and Selina showed every sign of progress, and Myles subdued his growing need of his wife and devoted himself to being what he felt she wanted of him most at this time: a man of strength to lean upon and to protect her, a man who demonstrated his love without demands. The rest must wait.

Georgina gradually let go of her dreadful fear of losing Selina, and the worst of her nightmares ceased to trouble her sleep. When the child was five months old, Myles had word from one of his tenants on a property he held far to the north near Scotland. The man begged him not to allow the steward to dispossess him of the farm his ancestors had tilled under the Barrowes family since anyone could remember, though he had fallen behind with the rent. He was sure, he wrote, he could make it up with this year's crop, which promised well.

This letter upset Myles dreadfully, and though he did not like to leave Georgina now and would not dream of allowing her to make such a tiring journey, he felt he must go himself and straighten out the problem.

"Of course you must go, Myles," protested Georgina, when he told her of the business. "I am perfectly fine now and have Mrs. Conyers for company, so you must go and not worry—and come back as quickly as you can," she added with a smile that caused him to wrap her in his arms.

So he went away, and Georgina and Mrs. Conyers were together more than ever. The weather turned delightfully warm, and they drove out to visit in the neighbourhood and, now that Georgina felt again equal to it, they rode every morning when it was cool.

During the afternoons they liked to sit beneath the trees on the grass or in the summerhouse with their sewing and books. Nurse Apple would join them with Selina when she had wakened from her nap, and Georgina would hold her while Mrs. Conyers read aloud. There were letters from Myles several times a week, reporting his progress, and letters from Lydia to report on the family and give them the news that Tarquin Ladbrook had returned to his regiment in Spain.

The days passed lazily, almost dreamily, and though Georgina missed Myles, she was not discontented.

CHAPTER

11

Georgina's carriage turned from the dust of the dry road onto the gravel drive of her old home, and she sighed gratefully as she patted her face, hoping she was not simply making streaks in the dust that had settled there. Not only there either, since her entire body felt coated dryly, as though the dust had filtered through her clothes. Prentiss took out a fresh handkerchief, soaked it in eau de cologne, and passed it across to her. "Just a bit again on your nose, m'lady. There now, you'll do, though you shall have a bath before dinner. I vow, I have never known such a dry August."

The carriage swept up to the door, and the footman jumped down to open the door and let down the steps. Georgina was ascending the front steps before the doors were thrown open and an astonished butler came hurrying out.

"M'lady! I had no idea—"

"I came without warning, Jelkins, as soon as I had Miss Lydia's letter. How are Mrs. Jelkins and young Jem?"

"Very well, m'lady, I thank you," the man replied, much gratified by her inquiry. He later confided to the staff, "M'lady has no side to her at all, though she is a countess now."

"Is Miss Lydia at home?"

Jelkins looked suddenly grim. "She is, m'lady, but very poorly to my way of thinking. Fair breaks my heart, she does."

"I will go straight up to her. My compliments to my papa and Lady Fitzhardinge, and tell them I will not see them until dinner, that is, if they dine at home tonight."

"They do, m'lady. I will tell them. Jakes"—he turned to

the hovering footman—"stop dawdling about and help m'lady's abigail upstairs with these cases."

Georgina hurried up the stairs, praying she would not encounter any members of her family, and scratched softly at Lydia's door. She heard a sighed "Come" from Lydia and thankfully slipped into the room and closed the door.

Lydia was reclining listlessly upon a chaise longue before the open windows, but when she saw Georgina, she started up with a cry and ran into her arms, where she immediately burst into tears and sobbed unrestrainedly against her breast. Georgina held her tightly until it seemed to her there was a diminution and then led her back to the chaise.

"There, darling, just lie back, and I will bring water to bathe your face." She stripped off her gloves and removed her bonnet, then fetched a basin of water and a cloth, and dropping to her knees beside Lydia, began tenderly washing her tear-stained face. "Goodness, the dust in my gown has been turned to mud, I fear, and smeared itself all over you."

"Oh, Georgie, did I ruin your gown?"

"Pooh, what of that? Now, that is something better, I think." She dropped the cloth into the basin and took Lydia's hands. "Dearest, I was so sorry to hear of poor Tarquin. Your letter came yesterday, and I came at once."

"Oh, Georgie, the baby—"

"Is very well with Nurse Apple," Georgina replied firmly, and with only the smallest pang of the fear she always felt when she thought of her frail little daughter. "You are the one who needs someone now."

"Dear Georgie, I did so long for you to come, but I did not like to ask you to travel in this wretched heat." Lydia sat up and blew her nose. "There, now, I feel so much better. That was the first time I have allowed myself to really cry, though I seem to sort of ooze tears when I am alone."

"But my darling child, why?"

"I could not bear for *them* to see me do so," sniffed Lydia. "They are all so—so—expecting and, well, hovering."

"But surely that is natural, Lydia. They are your family and—"

"Yes, perhaps I am being unreasonable, but still I could not. I cannot believe in their sympathy, when they were so indifferent to our love when Tarquin was alive. Mama only laughed and teased me, and Harry pouted and talked about pushing little girls trying to make themselves important, and Papa said Tarq was not a very stable type of young man if he preferred me to Harry. So I could not accept anything from them now.''

"Yes, I see," sighed Georgina, thinking how typical this was of her family. "Tell me, love, how did you learn of it?"

"His papa wrote and sent me a letter Tarq had left with him to send me if—if anything should happen to him.'' She reached into the pocket of her gown, extracted some folded pages, and passed them mutely to Georgina.

Georgina drew back. "Oh, no, I—"

"Please. I want you to read it, Georgie.''

Georgina took the letter reluctantly. It was but two pages and already soft from much handling, and when she opened it out, it proved to be blotched with tear stains. She began to read:

My Darling Lydia,

If you are reading this, it is because I will not be able to come to you myself ever again. That thought is unbearably painful to me now, and I know it will be grievously painful for you, and I wish I could think of some way to save you from it, but I cannot. I will not tell you not to grieve for me, little one, for it would be dishonest of me to make such a pretense of nobility. But after enough time has passed to ease your hurt, I hope you will remember our talk about being a soldier or the wife of a soldier and that we both must accept the possibility of sudden death, since it is an inherent part of the profession. We both agreed that prolonged grief was destructive. Do you remember, darling girl?

Now, though we may not yet have said our vows in church or known any of the joys of life together when you read this, I consider you my wife, a soldier's wife, who will allow sorrow its day and then return bravely to life. For you are so very young, my love, my beloved, and so obviously created to love and marry and have children. So do not allow grief to harden your heart. Open yourself to life, and someone will appear who is worthy of you. That is what I want for you.

Thank you for loving me and giving me the happiness of loving you.

Your Tarquin

* * *

The tears were running heedlessly down Georgina's cheeks by the time she had finished, and when she became aware of it, she turned away to hide them. Lydia's arms came about her and held her close. "It is all right, Georgie." And then somehow Georgina's head was on Lydia's breast, and Lydia was comforting *her*.

After a time Georgina sat up and dried her eyes. "What a help I am to you, to be sure."

"Do not say that, Georgie dear. It does help me, truly. I think it must help you also. You know, I do not remember ever seeing you cry before. I always wondered if you could."

"I—cried a great deal—once. It only made things worse for me."

"That must have been when your mother went away. Papa should have comforted you, but of course he would not be capable of that."

"No, of course he would not," Georgina agreed humbly, wondering how it was that Lydia could accept that fact so matter-of-factly when she had struggled against its truth all her life.

"Georgie, may I—could I—come to stay with you for a time?"

"For as long as you like, darling. That is exactly why I came. I made sure you would be better away from here."

"Did Myles come with you?"

"No, he was from home when your letter came. I brought only Prentiss. Now, it is late and I must go and rid myself of this dreadful dirt. I warn you the roads are hard as iron and the dust simply awful."

"I shan't mind anything," Lydia declared fervently. "I so look forward to seeing little Selina, and dear Mrs. Conyers again. I suppose if you are going down to dinner, I will also, though I warn you if that disagreeable Sir Vernon Braye is there, we shall both regret not asking for trays brought up to us."

"Why, who is he?"

"Another of Papa's attempts to rid himself of Harry. How he can even consider Braye, I shall never understand. The man is disgusting! He leers at me shamelessly, and if Harry is not looking, I make sure to keep well away from him, for he is always touching me." She shuddered. "I did warn Harry, but she accused me of making it up because he preferred her. I try not to think she deserves him."

Georgina smiled and went away to her room, where she found Prentiss waiting with her bath all filled. Georgina undressed and sank gratefully into the scented water. Before she could really enjoy it, however, there was a sharp rap at the door, immediately followed by the entrance of Lady Fitzhardinge.

"My dear, do forgive me, I could not get away sooner to come and greet you. How well you are looking."

"Thank you, Mama. I came to take Lydia back with me. I hope you and Papa will not object. I think she needs to get away."

"The very thing! How thoughtful of you. It will make everything so much easier here also, now that Sir Vernon is showing such a marked partiality for Harriet."

"Lydia mentioned him. Who on earth is he?"

"Oh, a charming man, I do assure you, and so eligible. Pots of money and a delightful estate not ten miles from here, though he has been abroad for years and years. The property came to him through his uncle, you remember old Billington? Well, his sister was Sir Vernon's mother."

"Lydia says he is not very nice."

"Oh, my dear, you know how sisters are. Always jealous of one another's beaux. And now, of course she simply casts a pall over any attempt to entertain the man."

Georgina wondered how it was possible for her papa and this empty-headed woman to have produced so wise and sensitive a soul as Lydia. "I think it must surely be understandable if she cannot hide her unhappiness after losing her fiancé."

"Yes, poor darling, too tragic," agreed Lady Fitzhardinge, her eyes filling with easy tears.

"How did it happen? Was it a battle?"

"No, no. Fitz says only some trifling skirmish, which makes it all the worse. Somewhere in the mountains of Spain. Did Lydia tell you Tarquin left her money?"

"No! Good heavens!"

"Yes, is not that wonderful? I do assure you your papa was pleased, for now he can make Harriet's portion larger. It seems Tarquin was left the money by his mother, so it is not part of the estate, which will now go to a cousin, since Tarquin had no brothers. His mother's money is not a fortune, but it is a tidy sum and will add enormously to Lydia's chances of attracting a really eligible husband. Now with

Harriet nearly off, I am thinking of bringing Lydia out next year.''

While Lady Fitzhardinge prattled on, Georgina stepped from the bath into the towel Prentiss held for her, aware that her stepmother ran a sharp eye over what she could see of her figure to assess the ravages of childbearing.

Let her, Georgina thought, though she resented it just the same. Such a trivial woman, only concerned with looks or clothes or money, and no depth of feeling at all with her shallow sympathy and facile tears. Yet kind to me and always patient, she recalled, trying to be fair. I never remember her losing her temper with me. Too much trouble, no doubt, she thought, reverting to irritation, because she was tired and wished the woman would go away and allow her a few moments of peace before dinner.

"Do you not change for dinner, Mama?"

"Oh, good heavens! What a goose I am. I shall never be dressed in time and I wanted Carstairs to do Harriet's hair. Oh dear, oh dear, and Braye coming too.'' She hurried away.

Georgina was helped into her sea-foam-green muslin, and when Prentiss had dressed her hair, she went to Lydia's room. The two went down the stairs arm in arm. As they reached the hall, Jelkins was just opening the door to an urgent rapping. Lydia winced back. "Braye! Oh, lord.''

But the gentleman who entered was evidently not Braye, for Lydia started with an inarticulate cry of happiness and ran forward to greet him, hands outstretched. When Georgina came up to them, he was holding Lydia's hands against his chest with both his own while she gazed mutely up at him, tears running down her face. He was murmuring, "Yes, my dear, I know. It must seem unbearable, but God does not send us unbearable trials. Take your grief to Him, and he will give you the strength to bear it.'' He released her hands to give her more practical help in the form of a handkerchief, which she accepted gratefully and began mopping at her face.

"How good of you to come, Adrian. I wrote only to you and Georgie, and now here you both are. I am truly blessed with good friends. Of, Georgina, you have not met Adrian Patterson, have you? He was my tutor, you remember. He is now the Vicar of St. Edward's in Toverton.''

"Mr. Patterson, very nice to make your acquaintance at last,'' Georgina responded warmly, for she liked the young man very well at once. She held out her hand, and he bent over it gallantly and returned the compliment.

Then Lady Fitzhardinge came down and greeted Mr. Patterson flirtatiously, congratulating him on his new appointment. It was clear that she found him attractive. He was a good-looking young man with dark hair and soft grey eyes and a clear, healthy-looking complexion, not tall, but very agreeably set up.

"Are you visiting in the neighbourhood, vicar?" Lady Fitzhardinge asked gaily.

"Why, not really, my lady. I came to see Lydia."

"Oh? Lydia?" Lady Fitzhardinge looked bewildered.

"She wrote to me about the death of young Ladbrook, and I came at once to offer my sympathy."

"Oh—oh, to be sure, the poor young man. How kind of you. I am sure Lydia is most grateful to you. You will stay to dinner, will you not?"

"I would not want to upset any arrangements."

"Not at all." Lady Fitzhardinge brightened. "It will be a favour to us all if you and dear Georgina can prevent Lydia from falling into a fit of the dismals at the dinner table. We have Sir Vernon Braye coming, you see, and I think it is so important to present a cheerful, happy family at table when a suitor comes to call. Do come along to the drawing room."

"Mama, I am sure Adrian would like to step upstairs and refresh himself before dinner," Lydia interjected.

"Oh, yes, of course. Jelkins, show Mr. Patterson to the Blue Room and have hot water brought to him at once. Now, do not take too long, Mr. Patterson. Lord Fitzhardinge becomes very irritable if he is kept waiting for his dinner." She tittuped away to order another place set at the table, and Adrian, with an engaging grin at the two girls, followed Jelkins up the stairs.

Lydia turned to Georgina. "Is he not the kindest creature in all the world to come to me at once?"

"Indeed he is. A very nice young man. Who are his people, do you know?"

"Not really, only that his father is a farmer."

"A farmer! Well, he certainly has done very well to get preferment so young, and only a farmer's son."

"Oh, he has a wealthy patron, remember I told you of it? Anyway, the man has several livings in his gift, and one came vacant not a month ago, so he gave it to Adrian. I am so pleased for him.''

As they turned away to the drawing room, Georgina wondered about Adrian Patterson, the farmer's son with finely bred features, and the mysterious wealthy patron who took such an interest in him and his advancement. She stopped herself from going any further with these thoughts when she realized it was the sort of idle speculation worthy of Lady Fitzhardinge.

The Fitzhardinge dinner table that evening was not to Georgina's way of thinking exactly cheerful, though Lady Fitzhardinge and Harriet kept up a steady barrage of empty chatter, each flirting openly with Sir Vernon, who sat between them. Georgina had loathed the man on sight, barely able to meet his eyes for fear he would see her distaste reflected in her expression. She knew Lydia was right and the man was not nice in the least. She was surprised her parents did not see this and hesitate to entrust their daughter to him. He was a muscular man of about five and twenty, and not ill-looking, but the cold, pale eyes and loose mouth spoke to Georgina of nastiness, even decadence. When introduced to her, he had pressed her hand significantly, his eyes raking deliberately down her figure. He had then looked up and smirked to show his approval and after that had eyed her openly all evening.

Lydia was barely civil to the man and confined her conversation exclusively to Adrian Patterson and Georgina. When the ladies withdrew to the drawing room, Harriet at once accused her of being rude to Sir Vernon.

''And ogling that curate all through dinner in that disgraceful way. The next thing you know he will be dangling at your shoestrings looking to marry up.''

Lydia looked at her sister contemptuously but refused to be drawn. Georgina, however, was outraged by her attack and faced up to her. ''How uncharitable you are, Harriet. Have you no sensibilities at all that you accuse your sister of such a thing when she is mourning the loss of her betrothed?''

''Betrothed? Ridiculous! Papa would not allow them to be betrothed until Lydia was at least out. She is only trying to make herself interesting with these die-away airs. But I think Braye is too clever to be taken in by such poses. He does not care for women who are not gay and animated.'' She gave her curls a triumphant toss and trilled an artificial little laugh, perhaps as an illustration of what Sir Vernon preferred.

Lydia gave her a look of disgust, rose from her seat beside Georgina, and moved down the room to the pianoforte, where she stood turning over pages of music with a pretense of interest until the gentlemen rejoined them.

Sir Vernon ignored the open invitation in the look with which Harriet greeted him and plumped himself down beside Georgina. "Well, at last I have the impatiently awaited opportunity to speak to you privately, Lady Trowbridge," he said, leaning toward her and speaking breathily into her ear.

She drew away. "How mysterious that sounds, sir. Are you passing on secret messages?"

"Indeed I am, dear lady, and my heart with it," he whispered. Harriet, a red spot of angry colour on each cheek, rose and flounced across the room to her mother, turning her back on them. Braye immediately put a damp hand on Georgina's bare arm and continued, "Your beauty has completely mesmerized me, fair one."

Georgina looked down at the hand and with great deliberation withdrew her arm. "I do not care for idle flirtations, sir."

"I made sure you did not the moment I saw you, and I assure you nor do I," he said eagerly. "I promise you I have never been more serious. Believe me, I never flirt with silly girls, dear lady. I prefer experienced, warm-blooded married ladies who know their way around," he said, smiling insinuatingly into her eyes.

She rose. "You must excuse me. I must speak to my father," she said freezingly. As she walked away, she saw Harriet cross at once and sit down beside Sir Vernon. Georgina went to her father who stood before the open French windows.

"Papa, walk with me on the terrace. I must speak to you." He led her out into the hot, still night. "It is about Harriet," she began at once. "You must not let her encourage that man. He is a shallow flirt, and unless I mistake the signs, a womanizer. He even tried with me just now. He will make any wife miserable."

"Please do not meddle in what does not concern you, Georgina," Lord Fitzhardinge replied coldly.

"But of course it concerns me. She is my sister!"

"She is my daughter, and you must allow me to know

what is best for her welfare. She must marry. She has had two Seasons and no offers at all. Sir Vernon is of good family, has a sizable fortune, and has shown decided interest. I cannot pretend to myself that he has fallen in love with her, but he wants to settle and set up his nursery, he says. If he offers for her, she will accept, and I will give them my approval. You approval is of no importance whatsoever.''

Georgina could think of nothing more to say after this, and they walked for a time in silence while she decided she truly disliked her father. When they turned at the end of the terrace, he said, ''Young Patterson has asked my permission to write to Lydia in his capacity of her spiritual advisor to offer her the support of religion in her sorrow. Very proper, of course, to apply to me first, and I see no reason to deny her such a comfort. Since she will be staying with you for a time, I thought you should know this and that I have allowed it. I would not care for it to be too frequent a correspondence, of course, so you must be vigilant. I will inform her that you or Trowbridge must be shown all his letters and her replies.''

''But I cannot. Letters between a vicar and—''

''Yes, I am sure they will be everything that is proper. I have found him to be an exceedingly sensible young man, who would not be so foolish as to look so high as a daughter of mine. It is not for him I take these precautions. It is for Lydia. She is of a volatile disposition, I fear, and much too precocious for her age in matters of the heart.''

''But she truly loved Tarquin Ladbrook and behaved very sensibly, not volatile in the least.''

''Pooh, a mere adolescent infatuation.''

''And what of him? Was his love for her only adolescent infatuation?''

''It was foolish and ill-advised.'' Lord Fitzhardinge snorted disapprovingly.

Georgina gave up. She could never understand this man who was her father. She would go away tomorrow, she decided suddenly, and take Lydia with her and leave Harriet to her fate. As her papa had reminded her, her opinion was of no moment to anyone.

CHAPTER

12

Though Lydia was not the gay, animated soul she had been on her previous visit to Falconley, her sore heart did find the peace there she had not been able to find in the midst of the unfeeling regard of her family. She threw herself into Mrs. Conyers's arms with obvious pleasure in renewing their friendship and was enchanted to make the acquaintance of her niece. She found she could spend quite long periods in the company of Selina without thinking once of Tarquin. She spoke openly of her loss when she felt it and allowed the tears to come when they would, and her speech was frequently interlarded with "Tarq always said" or "as Tarq used to tell me" in the most natural way.

The three women spent part of every day together, riding before breakfast through the cool morning mists, sitting together over their needlework in the beautiful little domed summer house on the south lawn, or dining together. Lydia saw few of her friends from her last visit, preferring not to air her loss around the neighbourhood. The heat of August slowly turned into September and eased its oppression, as the long, quiet days and understanding compassion of Georgina and Mrs. Conyers eased the hurt in Lydia's eyes.

She had received two letters from Adrian Patterson, to which she had replied. She had insisted Georgina must read his first letter, as she had promised her father she would, but Georgina had refused to read her reply or indeed any further correspondence between them. His first letter was for the most part a recital of his new duties as Vicar of St. Edward's. There had been gentle reminders of the solace of faith, and nothing at all that could possibly be deemed as rousing precocious passion in the heart of a grieving young girl.

Georgina felt a positive satisfaction in rebelling against her father's dictates in this matter.

Georgina also spent some time writing letters, for Myles wrote frequently, demanding news of her health and of Selina's progress. His letters were warm and loving and made her impatient for his return. When he was away from her, she always made serious resolves to be more loving with him, to indicate her willingness to receive him into her bed, for at the back of her mind was always an unexamined but nagging guilt about this aspect of their married life. Men, she knew, had these needs and appetites, and she was aware that Myles must feel deprived.

The quiet of the autumn days was disturbed by Cressy and her family, who descended upon Falconley suddenly and unannounced in an eruption of baggage and servants. They came in an impressively glittering yellow travelling carriage, surrounded by four liveried outriders and followed by a second, less ostentatious, carriage containing her abigail, his valet, the nurse with baby Simon, and piled inside and out with their boxes.

"Georgie, hello, hello!" Cressy cried gaily, waving out the window as the carriage came up the drive. Georgina and Lydia, warned by the footman's yard of tin when the carriage turned in at the gates, were standing on the steps, waiting to see who could be coming to visit them in such extravagant style.

Cressy descended from the carriage, still talking. "Are not you surprised? Oh, this is famous. If you could see your face! We have been visiting all summer, and I could not resist coming on here when we were so near. I adore visiting. I told Windy you would never forgive me if you learned we were but twenty miles away and did not take you in, did I not, Windy? Why, Lydie! I had no idea! How you have grown up!" Cressy kissed them both enthusiastically, bade her husband do the same, and prattled on unceasingly, at the same time issuing orders and counterorders to her servants and succeeding in creating a vast confusion.

Georgina sent Honeyman to sort out the chaos and quietly propelled the still-babbling Cressy into the house, while Windy followed, grinning proudly at his vivacious wife. When they were finally settled in the drawing room and Cressy was forced to draw breath in the middle of her catalogue of the houses they had been visiting and the fascinating people they had encountered, Windy made a shy reference to his son and the admiration he had elicited from all who saw him. It was only then that Georgina realized the child accompanied them, and she immediately rang for Honeyman to have him fetched down so that she could see him.

"If we are to have him, let us have your babe at the same time and have done with babies for a while," Cressy said, clearly of the opinion that the smallest amount of time spent in the company of children constituted a surfeit.

Simon Hughes-Jones, at six months, was a shock to Georgina, despite the forewarning she had had in a letter from Lydia at the time of his birth. He was a chubby, lively-looking child, but only those traits could have been said to relate him to either of his parents, Windy being chubby and Cressy lively. Otherwise, the child's black hair and huge, glowing dark eyes were in direct contrast to the blue-eyed fairness of his parents. Georgina stared at him in amazement as he was put into her arms. Fortunately Windy's entire attention was directed proudly upon his son, and he did not see Georgina's reaction, and Cressy, who did, was evidently beyond any feelings of embarrassment by now, for she only smiled blandly and turned her attention to Selina, still delicate-looking, with her father's grey eyes and her mother's auburn hair.

"Oh, what a beauty she is, Georgie," Cressy exclaimed generously.

Georgina had by now collected her wits enough to return the compliment. "And not only handsome but good, not to cry when handed to strangers. And such eyelashes! So unfair for a boy to—" She stopped suddenly as it struck her who had fathered this child. He was the spit of Dominick! She did rapid calculations in her mind and knew it must be so— that time in London when Cressy was slipping out of the house. Georgina's startled glance flew to Cressy, who only quirked an amused eyebrow.

"Well, well, they are both very sweet, and we are to be congratulated upon producing such handsome and pretty-behaved children, but surely they will be better off back in the nursery. Babies are after all the most boring creatures," Cressy said carelessly, earning an indignant stare from Nurse Apple. Mrs. Pomfret, Simon's nurse, was clearly inured to such remarks, for she dipped a curtsey at once, retrieved her charge from Georgina, and withdrew. Nurse Apple followed only after a nod from Georgina.

It was not until later that night, as Georgina prepared for bed, that she learned the real reason for Cressy's visit. She scratched briefly at the door and entered, at once insisting on taking the brush from Prentiss, who was just preparing to use it on Georgina's tresses as she sat before her dressing table.

"Oh, do let me. I adore doing it. Such hair, Georgina, and all grown out now. How I envied your Titus cut when you first met Myles, but I vow, I like it much better this way. That will be all, Prentiss, you may go now," she added peremptorily. Prentiss folded her mouth into a straight, disapproving line and stood her ground until Georgina, seeing that Cressy was determined to speak to her alone, smiled at Prentiss with a nod of dismissal.

Cressy, impervious to the impropriety of ordering her sister's servants about in such a high-handed way, began brushing out Georgina's hair with long, sweeping strokes, beginning an interminable monologue, which reminded Georgina of her stepmother with its intermingling of subjects, all trivial, until Cressy said, ". . . and so the Duke, Cumberland, you know, said that we must come to stay and he would not take no for an answer. Naturally I protested that I must take my child home after racketing about all over the country for the entire summer, but Windy was possessed to go to the Duke, so I was wondering, Georgie darling . . ." Aha, thought Georgina, now we come to it. ". . . if you would not think it too frightful an imposition if we left him here, only for the three weeks, mind, and then we would fetch him away on our way home."

"Well, of course you may leave him, Cressy, but—"

"Darling Georgie! So obliging. I knew you would understand."

"Cressy, about Simon." She raised a brow interrogatively at her sister's reflection in the glass.

Cressy giggled, not even pretending to misunderstand, and squeezed Georgina's shoulders. "Oh, what a slyboots it is. I might have known you would see everything at once. Dominick to the life, is he not, the darling sweet babe that he is. But Windy hasn't the least clue. Says his grandmother was part-French with just such eyes. Oh, he positively *dotes*, I assure you, and if he is happy, what does it matter. A child is a child, after all. And I am increasing again, and this one may very well be his.''

"Cressy! My God, how can you talk so?'' Georgina was horrified.

"Good lord, Georgie, what a maggoty creature you are, after all,'' Cressy said in the resigned tones of one who has had her worst fears realized.

"But this is beyond anything. You cannot just go about having affairs where you will and producing children who may or may not be your husband's and expect him to just go on in ignorance forever.''

"Why not?'' Cressy's bewilderment was unfeigned.

"But everyone will be bound to know sooner or later. Your reputation—''

"Pooh! What do I care of that? One cannot enjoy oneself if all one thinks of is saving one's reputation. Look at you. You have a virtuous reputation, and what has it got you? A husband with a string of mistresses in town while you live holed up here in the country with no amusements at all. I would stake my life you have never even thought of taking a lover to fill the boredom. I should simply be stifled to death with such a life. If you had ever—''

She stopped suddenly as she became aware of Georgina's wide, stricken eyes staring up at her in the glass. Oh, lord, she didn't know, Cressy thought, feeling guilty and pleased at the same time to have stirred up such a hornet's nest. She thrived on drama.

Guilt won out over her baser instincts, however, and she attempted to patch things over. "Now, really Georgie, it is of no great moment, you know. Nearly every man I know has a mistress, sometimes several.'' Then she ruined whatever good she might have done by adding, "Not Windy, of course. A man only takes a mistress when his wife does not satisfy him, and I would be ashamed if I could not satisfy my husband. Perhaps you would like me to tell you some tricks to—''

"Go away, Cressy,'' said Georgina flatly.

"Look, Georgie, I made sure you knew all about Myles. Why, everyone knows, even Windy, who never pays attention to anything. If I had—''

"Just go away, Cressy. Now.''

"Yes, of course, darling. But please do not—''

"Good night, Cressy."

"Yes. Well, good night."

Georgina heard the door close and sat staring blindly at herself in the glass, Cressy's words " a string of mistresses in town" echoing in her mind. Then she felt heat spreading through her body like a tide until her skin burned and a red film clouded her vision. With an inarticulate expression of rage she picked up a scent bottle and threw it with all the force at her command at the fireplace, where it exploded against the mantel, splattering scent over everything and causing the fire to spit and flare. In an excess of unspent anger she turned and swept her arm across the dressing table, sending bottles and pots flying across the carpet.

Prentiss's scared face appeared around the door. "M'lady," she gasped, "what—"

"Go away!" Georgina cried, her amber eyes blazing. The door closed abruptly. Georgina rose and strode about the room with long, driving steps, her heart pounding, while visions of herself hitting Myles in the face, plunging a knife into his stomach, firing a pistol at him point blank, presented themselves to her in a satisfying series. Blood, she thought, and agony and—

Abruptly in mid-stride she crumpled to the floor into blackness.

When she became aware of herself again, she could not for a moment think where she was. The room was filled with her scent, and there not an inch from her nose was a shard of glass. She stared at it uncomprehendingly, then rolled over and sat up dizzily. Slowly, working backward from the scent, the broken glass on the carpet, the scatter of pots and bottles from her dressing table, she arrived at the answer and began to tremble. Never in her life had she allowed her emotions to have full rein, and she was frightened to death of the unbridled anger she had unleashed. She huddled down onto the floor, her body shaking spasmodically, waiting for God to punish her.

Her body felt chilled through, and slowly it seemed to her that the walls of the room receded, leaving more and more space about her. The space grew larger and emptier, and she smaller and smaller. Away in the distance she seemed to see a door opening and her father standing there. Then Myles appeared beside him, and they both stared coldly at her for a moment, then withdrew without comment, leaving her in her cold, dark, infinite space. She knew it was her old nightmare come upon her again, but could not break its spell. Myles does not love me, she thought, I have lost him. She began to sob childishly.

Then soft arms were around her. "Georgie, darling, what is it? What has happened?" Lydia whispered anxiously. "Prentiss was frightened and came to me." When Georgina continued to cry and would not answer, Lydia thought it better not to press her further. She coaxed her to her feet and led her to her bed. When she had tucked her into it, she said, "Shall I bring you something warm to drink or some wine?" Georgina only shook her head. After a worried moment Lydia blew out the candles and went away.

Georgina sank at once into a sleep of total exhaustion. But she woke in the chill pre-dawn hours with instant and total recall of all that had passed. She closed her eyes again and felt, in fact encouraged, the space around her to expand emptily. After all, it was a familiar misery, and therefore more bearable than her present reality.

Then suddenly she was up and running to the windows. She threw the sash wide and leaned out, looking for something to establish her being, her size, in the world. It was that hour of vague lightening to the east presaging the sun, and the grounds were filled with a solid white mist. Then as she waited, her breath coming in gasps, a bird woke and chirped tentatively. In a moment others came awake, and the homeliness of their talk reassured and calmed her. It was another day and the world was going on as though nothing cataclysmic had happened. She had a shattering realization of the unimportance of her own life in relation to the world, which was soothing.

I have heard a dreadful truth, but nothing has changed. A man has been unfaithful to his wife. How many constant husbands are there in England today, I wonder? Windy, possibly. I released what I always suspected was a quite dreadful temper, but what has happened? I broke a scent bottle. No harm was done. I am still me, I still have my child, and if I have lost my husband to some bit of muslin— Here a familiar heat began to spread through her body, but she breathed deeply, and the September air seemed to cool her anger. There, she thought triumphantly, I can control it still.

She returned to bed, and when Prentiss came with her morning chocolate, she smiled at her, thanking her coolly and ignoring the scared, puzzled look in her abigail's eyes.

"I will have my blue riding dress, Prentiss," she said. "And my sister Hughes-Jones will be leaving this morning after breakfast. The child, however, will remain here for three weeks."

"Yes, m'lady."

"Air this room well after I am out. I broke a bottle of scent last night."

"Yes, my'lady."

Never explain, Georgina thought, never apologize. She dressed and went off for her ride. When she returned, she was just in time to bid Cressy and Windy good-bye. She looked her sister straight in the eye and bade her a firm farewell, giving nothing away, and watched the cavalcade whirl away down the drive with indescribable relief. She went into breakfast and found that Lydia was not yet down, and that too was a relief.

The morning post, however, brought a note from Lady Cunliffe to announce her imminent arrival, escorted by Dominick, for a long-planned visit to meet her namesake. Georgina stared at the letter in dismay. Lady Cunliffe now! How on earth was she to face the old lady and hide this cold rage that filled her to the exclusion of all other feelings? And Dominick! His own son here to greet him and come under the all-knowing eyes of Lady Cunliffe, who would at once spot the resemblance and know all. Oh, lord, what am I to do? she thought wildly, feeling most unfairly beset.

"Good-morning, Georgina," said Mrs. Conyers from the doorway, "I hope you do not mind that I have shown myself in."

Georgina sprang to her feet and rushed over to clasp Mrs. Conyers's hands. "Oh, thank heaven, just the person I need. You must tell me what I am to do. Cressy has just left."

"Oh, was that who it was? I passed them in the drive. A most impressive equipage, I must say. They made a very short stay, surely."

"Yes, just long enough to deposit their son while they make a three-week visit to the Duke of Cumberland. And that is just the problem. The boy is not—not Windy's. One has only to see him to know he was sired by Dominick Barrowes."

"Your brother-in-law?"

"Yes, and I have just had a note from his aunt, Lady Cunliffe, to tell me she is coming, escorted by Dominick. She will see the child and know at once."

"Does that really matter? She is outspoken but not a gossip."

"Do you know her?" Georgina asked in some surprise.

"Ah—well—no. I have heard of her. In any case, this is not something that can be kept a secret from her. She would be bound to encounter him another time, if not here. You cannot allow these things to overset you so, Georgina. After all, it is not your problem."

"I suppose you are right, but I would have preferred it if she had encountered him some other place than here."

"You are very pale this morning. I hope you are not sickening for something."

"No, no. It is nothing. Will you have some breakfast?"

"Just some chocolate, thank you. When do they arrive?"

"Tomorrow, I believe. Oh, you will like Lady Cunliffe, Mrs. Conyers. She is so amusing."

"I am sure I should, but I am afraid I will not be here to meet her. I must go away myself tomorrow, you see."

"Oh, no! What shall I do without you? And Lydia will be so sad. Must you go now?"

"Yes, I fear I must. A friend in—ah—Bath has written to ask me to come at once. She is—ill, you see and——needs me." Mrs. Conyers ended rather breathlessly, as though she had been running a race.

If Georgina had not been so bemused by her own problems, she might have wondered at this speech, so unlike Mrs. Conyers's usual smooth, precise delivery.

CHAPTER

13

"Did you say Mrs. Conyers?" barked Lady Cunliffe, her head raised alertly from the dressed lobster on her plate that had hitherto claimed her riveted concentration.

"Yes, Lady Cunliffe," replied Lydia. "She is a neighbour of Georgina's. We are both exceedingly fond of her."

"Mrs. who Conyers?" queried Lady Cunliffe.

"Why, Blanche, though no one calls her that. She is simply Mrs.—"

"Blanche?" Lady Cunliffe dropped her fork.

"Well, well, Auntie, that is surely a most dramatic reaction," drawled Dominick with a lift of sardonic eyebrows. "I hope you have an intriguing tale to tell us."

"What was her husband's name?" demanded Lady Cunliffe of Lydia, ignoring her nephew.

"I cannot say that I ever heard. One somehow does not ask her such things, or at least I could not. Did you, Georgina?"

"No. She is a very private person, and never pries into one's own personal life. I respect her for it very much. It makes her such a soothing friend."

"Well, Auntie?" persisted Dominick.

"Well, nothing," snapped Lady Cunliffe, resuming her fork and addressing herself again to her plate.

"How cruel of you to tease us," laughed Dominick.

"Nothing of the sort! I only thought the name seemed familiar. No doubt someone I once met." She changed the subject firmly. "I shall want to see the child later, Georgina."

"Of course. I will have Nurse Apple bring her down to the drawing room," said Georgina nervously. She had been fortunate till now that Lady Cunliffe had not visited the nursery and discovered Simon. Immediately after her arrival several hours ago she had gone straight to her bed to recover from the rigours of the trip from London. Then, awakening with ravenous appetite, she had sent word that she would appreciate it if dinner could be put forward three quarters of an hour.

Georgina knew it would be foolish to hope she could keep Simon's presence from the old lady for her entire stay, but she desperately needed a few more days to become inured to the emotional state Cressy's revelation had roused in her before having to deal with any possible to-do over Dominick's lovechild now residing at Falconley under the name Hughes-Jones. Dominick, of course, would take the news without a blink, no doubt already aware that the child was his.

She studied him covertly, noting again the heavy fringe of lashes so like Simon's, the dark, brooding eyes, the perfect profile. He must surely be the father of many unacknowledged children, Georgina thought, with such devilish good looks. He can never have found much difficulty in having his way with whatever women take his fancy.

He looked up suddenly and met her glance with something so compelling in his eyes that it was a moment before she could drag hers away. She felt that he knew what she was thinking, and an uncomfortable blush mounted her cheeks. She took up her wine and drained the goblet to cover her confusion.

She had never had so much difficulty in maintaining her usual cool manner. It was as though her fit of temper the previous night had broken down all the carefully built walls that had protected her so well all these years against any attacks upon her fragile emotions. She knew she owed Lydia some explanation, but had assiduously avoided any tête-á-tête meetings with her, feeling as yet unprepared to cope with the problem.

She became aware now of what Lydia was saying and realized she would have done better to have found some private time with her sister, if only to take her into her confidence in at least one area, for Lydia was saying, "Oh, and you must see Simon also, Lady Cunliffe. Cressy's son, you know. She and Windy left him here yesterday to visit Cumberland, and Simon is staying here until they fetch him on their way home. He is a beautiful child."

"Ah, your sister Hughes-Jones. Rackety sort of creature, one hears. She will not be received anywhere if she carries on as she has done. One hears the boy is not even her husband's," pronounced Lady Cunliffe, never caring whether she gave offense or not.

Georgina could not keep her horrified gaze from flying to Dominick, and he gave her a lazy smile in return. Again she felt the blood heating her face, and she dropped her eyes and reached for her wineglass, which Honeywell had refilled.

Lydia laughed outright at Lady Cunliffe's bluntness, a quality she preferred to the polite innuendo that prevailed among the *ton*. "I fear you may be right, though Windy has no notion of the truth and adores the child."

"Bah! I have never felt any sympathy for betrayed husbands. Allowing themelves to become the objects of Society's gibes. No real gentleman would allow it," declared Lady Cunliffe scornfully.

"I suppose they cannot help themselves, any more than betrayed wives can," Georgina was horrified to hear herself rejoining heatedly. It must be the wine loosening my tongue, she thought, noticing only now, rather fuzzily, that her glass was being refilled yet again by Honeyman. Every eye was now fixed upon her, and she could think of nothing to do but pick up the glass again.

"Oh," Lady Cunliffe waved a dismissive hand, "that is not the same thing at all. Men are expected to behave so."

"Then why should not women have the same privilege?" demanded Lydia militantly.

"Sauce for the goose, you mean," Lady Cunliffe replied with a wicked cackle, "and so they may. Only they are expected to be more discreet about it. Otherwise there would be no order in Society at all."

"But how monstrously unfair!" cried Lydia. "Men may not only behave in a way that can only be called sinful, but they are expected, even encouraged, to do so, and *they* are never condemned for it or refused admittance to the *ton* drawing rooms, while women must be underhanded and sneaky if they do the same thing and become outcasts of Society if they are caught at it."

Georgina rose unsteadily, realizing rather belatedly that the conversation was perhaps not one a young, unmarried girl should be taking part in. "Shall we withdraw? Dominick, do you want—"

"No," he said decisively, rising himself. "I see no reason

to remain here alone." He helped his aunt to her feet and led her out, with Georgina and Lydia following. Once he had settled the old lady before the drawing room fire with Lydia on a stool at her knees preparing to resume her debate, he held out his arm to Georgina and suggested a walk on the terrace.

She, seemingly without volition of her own, took his arm and allowed herself to be led out the French windows. It was a warm, still September night, with a full moon well up pouring light over the gardens. They strolled without speaking to the end of the terrace and halted there. Georgina stared out over the moon-rapt gardens, willing her head to stop spinning.

Dominick stared at her. At last he said softly, "Ah, Georgina, you are much too beautiful." He put his hand over hers where it rested on the balustrade. She did not feel inclined to speak nor, surprisingly, to remove her hand. His palm was warm and dry and comforting. He raised her hand to his lips, brushing it back and forth over his mouth, then turning it to kiss her palm. She felt her knees weaken and she gasped. "A man could not be blamed for losing his head completely over you," he continued, his voice a low, almost lulling, murmur.

He gently turned her face to him and ran his finger slowly down her cheek. "Like white marble in the moonlight, but so infinitely soft and warm." His finger came beneath her chin, tilting her face up to his, and he touched his lips lightly to hers.

Georgina, flown with wine, felt in an almost dreamlike state, with his low voice murmuring words that poured through her like warm honey, healing the raw hurt inside her, and his touch, light and undemanding, yet stirring her senses.

"Georgie, Dominick," came Lydia's voice from the doorway, "are you there? Lady Cunliffe wants to see Selina now. Shall I ring for Nurse Apple?"

Dominick pulled Georgina's hand through his arm and calmly walked her back to the drawing room. Georgina wondered if her dazed condition could possibly escape Lady Cunliffe's notice. She could not look at the old lady as she went to ring for Honeyman and tell him to summon Nurse Apple with the baby.

"Just the one, mind," ordered Lady Cunliffe. "I canno

take two infants tonight. I will see the boy tomorrow.''

Nurse Apple arrived, and Selina was examined and admired. Dominick watched with his usual sardonic smile, not bothering to move from his stance at the fireplace where he leaned casually against the mantel, hands in pockets, one leg crossed nonchalantly over the other.

Georgina, smiling dreamily, took the child from Lady Cunliffe and gazed down into the sleeping face framed in dark-red curls and kissed the tiny, soft mouth for the first time, all the held-back love for her baby swelling up inside her into something very near pain. The child woke and began to whimper, and Nurse Apple clucked reprovingly and took her back.

"There now, m'lady, you've waked her," she chided. Georgina only smiled as Nurse Apple bustled out of the room. Lady Cunliffe declared she was for her bed now also, and Georgina was glad to accompany her up the stairs, bidding the other two good night almost absently, though Lydia came along immediately behind her.

Dominick watched them go, not moving from his stance at the fireplace, as he mulled over Georgina's puzzling behaviour this evening. He had never had any real hopes of seducing his sister-in-law. Her attitude towards him from the first had been cold, almost aloof, as though she considered him beneath her notice. He truly found her beautiful, but there were so many beautiful women who were more giving, so he had shrugged and remembered her only when he was with her. It was clear, however, that something had happened since he had seen her last to shake her out of her usual composure. He had sensed it at once and sensed the possibility that she might be more receptive. And see how right he had been!

He was not displeased that Lydia had interrrupted them when she had. The ground had been laid, and he could only congratulate himself on his handling of her, for she was not the sort of woman who would rush headlong into an affair but must be teased along with small sips at pleasure until the climactic moment happened almost without her being aware that it was upon her. He contemplated the prospect with great pleasure, for he enjoyed seduction in all its variety.

In her bed at last Georgina felt the room spinning the moment she closed her eyes. As sleep overcame her in a rush, she felt as though she were being sucked down into the eye of a whirlpool and she went gladly, unwilling to think.

She was rudely awakened, it seemed almost immediately, by the crack of the drapes being thrown back to admit a blinding flood of sunlight and Lady Cunliffe's irate voice demanding that she wake up immediately.

"What? What on earth—" Georgina blinked bemusedly.

"Are you preparing to sleep all day?"

"Where is Prentiss? What hour is it?"

"It is past nine. I had no idea such hours were kept in the country these days. When I was a girl we—but never mind that. That is not what I wanted speak to you about."

"I should like to have Prentiss bring my—"

"Chocolate? Here it is. I had her bring it up and leave it with you. Now, I want to know if you had realized whose boy that is in your nursery."

"Boy?"

"That Hughes-Jones child."

"Well, I—" Georgina delayed, taking a cautious sip of her chocolate.

"Do not pretend to me, Georgina. You must have seen at once, as I did, that that boy is Dominick's. If you did not, you are more of a slow-top than I credited you. Why, one has only to set eyes on him to know."

"Yes." Georgina drank her chocolate greedily, for it seemed to be doing wonders for the slight headache she had.

"Is that all you have to say?"

"I cannot for the moment think of anything else."

"But you must have known I would guess at once."

"Of course, but what would you have me do? Hide him in the attic or pitch him out?"

"Sauce!" snapped Lady Cunliffe warningly.

"I beg your pardon, darling Aunt Selina. I realize you are upset and I would not have you so, but when I agreed to have him here, I had not yet received your note."

"Well, of course I do not blame *you*, child," said Lady Cunliffe, somewhat mollified, "but it is an untidy situation, and I dislike untidiness. The child and Dominick here at the same time . . ."

"He will not care."

"No doubt. But what of that innocent child Lydia? And what if Myles should return?"

"Myles should long since have lost his illusions about his brother," Georgina replied, her voice hardening.

Lady Cunliffe shot a shrewd glance at her. "What is wrong? Have you and Myles quarreled? I thought you were behaving peculiarly the moment I arrived."

"Fiddle! There is nothing wrong in the least. Will you pull that bell? I think I will get up now and have a long ride."

Lady Cunliffe gave her a long, calculating look, but pulled the bell to summon Prentiss and stumped away, saying she supposed she would be obliged to breakfast alone.

In that she was mistaken, for Lydia joined her at the table, and before they rose from it Lady Cunliffe had drawn out from Lydia the whole tale of her tragic loss and they had become fast friends. When Georgina returned from her ride, they still lingered there and stayed on with her while she ate baked eggs with good appetite. Dominick did not appear, for which Georgina was grateful. She was not yet ready to deal with him or even to examine her behaviour the previous evening. She felt suspended, awaiting events.

She visited the nursery and gave herself over to her baby completely, allowing herself to feel again that wondrous love she had experienced last night as she had kissed her, refusing to admit caution or fear of consequence to come between her and the child, not with conscious decision, but as part of the unreal state she found herself in where it seemed safe to expose her feelings.

She wore a gown of blush-pink and fussed uncharacteristically over the way Prentiss dressed her hair for dinner. When she came down, she was much gratified by the look that came into Dominick's eyes. During the meal, though she had resolved to be more careful with her wine, she found herself sipping away almost deliberately, as though eager to induce the hypnotic state of the evening before.

Lady Cunliffe said casually, "Perhaps you might invite your friend Mrs. Conyers for dinner tomorrow, Georgina. I should like to thank her for her kindness to you."

"Oh, I am sorry, but she is away now. She was called to Bath to attend a friend who is ill."

"Really. When did she leave?"

"Why, let me think, it was the day you arrived, as a matter of fact, for she told me of her trip at the time I told her of your message that you were coming for a visit."

"Hm-m-m," was Lady Cunliffe's noncommittal reply to this information. "I should go more carefully with that wine, if I were you, child."

"Why, that from you, madam," laughed Georgina, "who practically thrust a glass into my hand the moment we first met and told me to drink it up, it was good for me."

"In moderation, girl, in moderation."

Georgina only laughed and saw Dominick raise his glass to her. She raised her own, and they drank, eyes meeting steadily over the rim of their glasses. She felt a slow surge of warmth through her body and a blush rising up her neck. She forced herself to look away from him and pick up the conversation again between Lydia and Lady Cunliffe.

After dinner, as though ordained, she again found herself walking the terrace with Dominick, while Lydia played the pianoforte for Lady Cunliffe. They again paced silently through the heady warmth of the moonlight and halted at the balustrade as before, only this time she turned to him, staring wordlessly, waiting.

"My God, Georgina, you will drive me mad!" he whispered, his dark eyes glowing, not touching her yet, wooing her with words. "I had to go clear away from you today or I do not know what I might have done. My fingers ache to touch that white skin. I dream of your eyes, your mouth, of touching your hair. You are like some enchanted princess from a fairy tale. I cannot believe in so much beauty. I have surely dreamed you and in a moment I will wake up and you will be gone—and I shall be desolate."

Again she felt the healing words salving her wounds. She was not unlovable after all. Here was a man who could have any woman he wanted, who yet found her desirable, as Myles, apparently, no longer did. She swayed forward, her eyes locked to his, her lips apart, wanting him to kiss her again as he had before.

He slowly cupped her face in both his hands and very deliberately brushed his lips against hers, then again more and more lingeringly. He put his arms about her with great care and pulled her close, not loosing his mouth from hers.

Then without warning Georgina felt the white-hot explosion inside her she had known only once before, when Myles had kissed her that first time. Now, however, she did not smother it. She could not have done so, for the controls she had so carefully exercised over herself so far in her life were shattered.

Her arms came up to hold him, her lips softened and fused to his, her heart pounded as she pressed closer, closer. Then he was holding her away with a soft, exultant laugh.

"Come, darling girl, we must walk back. Auntie is a suspicious old bird, and we must not give her cause to wonder." And then he was leading her back along the terrace. She clung to his arm, her knees trembling so that she feared she might collapse.

The transition was too abrupt. She felt dazed, disoriented. He walked slowly, seeing her condition, murmuring to her, "Breathe deeply, sweetheart. There, now, is not that better?" He tucked back a curl that had become dislodged, and as they passed the lighted doorway he laughed politely, as though responding to something she had said, and said, "Yes, no doubt you are right, but I am sure Myles will see to it when he returns."

By the time they had reached the other end of the terrace, turned, and were approaching the door again, she had recovered herself. All she wanted now was the privacy of her room.

Before they reentered the room, he breathed, "I will think of a way to see you, sweeting, have no fear."

CHAPTER

14

Georgina drifted into the dining room the following morning to find Lady Cunliffe and Lydia, dressed for riding, there before her. She greeted them absentmindedly as she sank into her chair and asked Honeyman for toast and tea. Lydia eyed her curiously, exchanged a glance with Lady Cunliffe, and said, "A letter from Mama today. I am sure you can guess the dire news."

Georgina thought for a moment before she said, "Harriet, of course, has accepted the despicable Braye."

"Yes, and they are to be married in a month. Papa no doubt arranged that to be sure Braye did not get away."

"Who is this Braye?" demanded Lady Cunliffe.

Georgina, seeming to lose interest in the subject, only shrugged and bit into her toast, leaving explanations to Lydia, who answered Lady Cunliffe with a vivid and contemptuous description of Sir Vernon.

"Ah, that Braye. I knew his mother. A detestable creature. Still, I suppose your sister must marry someone, and if no one else will have her, she had best have Braye."

"But he will be sure to make her miserable," protested Lydia.

"She will be even more miserable unmarried, since Society offers women little else. No woman is considered successful until she has achieved the honour of bearing some man's name."

"That is certainly true for Harry, though I think the name is all she wants of marriage. Would you agree, Georgie?"

"I suppose so," Georgina replied without interest.

Lady Cunliffe eyed her at length and said at last, "What ails you, girl? Are you breeding again?"

This shook Georgina out of her abstraction, and she looked up, startled. "Good heavens, no!"

"I cannot think why you should look so astonished," retorted Lady Cunliffe. "It is a perfectly normal thing to happen to a married woman. Well, if you are not breeding, perhaps you need a tonic. Send for your doctor.

"I have no need to send for him. His sovereign remedy for all ailments is beef tea and port. Besides, there is nothing wrong with me at all."

"I am happy to hear it, for I have wondered if you do not mean to entertain me at all while I am here."

"Entertain—Oh, Aunt Selina, I am sorry. How selfish I have been. I have done so little entertaining lately that I have quite got out of the habit of even thinking of it. If only Mrs. Conyers were here, you would enjoy her company, I know, but our other neighbours are not, I fear, very interesting—with the exception of Lady Venables. She is amusing—"

"Sally Venables? Good lord, I had thought she was dead this age! Well, I should like to see her again. Who else? Are there no young people? Perhaps we could have dancing if there are enough couples to stand up. I enjoy watching young people dancing."

"Well, perhaps that would not be quite the thing," She cast her eyes significantly toward Lydia, hoping Lady Cunliffe would take her meaning without need of further explanation.

Lady Cunliffe was impervious to such subtleties. "If you mean Lydia, that is all nonsense to my way of thinking. One cannot allow a girl of fifteen to drown in her sorrow. And there is nothing improper in a private dance. I would not advocate a ball, or even the Assembly, but within her home is quite a different matter. She is not in official mourning, as there was no betrothal announced. What she needs is something to take her mind off it. That young man of hers sounds to have been too sensible to have wanted her moping about dwelling on her unhappiness."

Lydia, who had been about to protest that the last thing she wanted was gaiety, was much struck by this, for she thought it was exactly what Tarq *would* have said. "If Lady Cunliffe wants to meet some of your neighbours, I have no objection, Georgina," she said bravely.

"No objection to what?" drawled Dominick as he strolled into the room.

"To a dinner party," said Lydia.

"Oh." Dominick shrugged, took a cup of chocolate, and walked over to the window. "I thought you would ride this morning, Georgina," he said casually.

"Oh, I, I had not thought to . . ." Georgina faltered.

"Take Lydia," ordered Lady Cunliffe. "She is already dressed for it, and Georgina and I will begin the invitations for the party."

"I shall be delighted to do so, of course," Dominick said politely, turning to Lydia with a smile that concealed his irritation with his aunt for her interference. He had planned this ride to be alone with Georgina, perhaps to find a secluded glade where he could progress to the next step in his seduction of her.

When they had gone, Lady Cunliffe and Georgina repaired to the back drawing room. Georgina forced herself to enter into the affair with a great deal more enthusiasm than she was actually able to muster within herself. She had no desire to see anyone, she thought, as she picked up a pen to begin a list. Who must they ask? Lady Venables for Aunt Selina, of course, and the two elderly widowers who were of the same age as partners for them; but what of young people? She supposed Hester Knyvet must be asked, though the thought did nothing to cheer her. However, since Myles was not to be of the party, Hester might be less disagreeable to her hostess than she had been on previous occasions.

A list was made at last, and the date was settled for three nights hence. Georgina sat down resignedly to write out the invitations while Lady Cunliffe watched.

"I like your sister very well. A great deal of backbone there," she commented.

"She is a darling," Georgina agreed, scratching away busily at her escritoire.

"I think the best thing for her would be to marry soon. Musn't allow her to get in the way of thinking of herself as a martyr to love."

"Marry? But she is only fifteen."

"I make no doubt she would have contrived to marry her young man before too much time had passed had he not been taken. She is mature for her age."

"Yes, but I doubt she will be ready to consider such things for some time yet. She did not love Tarquin Ladbrook lightly, you know."

"No, she would not do so. She is a girl of deep sensibilities. But she is also sensible and not given to languishing," Lady Cunliffe said approvingly. For a time there was silence, then she added, "I should like to see Dominick married."

"Dominick!" Georgina dropped her pen and turned around in astonishment.

"I suppose he may marry as other men do," Lady Cunliffe snapped.

"He *may,* but I doubt he *will.*"

"If he will not see what is good for him, I shall have to show him. He will listen to me."

"I cannot give much for your chance of success."

"We shall see," Lady Cunliffe replied stubbornly.

Georgina studied her suspiciously. "Now what are you up to? Have you someone in your eye for him?"

"Yes, as a matter of fact, I have."

"May I know who?"

"Lydia."

Georgina gaped at her, too taken aback to speak for a moment. Then, with something like awe in her voice, she said, "You must be mad!"

"I fail to understand your attitude, Georgina," Lady Cunliffe replied stiffly, clearly offended.

"Forgive me, dearest. It was just that I was so thunderstruck. They are so entirely unsuited. He is an unprincipled hedonist, by your own admission, while Lydia is—the opposite," she finished lamely.

"Exactly why I thought of it. She would settle him down."

"I doubt she would care for the job, or that he would care for it even if she could be persuaded to try. Oh, don't you see, darling, he would break her heart again and again. He would any woman's who was unwise enough to marry him. I could not bear for her to be hurt in such a way. She is so good, so rare."

Lady Cunliffe was not to be persuaded to give up her inspiration so easily, however. "The proper wife could change Dominick," she maintained stoutly.

Georgina shrugged and turned back to the invitations, seeing that further argument was a waste of time. Nothing would come of the scheme in any case. Lydia was hardly likely to fall in love now, especially with a man like Dominick—unless he could be persuaded to the idea by Lady Cunliffe and made love to Lydia. He could be most persuasive, as Georgina had reason to know. The remembrance of his lips against her own the night before flashed through her mind, and she shivered. Why had she allowed this to happen between them? He was not a man *she* could fall in love with either, but—yes, *but*. In spite of all she knew of him, she had not repulsed him; had, rather, encouraged his advances, and the resulting explosion of sensations she had experienced in her body had been pleasant rather than destroying as she had always feared. But why had she allowed it to happen with Dominick?

The terrible anger Cressy's slip of the tongue had released in Georgina had laid bare her deepest fear, the seed of which had been planted by her mother's desertion, nurtured by her father's neglect, and finally confirmed by her husband's betrayal: that she was not lovable. Dominick had arrived at this crucial stage, and the admiration and invitation in his eyes had been like a welcome rain soaking into barren soil. She had not decided upon what followed, only allowed it, and not a small part of her doing so was her knowledge that for Dominick it would never be a serious affair. He had no thoughts of anything beyond providing himself with some amusement to pass the time on what must be for him the boring duty of escorting his aunt on this visit to his childhood home. Thus she was safe from the need to think of any future demands he might make. There was no future in any of Dominick's affairs. Would she allow herself to go on with this?

She was staring blankly before her, her pen still on the paper. She became aware slowly that Lady Cunliffe was watching her intently. She resolutely set her pen in motion again.

Lady Cunliffe, meanwhile, put her mind to what might be Georgina's problem. She was not so unseeing as Dominick had hoped and had been very much aware of the adroit way he had maneuvered Georgina out onto the terrace the past two evenings. She knew her nephew very well and adored him despite all the unpleasant truths she had had to face about him, not the least of these being the latest to be revealed to her, that he had seduced Georgina's sister Cressida, a seventeen-year-old-girl of good family. Lady Cunliffe shuddered at the thought of the scandal that might have ensued from that escapade. Now it seemed he was applying his wiles to Georgina. Lady Cunliffe had no idea if he had had any success so far, but Georgina was behaving peculiarly, so it behooved Lady Cunliffe to put a spoke in his wheel whenever possible.

That evening, therefore, and the following one, she found Georgina's attendance upon herself an absolute necessity. Lady Cunliffe suggested with a sly look at Georgina that Dominick walk on the terrace with Lydia, which he was obliged to do. On the second evening Lydia declined, and Dominick was left to contemplate with distaste a book of sermons pressed upon him by his solicitous aunt.

Then came the evening of the dinner party. Several young men and women, including Hester Knyvet, had been invited, as well as Lady Venables and the two elderly widowers. Hester, looking extraordinarily fetching in hyacinth-blue silk, greeted Georgina with condescension, dropped a respectful curtsey to Lady Cunliffe, and dimpled shyly at Dominick, whom she had not seen much of even when he had been a child at Falconley. She had never had much time for him then, since Myles had filled her every thought. As she remembered him, Dominick had been a disagreeable little boy, dark-browed and sullen. Who would have dreamed he would grow into so handsome a man? She held out her hand, and he bent gallantly over it. He then raised an appreciative eyebrow at her and declared he had had no idea she would grow up to be so pretty or he would have made sure to be nicer to her when they were children. She smiled and lowered her eyes demurely before moving away. After a moment he followed her.

"Well, that seems a pretty-behaved child," commented Lady Cunliffe, watching them with a speculative gleam.

"If you are nursing any hopes for marriage, I think it only fair to warn you that Miss Knyvet has been head over ears in love with Myles for years," replied Georgina drily.

The dinner was lively with conversation. Lady Cunliffe and Lady Venables were delighted to meet again and had years of gossip to catch up on, Lydia had captured the hearts of the two widowers, who outdid each other in practicing their antiquated gallantries on her, and Hester seemed effervescent with charm toward everyone, particularly Dominick. Georgina entered into the spirit of the occasion as best she could, but felt strangely apart from her guests, as though watching them detachedly from a distance.

Lady Cunliffe demanded dancing afterwards, and Georgina obediently ordered Honeyman to have the carpets rolled back and sat herself at the pianoforte. Lydia settled down on a sofa between her two elderly admirers, declaring she would not dance this evening. Lady Cunliffe made only a token protest, though the original reason for her suggestion to have this party had been to promote a romance between Lydia and Dominick. Since then she had had a private word with him, however, and her none-too-subtle hints had fallen on flinty ground. She had been forced to realize he could not be pushed in Lydia's direction and had reluctantly given up her plan. Never mind, she thought, she would give her attention to the problem. Someone suitable could more likely be found in London. She would have to look about when they returned. Meantime here he was leading out that pretty Knyvet girl, as she might have known he would. Ah, what a handsome devil he was, to be sure.

Georgina played on automatically, noticed that Dominick was flirting with Hester and that Hester was not displeased in the least, and felt no resentment at all, any more than she had resented Lady Cunliffe's maneuverings these past two evenings. Georgina simply accepted whatever befell her, incapable of planning meetings with Dominick or of resisting them if they came about. She had given up all control of events, floating along will-lessly with any current. It was not an unpleasant sensation.

Lady Cunliffe and Dominick stayed for a further week. In that week Dominick came down, breakfasted, left very early each morning, and generally did not return until late afternoon. He never mentioned the child in the nursery that he knew to be his own or made any request to see it. He simply had no interest in it at all. He continued to show Georgina his admiration whenever possible, but only obliquely, for, except for one evening when Lady Cunliffe said she had the headache and retired to bed immediately after dinner, they had no opportunity to be alone. On that evening, as Lydia sat down to the pianoforte, Dominick held out his arm in silent invitation to Georgina, and they were once more on the terrace.

The night was cloudy, however, with sharp, scudding little whips of wind that caused them to walk rather more briskly than before, and was not in the least romantic. When they reached the balustrade at the end of the terrace, he took her rather perfunctorily into his arms and kissed her. She felt nothing and after a moment turned away and pulled her shawl closer about her shoulders. Without speaking, they returned to the drawing room.

How strange, she thought, that I should feel nothing now, when only a few days ago his kiss made me go weak in the knees. Perhaps it is the weather. It is too chilly for dalliance on the terrace. Or more probably it is something in me, she thought in despair. I am too passive, too unresponsive, and I have disgusted him, as I have—No! I will not think about Myles tonight, she told herself fiercely.

Lydia was relieved when Dominick and Lady Cunliffe were gone back to London, for though she liked Lady Cunliffe very well, she had found wearing the necessity to be in attendance on her as well as the necessity to conceal her unhappiness in order not to cast a pall over their visit. She was also very uneasy about her sister. Georgina had been most unlike herself since the evening Lydia had found her on the floor of her bedroom, surrounded by broken glass.

Lydia had intercepted several exchanges of glances between Georgina and Dominick and was not long in deciphering their meaning, at least on Dominick's part. She had been aware too of Lady Cunliffe's stratagems to frustrate her nephew's plans concerning Georgina and had applauded them, for she despised Dominick. She saw him as a shallow sensualist with no character or purpose or ideals, and she had no use for such men. She had seen at once that Simon must be his child and had loathed him even more for his total lack of interest. She was amazed that Georgina could tolerate the man even to the extent of walking alone with him on the terrace, much less allow him to flirt with her.

Since such behaviour was foreign to all she knew of Georgina, Lydia was certain something was dreadfully wrong with her, though she could not bring herself to probe into the matter. Georgina was so intently a private person that Lydia could think of no way to speak of it to her. She wished she were older and wiser or had someone old and wise to consult.

Then she remembered that Mrs. Conyers was to return the next day, and her heart felt lighter. Mrs. Conyers would know what to do.

CHAPTER

15

Myles stepped down from his carriage before his aunt's house in London with a weary sigh of relief. He had traveled for days from the farthest-removed of his properties, located in the north near the border with Scotland, where his bailiff had been lining his pockets richly at the estate's expense. He had had weeks of setting things to rights, finding a new man and settling him in, and listening to all the petty complaints of his many tenants. Now all was well in hand, and he was eager to return home. He had missed Georgina and found himself thinking of her at every moment his mind was not occupied with business. He had not wanted to leave her at all now after the closeness they had achieved, for he had realized at the same time that he really knew very little about her inward self and he longed to explore it. She revealed so little voluntarily that he knew the task would not be an easy one, but he was determined to learn, to start anew with her, court her, woo her if possible, until she opened herself to him.

He had given up his last mistress after the birth of his daughter and found in himself no inclination for another or indeed for more casual affairs. This made him even more eager to return to his wife. Tomorrow, he thought, tomorrow I will be with her again.

He planned to break his journey at his aunt's town house rather than at his own, where everything would be under holland covers, the bed unaired, and the housekeeper sure to get into a state of hysteria at his unannounced arrival. His Aunt Selina would be happy to give him dinner, and if she dined out, her cook would prepare something for him. He would not mind dining alone and retiring early.

"Ah, Trott, good evening," he said to the butler, who bowed him in deferentially. "Is my aunt at home?"

"Good evening, my lord. Lady Cunliffe is dressing for dinner."

"She dines at home?"

"She does, my lord. I will just go up and apprise her of your visit. You will be staying, my lord?"

"Yes. Have my man take my case up and lay out my evening clothes. I will go up as soon as I have taken a glass of wine."

When he came down, his aunt was waiting for him. "My dear boy, how good to see you," she exclaimed with real pleasure. "Where have you come from?"

"Blostwick. Had to get rid of the man I had there. Messy business, but all in hand now, thank God. I came to beg a meal and a bed from you. I'm for Falconley tomorrow at first light."

"Happily, dear boy, happily. I have just returned from Falconley, by the by. I went to inspect my namesake."

"Did you indeed? I wish I might have been there. What do you think of my daughter?"

"She is beautiful. She will look exactly like her mother, thank heaven."

Myles laughed delightedly. "I join your thanks. And how did you find my beautiful wife?"

Lady Cunliffe hesitated and then said carefully, "She seemed well physically, but it seemed to me she was troubled in her mind about something."

"Did you ask her what was troubling her?"

"Georgina? No, I did not. She is not at all a confiding sort of girl, which makes it difficult to question her. And no wonder that she is so if even part of what Lydia told me about Fitzhardinge is true. Devilish cold sort of man. Neglected Georgina dreadfully just when she needed him most after that business with her mother. Speaking of which, I—" She stopped abruptly. Not yet, she thought, I must think of this more before I decide what I want to do.

"Yes?" Myles prompted.

"Oh, nothing. It is an old story. No need to rake it over again. Let us go in to dinner. I am sure you must be famished."

Over the meal they spoke generally, but when the table was cleared, the port set before Myles, and the servants withdrawn, Lady Cunliffe, who had elected to remain with the port, leaned forward to pour herself some wine.

"I am very partial to port and see no reason to leave you here to enjoy it alone. Besides, there is something I wish to discuss with you." She took a sip of the wine and said, "That Hughes-Jones creature was at Falconley before me, with husband and child. They left the child there while they went off to stay with Cumberland. Have you ever seen the child?"

"No. Lydia wrote that he does not resemble either parent, but that is all I know."

"Well, you had best be prepared for it, so I will tell you. The child is Dominick's."

"What? You cannot be serious!"

"I am very much so. You will know it at once yourself, as will everyone who sees him and is acquainted with Dominick, and it will become even more apparent as the boy grows. It is disgraceful!"

Myles was too stunned to speak. He was not unaware of his brother's reputation as a womanizer, but he had discounted most of the gossip as untrue and had certainly never heard Dominick called a dispoiler of virgins even by the worst scandalmongers in London. But if Aunt Selina said it was so, it must be so. My God, he thought, Georgina's own sister! And it must have occurred when she was a guest under my roof! He rose abruptly.

"Dear Aunt Selina, please forgive me if I leave you now. I must find Dom."

"Rather late in the day to ring a peal over his head for that now, Myles. I only told you because you have always refused to recognize what a truly wicked man he is. Perhaps in future you will be more awake on that suit."

She had told him because she wanted him not to be so trusting where his own wife was concerned when his brother was near. Unless she was very much mistaken, Dominick would not hesitate a moment to seduce his own brother's wife if the opportunity presented itself. She bade Myles good-night and went off to the drawing room for a game of patience until the tea tray was brought in and also to think some more about Blanche Conyers.

Myles tracked down his brother to White's, where he was engaged at cards with some of his cronies. He waited patiently until Dominick could withdraw from the game and then carried him off to Dominick's own house, telling him they must talk with great privacy. When they were settled before the fire with brandy, Myles faced his brother with the news he had just learned from his aunt.

Dominick heard him out without interruption, then said lazily, "Well, and what of it? Good lord, Myles, the girl herself was absolutely determined on it. Even you must have sensed it. If it had not been I, it would have been the next man she took a fancy to. Why should I not have taken what was being so freely offered? Still is, if what one hears is true."

Myles, aware of the problems her parents had had with Cressida that had caused them to leave her in London in the first place, could hardly deny this, however. Another man would at least have offered to marry her," he said.

"Please do not be so ridiculous. I have no wish to be leg-shackled, least of all to such a girl as Cressida. Why, she has had at least thirty lovers since then by latest count. Besides, I found her a husband."

"But think if Fitzhardinge had learned of this! She was in my charge, she was but seventeen, and Georgina's own sister! Good God, did not any of these things trouble you at all?"

"Why, no," Dominick replied, genuinely puzzled, "and you must not allow them to trouble you. I assure you Cressy is perfectly happy, and everything has turned out very well."

"And the boy?"

"What boy?"

"Your *son!*" Myles shouted in exasperation.

"Oh, he will do very well. After all, he is Windy's heir and will come into pots of money. Nothing to be concerned about there. Most fellows have a child or two here and there along the way. Even you." He slanted a look of malicious amusement at his brother.

The shot went home, and Myles turned his back abruptly. He realized he had never really understood his brother at all. They had always gone along together very well, never quarrelled, and Myles was genuinely fond of Dominick and knew his feelings were reciprocated. Beyond this the only thing he was still certain of was that Dominick did not resent his brother's seniority, title, or inheritance.

To his credit Dominick did not. He had no desire for Myles's responsibilities. He had inherited a fortune from his mother sufficient to enable him to live just as he liked and had every intention of continuing just as he always had, with no one to make any demands upon him. He had only one interest in life: the pursuit of his own pleasure. He had, he felt, arranged his life very well.

"Well, my boy," Myles said at length, "I cannot make you understand my position, I suppose. But please oblige me by taking greater care in future about who you become entangled with. Another time you may not come out of the matter so easily."

He went on his way the next morning, and as the miles passed, separating him from London, the business of his brother and Cressy faded from his mind. It was over now, and there was nothing to be done about it. He thought about the child he himself had fathered so many years ago, however, and wondered uneasily if he had done enough for it. Perhaps he should settle some money on the child, a goodly amount that would assure a respectable income. Yes, he would do so. Then he need not think of having to include the child's name in his will and create possible pain for Georgina.

When he arrived at Falconley, he was informed by Honeyman that m'lady and Miss Fitzhardinge were in the back drawing room and made his way there quickly, his heart beating harder with expectation.

Georgina sat before the fire with Selina in her lap, while Lydia knelt adoringly before them. They both looked around in surprise at his entrance, their faces still smiling with delight in the baby.

"Why, Myles!" Lydia cried, rising at once and coming forward to kiss his cheek in greeting. He returned the greeting, but his attention was all for Georgina. He thought he had never seen her lovelier than at this moment, the fire lighting her face rosily and sparking her hair, her eyes soft and loving. But as he watched, he saw her smile fade and her eyes turn hard and cold.

He crossed to her and bent to kiss her, but she turned her head down so that his kiss landed on the top of her head. "Georgina, my love, you are looking so well I need not ask how you are keeping," he said softly, refusing to accept what she was showing him, willing it not to be so.

"I am well," she said, shrugging her shoulder away from his hand. He took the child from her and cuddled it against his neck, murmuring to it the senseless things ones does to babies. The baby, so suddenly dislodged from the familiar, began to fret, and Lydia, thinking to leave them alone, came forward.

"Shall I take her back to Nurse Apple, Georgina?"

"Thank you, no. I will take her. There is something I must speak to Nurse Apple about. Shall I put dinner forward, Myles?"

"Why no, my love. The usual time will do me fine."

Without any further comment Georgina left, and Myles stared after her for a moment before turning to Lydia, his eyes questioning.

"I do not know, Myles. Something has happened, but she has said nothing."

"All seemed well when I left. She was happy, or so I thought."

"Well, so she seemed to me. She came for me, you know, when . . ." She faltered.

He went to her at once and took her hands. "My dear child, forgive me. It slipped my mind for the moment. She wrote me about young Ladbrook, and I was so sorry. Such a tragedy for you both."

"Thank you, Myles. It is all right." She swallowed several times, then went on. "Anyway, we came back here and all was well. Then Cressy and Windy came, and it was after that that she seemed—changed." She pondered describing Georgina's condition the night she had found her lying on her bedroom floor, but decided against speaking of it. It was too disturbing and inexplicable. Lydia felt again her youth and inexperience. If only she had had the chance to speak to Mrs. Conyers, who had returned only this morning and sent word she would visit tomorrow morning. She continued, "And then Mrs. Conyers went away and Lady Cunliffe and your brother arrived, so there has been no chance at all to talk, though I cannot be sure she would have told me in any case. Georgina does not discuss her feelings much, you know."

Myles only stared into the fire. Presently Lydia said she would go change for dinner and went away feeling confused and unhappy. When she had changed, she had a sudden inspiration and penned a quick note to Mrs. Conyers and told a footman to take it to her at once.

Dinner was an excruciating session for all concerned. Conversation was carried forward exclusively by Lydia and Myles, with Georgina responding only when addressed directly. All of them declared an urgent need for sleep even before the tea tray was carried in and retired to their separate rooms with alacrity and exquisite politeness. Myles could not entertain even for a moment the hope that his presence in his wife's bed would be welcome and spent a mostly sleepless night trying to fathom what could have happened to turn his wife from the soft, nestling girl he had left into the frozen automaton he had returned to.

The following morning Lydia greeted them with the news that Mrs. Conyers was feeling unwell and had written begging that Lydia be allowed to come to her for a few days. Georgina could not deny Mrs. Conyers this small favor, especially when it was clear that Lydia was more than eager to go.

With immeasurable relief Lydia went away to pack a small case, for this was what her note had asked of Mrs. Conyers. Lydia felt that whatever was wrong between Georgina and Myles could best be sorted out without her presence.

CHAPTER

16

"Was she crying?" Mrs. Conyers asked.

"Yes, just lying there in a heap. She was not unconscious or asleep. She did not speak, but when I urged her to get up, she did so immediately and went to her bed. She closed her eyes at once as though going to sleep, so I went away. Perhaps I should have stayed with her, talked to her, tried to find out what had happened."

"I doubt she would have told you. It is very strange, to be sure. Did she and Cressy have words, do you suppose?"

"Why Cressy?"

"Well, you say she was all right when she said goodnight to all of you. You did not speak to her after that, and I doubt Mr. Hughes-Jones would go to her room, so that leaves Cressy. She must have come to ask if she might leave the baby at Falconley," guessed Mrs. Conyers, feeling her way, "and then said something that completely overset Georgina."

"I should think she must have, if the state of Georgina's room is anything to go by. And yesterday with Myles"—Lydia shuddered—"she cannot have addressed two sentences to him."

"Then it must have something to do with Myles."

"Will you talk to her, Mrs. Conyers? Perhaps she will confide in you."

Mrs. Conyers looked doubtful at this, but said she would call on Georgina and give her the opportunity if she felt inclined toward confidences. The following day, therefore, Mrs. Conyers and Lydia drove to Falconley, ostensibly to request that Lydia be allowed to stay on until the end of the week. Georgina greeted her old friend warmly and with many anxious inquiries about her health, which caused Mrs. Conyers some embarrassment. She turned the inquiries aside by saying it was only a slight thing and made her request for Lydia's company for a few extra days. Georgina agreed, and Lydia rose at once, saying in that case she must fetch another gown and kiss darling Selina, and sped out of the room.

Mrs. Conyers turned to survey Georgina's pale face. "You are looking tired, my dear. Has all this company been too much for you?"

"No, no, not at all. I did little enough to entertain them. Aunt Selina had to remind me of my neglect. We had a dinner with some dancing, and oh, how I wished you might have been here. You would have adored Aunt Selina, I assure you."

There was something almost feverish in this spate of words from the usually less voluble Georgina. Mrs. Conyers became if anything even more concerned, and this made it easy to ask in the most natural way, "My love, is something troubling you?"

Georgina looked at her hands in her lap for a moment, then looked up into Mrs. Conyers' eyes, and for just an instant Mrs. Conyers saw a bleakness there that caused her heart to turn over with pity.

"Georgina," she gasped, despite her firm resolve never to probe, "what has happened?" Georgina immediately dropped her eyes again. "My dear, I have always respected other people's privacy, but there are times when it is better to share one's troubles. Can you not tell me about it? I want to help, if you will let me." Georgina did not respond or look up, and the silence lengthened. At last Mrs. Conyers said, "Very well, my dear, I will not tease you more, but if you should ever want to talk to me, I will be there. I am a very good listener and I never scold or lecture." She patted Georgina's cold hands and rose. "Is Myles about? I should like to say hello."

"Perhaps Honeyman will know," Georgina replied indifferently. "Thank you for coming, Mrs. Conyers, though it should have been I who called on you since you have been ill. I will come to you soon and bring Selina, if I may."

"I will look forward to it."

Mrs. Conyers went away to find Myles, feeling such depression that she ached with it. Honeyman directed her to the estate office, which was part of the stables. She rapped at the door and was bade to enter.

Myles rose at once when he saw her and came around his desk to greet her. "My dear Mrs. Conyers, how good to see you. But you should have sent Honeyman for me. I would have come at once, had I been informed you were here. Are you feeling better?"

She gave him the explanation she had offered Georgina. "But I have sought you out on purpose to speak alone with you, my lord. I am most distressed about Georgina. Lydia tells me she has not been herself for some time. Not since her sister Hughes-Jones's visit, in fact."

Myles frowned and ran a hand roughly through his dark hair. "She will not speak to me at all, except for the barest civilities, so there is little I can tell you."

"Do you speak to *her,* my lord?"

"I try, but it is a discouraging procedure."

"I do not mean commonplace conversation. I mean have you attempted to speak to her about what is troubling her?"

"No, I—it is so nearly impossible. She is not the sort to encourage—"

"No, I know," she interrupted him with a trace of impatience, "but sometimes one must force such things. Georgina has got into the habit of retiring into her mind with her troubles and closing the doors. She had a very lonely childhood, as you must know. Oh, there were people around her, but no one *for her,* if you take my meaning, with her mother gone and her father—well Fitzhardinge was always a cold, ungiving sort of man." He gave her a puzzled look, and she added hastily, "So Lydia tells me. At any rate, in her loneliness she had only her pride to hold her up. She refused to cry or make demands, to speak of her unhappiness. Now she cannot. Do you see?"

"Could not you—"

"I have not the right. I wish I did," she said with some wistfulness. Then she became brisk again to cover her lapse. "No, it must be you. She is your wife and it your responsibility, for I do not believe there can be any doubt that whatever is wrong has to do with you." He began to protest, but she held up her hand. "Hear me out, please. From what Lydia and I can piece together it must have been something Cressida said to her, and since you are the one person she will not speak to,

I think it must be something she learned regarding you.''

"But there is nothing—''

"Cressida moves among the *ton* in London, and they are great gossips, as you must know. I doubt that any slightest indiscretion escapes their notice." She paused suggestively and looked inquiringly at him. He turned away to the window as he felt himself reddening in embarrassment. She continued gently, "Forgive me, my lord. I am aware that gossip is not necessarily the truth, but it can do a great deal of harm just the same. If she will not tell you what it is, then you must bring the issue into the open yourself. I am sure if there has ever been anything to cause gossip about yourself, it is now all in the past."

"I cannot. I cannot," he muttered distractedly.

"I think you must, if you love her and want some prospect of happiness in your marriage." She came up behind him to pat his shoulder and then left without any further words.

Myles stayed where she had left him while his mind whirled in a chaos of contradicting thoughts: a few pithy words he would like to be delivering to Cressy personally, stray bits of sentences Mrs. Conyers had spoken, pictures of Georgina's icy eyes, the memory of his own smug rectitude when he had given up his last mistress.

He rubbed his face vigorously to wipe them all away. He could not do it, he thought. How could she expect a man to ask his wife if she was angry with him because she has heard he kept a mistress? Men just did not discuss such things with their wives! For a moment he allowed himself to feel indignation with Mrs. Conyers, but then he had a vision of the years stretching bleakly ahead while he and Georgina proceeded with their lives almost silently. It was horrible! Mrs. Conyers was right, he did not want that. Damnation! Had he not given up his previous life, determined to devote himself to his wife and win her love at any cost? he thought virtuously. He wanted more than anything in the world to make her happy, to cultivate that brief, growing intimacy that was beginning before he had been forced to go away to Blostwick. Perhaps if he had not gone . . .

He sighed and turned back to sit at his desk. He felt tired suddenly, too dispirited to move. I am too old for this, he thought drearily. I have reached the time of life when one wants peace, not endless scenes and misunderstandings with a volatile young girl. I should have married closer to my own age or even an older woman—like Mrs. Conyers. He tried to imagine a life, surely calm, with Mrs. Conyers, a life without Georgina in it, and the thought created a pain as though a hand had squeezed his heart.

Oh God, he thought in despair, what am I to do? I cannot live without her and I cannot live with her as things are. So what is left?

He rose resolutely and went to find his wife. He learned from Honeyman with no small relief that m'lady had gone for a drive with Lady Selina and Nurse Apple. He returned to the estate office and attacked the work awaiting him with the energy of reprieve.

At dinner he contrived some sort of conversation for the benefit of the servants, to which Georgina replied politely. She left him to his port, and he used the time alone to strengthen his resolve to follow Mrs. Conyers' advice. He drank rather more wine than was his wont before rejoining Georgina in the drawing room.

She was working at her embroidery and glanced up only briefly to acknowledge his presence, not meeting his eyes. He allowed himself to become mesmerized by the movement of her slim, white fingers plying her needle industriously, and silence reigned until a burning log fell, sending up a shower of sparks. He started and sat up straighter.

"We are very quiet here," he remarked lightly.

"Yes."

"I wonder if it is not too quiet for you, my love. You are so young. Shall we go to London for some gaiety?"

She looked at him levelly. "*I* have little liking for London, sir, and have no friends there at all besides your aunt. If *you* are missing town, I hope you will feel free to go up at any time you care to."

There was an edge of bitterness to her words that was not lost upon him. "I do not care to at all," he said, rather too heartily he realized at once, as one who protests too much. "No, I am content here by my own fire, and there is much to be attended to here at Falconley." He watched her carefully, but she made no response, not even looking up from her work. "You are very silent tonight," he probed, trying to find a way to open up the subject Mrs. Conyers had said he must.

"I have never been good at idle conversation," she replied, her hand plying her needle steadily.

"Surely our conversation need not be idle. One of the great advantages in marriage is that one has someone to share one's troubles with—as well as the joys, of course," he added. He waited a bit, but she did not respond to this, and at last he said carefully, "Is anything troubling you, Georgina?"

"No."

He looked at her helplessly. He knew that now he should ask her point blank if her sister had said anything about him, and he tried, but could not make the words come out of his mouth.

Oh lord, he thought, I cannot do it. I will have to think of another way. Maybe tomorrow I will think of something. Yes, that is it. Give the matter more thought. Do it right, if it must be done.

He pushed the matter away with some relief. "Would you like me to read to you, my love?"

"If you like."

He picked up a book lying beside him on a table—as it happened, the very one Lady Cunliffe had recommended to Dominick—and without realizing what it was, Myles opened it and began to read aloud from what he was well into before he really attended to the words. To his horror it was on the topic of infidelity in marriage. He clapped the book closed hastily. "How very boring. Sermons are hardly entertaining reading. I will fetch something else." He hurried off to his library and returned with *Ambrosio* by Mr. Monk Lewis.

The picture they presented was one of great intimacy. A man and his wife on either side of the fire, she doing her needlework while he read aloud to her. But they might as well have been sitting on either side of a deep gorge.

In the next few days Myles managed each time the matter came to mind to find further reasons to put off questioning Georgina. Her attitude, while not warm, thawed enough as the days passed to encourage him in the belief that with patience and love he could eventually win her back to the intimacy he craved without a confrontation.

Lydia's return from Mrs. Conyers's eased the strain between them considerably, especially for Georgina, since her sister's presence evidently allowed Myles to feel released from his obligation to spend his days with Georgina, and he returned to estate business.

One morning, when he had taken his breakfast with Lydia and gone before Georgina put in an appearance, Lydia with a happy sigh opened the letter she had just received from Adrian Patterson. When Georgina came in, she looked up with a glad smile. "Look, Georgie, a letter from Adrian. Will you read it?"

"I will not," Georgina replied decidedly.

"Shall I show it to Myles then? Papa will be sure to ask me if I obeyed him in this. He never forgets such things," she added gloomily.

"Then you may tell him truthfully that each letter between you was offered to me. What has Mr. Patterson to say?"

"That he has business in this direction and will contrive to pay us a visit, though he is unable to make the time more specific than the next few days. Oh, I shall like to see him again!"

Lydia resolutely refused all outings for the next two days for fear she might miss his visit, and on the third day was rewarded when he arrived in a hired chaise, looking somewhat travel-stained but calm and smiling as always.

He was shown into the drawing room by Honeyman, and Lydia rose with a huge smile and went to greet him. Georgina saw him take her hands, bend to kiss each one, and then look for a long, searching moment into her eyes. What he saw apparently satisfied him, for he said, "You are healing, little one. I am glad."

"Adrian, it is so good to see you again," she said artlessly.

"How kind of you to say so. I had thought your days here would be so full you would have little inclination to welcome a simple country parson between your engagements."

She laughed. "You are teasing me. We live very quietly here, do not we, Georgina?"

Adrian released Lydia's hands hastily, as though he had not been aware of Georgina's presence until now, as indeed he had not been. "My dear Lady Trowbridge, forgive me! I did not see, I mean I was not aware . . ." He floundered to a stop.

Georgina smiled mischievously. "So I noticed. But do not concern yourself, sir. Now, please sit down and I will fetch some wine."

There was no reason for her to leave the room to do so with the bell rope hanging there to summon a servant, but she wanted to give them some time alone together. She knew her stepmother would find such conduct reprehensible if she learned of it, but Georgina had always thought the idea that two people of the opposite sex could not be left alone without attacking each other carnally too ridiculous.

When she returned ten minutes later, followed by Honeyman and a tray, she found them seated across from each other chatting easily together, with not a single blush from Lydia to indicate that anything untoward had been said or done. Georgina sat down and joined in the conversation, and they were still there when Myles came in.

He took two steps into the room and halted abruptly as Adrian rose and turned courteously to greet him. Myles looked as though turned to stone as all the colour drained slowly from his face.

Adrian advanced with a beaming smile, his hand extended. "Why, Mr. Barrowes! This is indeed a surprise. I had no idea you came from this part of the country."

Myles seemed to sway.

"Adrian, you have made a mistake," said Lydia, looking with some concern at her brother-in-law. "This is Lord Trowbridge."

"I beg your pardon, sir, surely—are you not Mr. Barrowes?"

Myles braced himself with an effort. "How do you do, Mr. Patterson. You took me by surprise. I sometimes prefer not to use my title, you see, but only my family name. What brings you to Falconley?"

While Adrian explained and informed Lydia eagerly that here was his patron, the man who had advanced his career, Georgina, who had been shocked by her husband's violent reaction to Mr. Patterson, looked from one to the other, something nudging persistently at her mind.

It was only later during dinner, to which Adrian had been invited as well as invited to spend some days as their guest, that it came crashing into Georgina's consciousness. She glanced up at some sally of Lydia's to see Adrian raising an eyebrow and smiling. She had seen that expression often on Myles's face. She studied them both more carefully and remembered Myles's strange conduct when he had walked into the drawing room and found Adrian there. She put together with that the news that "Mr. Barrowes" was Adrian's patron. Adrian quite obviously did not realize the truth, but Georgina did! Adrian Patterson was—must be—Myles's own son!

The dinner table tilted sickeningly for a moment as this conviction sank into her mind. When it had settled again, she reached for her wineglass and by the time she and Lydia withdrew she was definitely feeling the wine. She felt a hot wash of fury sweep through her as the wine loosened her control, and terrified at what she might say or do, told Lydia that she felt quite wretched with headache and would go to her bed. She fled upstairs to her room and, head reeling, hastened to bed, where she resolutely slammed the door on all her swarming thoughts and sank gratefully into wine-induced unconsciousness.

Myles, left alone with his son, could not help feeling that fate had dealt rather unkindly with him. It was surely unfair that this young man should be deposited on his very doorstep through so wild and unlikely a coincidence. After all, Myles thought aggrievedly, he had made up for his youthful indiscretion as best he could and meant to do more for the boy.

Myles had been but sixteen. When the woman, Dominick's governess, had come to him in tears to confess her condition, he had gone straight to his father and stoutly declared that he would of course marry her. His father had rung such a peal over his head that his ears had rung for days. What? A sixteen-year-old boy to be trapped into marriage by a woman ten years his senior who should have known better? The heir to the earldom to marry a governess whose father was a greengrocer? And on and on. The upshot was that the governess was dismissed in disgrace. But Myles had not let the matter rest there. He had followed her and in further conversation learned of one Moses Patterson, an ambitious young farmer, who had shown a definite interest in her but who had been deterred from a proposal by her lack of dowry. Out of his own pocket, well-lined even at sixteen, Myles had presented her with five thousand pounds and urged her to waste no time in acquainting Mr. Patterson of it. She followed his advice and was married one month later, bringing Adrian into the world somewhat prematurely as far as the neighbours were concerned. Whether Mr. Patterson ever knew the true state of affairs Myles did not know. He had visited them from time to time, claiming for a reason his gratitude to the woman for her efforts in educating Dominick, helped the boy's ambition later by making it possible for him to go to Oxford, and promised when the boy decided to take orders that he would have one of the livings in his gift when he was ready for it.

Mrs. Patterson had quite obviously never divulged Myles's true relationship to her son any more than she had divulged his real name, and Myles had never had any trouble with keeping his secret to himself; but now, with the boy at his own table, he was assailed by an overwhelming urge to tell him the truth. He knew this was a compound of guilt and pride, for he could not suppress his self-congratulation at having sired such a handsome, upstanding young man.

He swallowed down his foolish impulse and said, "Do you make a long visit, Mr. Patterson?"

Adrian smiled easily, "No, Mr.—ah—Lord Trowbridge, I must return to my duties at St. Edward's. I came only to reassure myself about Miss Fitzhardinge. She was much hurt by Ladbrook's death, as you must know, and I have worried about her."

"That was very kind of you, Mr. Patterson. I know her family will appreciate your concern."

"It was not so much kindness on my part, I must confess, as it was need. Miss Fitzhardinge's welfare is a matter of great moment to me, you see."

He looked straight at Myles as he said this, and Myles took his meaning with dismay.

Good lord, he thought, another complication. The boy's in love with Lydia and means to have her if he can, and I would lay money on it that he will win her in the end if he is patient. He wondered in some amusement how Lord Fitzhardinge might react to such a match. By the Lord, he should be grateful to have such a husband for his daughter!

Myles realized Adrian was still awaiting some reply and pulled himself together. "Well, Mr. Patterson, if I understand you correctly, I fear you have set a difficult goal for yourself. The girl is still too young for marriage and still in mourning for Ladbrook, and I cannot be sanguine regarding her father's consent to such a match. Very high in the instep is Lord Fitzhardinge."

"I have thought of all those things, my lord. Naturally, she must have time to recover from her grief, and I know her parents will want to bring her out properly and all that business. I would not want to deny her the chance to enjoy her youth and know something of the world. As for Lord Fitzhardinge, well, we shall see.''

Myles could think of nothing to say to such superb confidence, and he was more than ever convinced the boy would have his way. In view of that, it would perhaps be better to allow Adrian to continue in ignorance of his origins. To learn at this point of his illegitimacy might not undermine his admirable character, but why take such a chance? Damned if he didn't wish the boy luck!

Then it struck him that if Adrian had his way, some day his son would become his brother-in-law.

CHAPTER

17

Georgina woke at dawn with a genuine headache and a churning need to get away from the house. She could not face Myles this morning, nor Mr. Patterson, for that matter. Not that she blamed him for what he was so clearly not responsible for, but to sit talking politely to him was a feat beyond her capabilities. She therefore rang for Prentiss, dressed in her habit, and crept quietly out of the house.

She rode furiously for an hour, the air flowing in a cold stream past her face, holding thought at bay. Still reluctant to return home, she turned her horse toward the Priory, thinking a visit with Mrs. Conyers might calm her.

She was shown into the breakfast room, where Mrs. Conyers was reading her morning post.

"My dear! What a lovely surprise. You have had an early ride, have you not? Are you famished?"

She led Georgina to a chair and overrode her protestations by ordering toast and a fresh pot of chocolate to be brought at once. "You must take something, I insist. Was Lydia too lazy to ride this morning?"

"I did not inquire. I wanted to be alone, so I just came away. Besides, she would want to stay to entertain Adrian Patterson."

"Ah, Mr. Patterson. How do you like him, now that you know him better?"

There was a marked hesitation before Georgina replied, as though forcing the words out, "I like him very well."

"But?" prompted Mrs. Conyers.

Georgina turned away to look stonily out the window and after a moment said in a strained voice, "He is Myles's son."

"Myles—Why, my love, what are you saying? Has Myles told you this?"

"It was not necessary for him to tell me. If you could have seen his face when he walked in and found Adrian there! I thought he would faint he turned so pale. And Adrian knew him. Greeted him as Mr. Barrowes, and Myles became flustered and looked as though he wished the floor would open up and swallow him. Then, they are alike in so many ways. Oh, it is perfectly obvious."

"Does the boy know?"

"Not he! Myles would make sure to buy everyone's silence," Georgina exclaimed bitterly.

"Well, it is not exactly a thing a man would advertise," Mrs. Conyers reminded her gently. "How old is Mr. Patterson?"

"Lydia says he is two and twenty."

"Very young to be a vicar."

"Oh, that is Myles's doing, of course. He is the famous patron Mr. Patterson speaks of."

"Then he has certainly done very well by the boy, even though not acknowledging him."

"He can well afford it."

"Georgina, you are not being fair. By my calculations your husband cannot have been more than a boy himself when his son was conceived, seventeen at most. As his father's heir, he would not have been allowed to marry at so young an age and certainly not to someone below his station. I think you must admit that he has behaved very responsibly in a situation in which he could not have been forced to do anything for the boy had he not wished to do so. And after all, it happened so long ago, before you were even born. Surely this is not what has been troubling you these past weeks."

"No, I only learned *this* last night."

"Do you mean there is more?"

"Oh, much more! But all of a piece."

Mrs. Conyers waited patiently after this acid statement, while Georgina stared into her cup, her mouth drawn into a tight, hard line.

She continued after some moments in an anguished voice, "He keeps a mistress."

Mrs. Conyers felt her heart plummet in dismay at the accuracy of her guess. "Oh, my dear, how—"

"Cressy told me when she was here. Oh, she did not mean to, it slipped out. She never thinks before she speaks. I could tell it was the truth by her behaviour when she realized what she had said."

"Have you spoken to Myles about it?"

"Of course I have not!" Georgina was scornful at such a question.

"But then what do you mean to do?"

"Do? Why, nothing. What can I do about it?"

"It may very well be that Cressy was only repeating some gossip she had heard and knows nothing really herself. You should at least give Myles a chance to refute it."

"I would not demean myself by discussing his mistress with him. If he wants to behave in such a disgusting way, he may do so. I would not allow him to think I care. After all, it is only one more in a long list of betrayals. I am hardened to them by now."

"And revel in them, it seems," replied Mrs. Conyers with unusual sharpness.

"What?"

"I mean that you hoard up your hurts and brood over them in private, counting them over in your mind, almost pleased to have another to add to your collection. You tell yourself it is your pride that will not allow you to acknowledge wrongs done to you, to confront the perpetrators, but I begin to think it is something quite other."

Georgina looked bewildered and hurt. "No, that is not true. I do not hoard them."

"Then you are afraid."

Stung, Georgina cried out, "I am *not* afraid. How can you say so? It is only that I think it is disgusting to be forever parading one's feelings before the world."

"I do not advocate taking the world into your confidence, Georgina, but I think it unfair to those who love you to clutch your resentments to you. If you will not tell us how we have hurt you, how can we hope to apologize, to change, to stop hurting you?"

"If all those who claim to love me truly did so, they would not hurt me."

"But sometimes we act out of some need more urgent than can be resisted, not wanting to hurt others, but—"

"Myles's need for a mistress was too urgent to take his marriage vows into account, is that what you mean?" asked Georgina scornfully.

"Perhaps. You should think about it, child. Can you honestly say you have met his needs? Do you even know what they are?"

"I have always done my duty."

"Ah, duty, the most dreadful word in the English language, a grudging, cold sort of word. To my mind one should never act from duty but from love. Where love is, duty has no place."

"I *have* loved Myles!"

"Then you should know his needs."

"His? What of mine?" Georgina stormed.

"Very well, what are yours?"

"Not to be betrayed and decieved."

"I am saddened to learn they are such negative ones."

"What do you mean?"

"I would rather hear of more positive yearnings than what you need *not* to be done to you."

"Oh, you speak in riddles, I do not understand you. Why are you trying to make me feel as though I have done something wrong, that I am stupid? It is Myles who has behaved shamefully."

"You are being overly dramatic, my dear. The bit of gossip you heard from Cressy may be years old. After all, your husband was unmarried for many years. It would be no great thing if he had a mistress or even several during that time. There is no proof he has had one since he married you, and I for one would be inclined to doubt that he has, since it is clear he adores you. And since," she added drily, "you say you have always done your duty."

Suddenly Georgina remembered with discomfort a certain conversation with Lady Cunliffe about the joys of the marriage bed. She had never been able to bring herself to admit the guilt this conversation had roused in her, but she had always known, despite everything, that she had failed Myles there.

But it is not my fault, she cried silently. Surely I cannot be blamed for disliking that! I have never denied him his rights. I have done my duty. Duty. She heard again the scorn Mrs. Conyers had invested in the word. A grudging word, she had said. Had she allowed Myles to make love to her grudgingly?

A lump formed in her throat, and she turned her head away sharply and lifted her chin. No tears, she ordered herself. In a hard voice she said, "It seems it is always I who am at fault, I who must change. Myles, naturally, is blameless."

"Oh, darling girl, I am not trying to apportion blame for anything. But you must learn not to be so unforgiving, that is all I am trying to show you. Have you never done anything you regretted?"

"Nothing I would be ashamed to confess," Georgina said proudly.

"A pity," returned Mrs. Conyers succinctly.

"I think it extraordinary that you should find it pitiful that I have behaved as I ought. I had not thought I would be condemned for it."

"I only meant that sitting upon such a peak of virtue prevents you from understanding the imperfections of the more frail of your fellow men."

Georgina rose stiffly. "I will bid you good day, Mrs. Conyers."

"Georgina! Forgive me. I have made you angry and I only wanted to help," Mrs. Conyers cried repentantly, rising to come swiftly around the table to take Georgina's cold hands into her own. "I hope you will not hate me for it, for I care for you so deeply."

Georgina felt her throat constricting with tears and pressed Mrs. Conyers's hands before turning away and hurrying out of the room.

As she rode home, the words they had spoken jostled in her mind, tumbling and overlapping one another meaninglessly, until quite clearly she heard herself saying, "Nothing I would be ashamed to confess," and with the words came the memory of melting beneath Dominick's kiss. Would she be willing to confess that to anyone? But nothing happened, she protested silently, nothing at all! So there is no reason to confess it to Myles. There was nothing in it after all, and to tell him of it would only cause bad feeling between the two brothers needlessly. I hope I am not such a make-mischief as that.

Feeling comforted by this self-serving virtuousness, she

arrived home to find the house a hive of activity, with servants hurrying up and down the stairs, carrying piles of clothing and traveling cases. Myles came out of his library as she started up the stairs.

"My dear, I wondered where you had gone for so long. I have had the most dreadful news from Dorset. There has been a fire at Hallowhill, and I must go at once. Would you like to accompany me?"

"No, I thank you. You will want to leave quickly, and I should only hold you back. Then there is Lydia."

"Lydia had a letter from her mother this morning, bidding her come home at once for Harriet's wedding. We were asked to come also, but of course I cannot."

They were interrupted by Nurse Pomfret, holding young Simon and leading down the stairs a procession of a maid, Honeyman, and a footman carrying baggage.

"Oh, my lady," cried Mrs. Pomfret, "Madam has sent the carriage for us, and we are to go home at once. She and the master have gone on and now we must travel alone. I am that afraid to be travelling the roads with no man to protect us."

"You will have the coachman, Mrs. Pomfret, but I will send one of the stable lads to ride beside the carriage. Honeyman, send word out to young Tom to make ready."

"Oh, my lord, such kindness. I thank you, indeed I do," she bobbed a curtsey, and still babbling of highwaymen and the evils of coaching inns and unaired sheets, hurried out to the waiting carriage.

"Really, Cressy might have come for her own child. I suppose they were invited some place else to stay along the way. I will go up to Lydia."

Myles thought grimly that it was more likely Cressy decided to postpone a meeting with himself after the mischief she had caused, but he only said, "My dear, I shall be leaving almost at once, I think, if you do not care to come. But I cannot like leaving you here alone."

"I will accompany Lydia," she said with sudden decision. "She cannot travel alone."

"Well, as to that, I believe Mr. Patterson means to escort her."

"Good lord, I had forgotten him altogether," she exclaimed. "Well, he shall escort us both."

"Will you take Selina?"

"No. She will do much better here than jolting about the roads. I will not be away that long."

"Then I shall make sure to finish my business at Hallowhill as soon as possible and come to escort you home," he said, putting a hand over hers where it rested on the banister.

"As you wish. I will bid you good-bye until then." She carefully extricated her hand and turned away up the stairs, feeling secretly relieved that she could not be expected to speak to him about anything when he was so troubled by the business at Hallowhill.

Myles watched her retreating back, experiencing very much the same feeling, though mixed with guilt. He resolved that when they were both back home he would force himself to speak, by God he would!

CHAPTER

18

A week later Georgina and Lydia stood arm in arm on the Fitzhardinges' steps and waved good-bye as Sir Vernon's carriage disappeared down the drive, bearing him and his bride the ten miles to his own estate. They were to begin their wedding trip three days hence.

"To the Lake Country only," sniffed Lydia contemptuously, when she learned of it, "I suspect he is very mean with money, or he would take her abroad."

Harriet had looked nearly beautiful as she had followed Lydia down the aisle on her father's arm, expertly gowned by Lady Fitzhardinge in a robe of real Brussels point lace and a cottage bonnet of Brussels lace with two ostrich feathers, with a deep lace veil and a white satin pelisse trimmed with swansdown. She made no effort to conceal the blazing smile of triumph that lit her face.

"You would think she'd captured the Crown Prince!" whispered the irrepressible Lydia, "instead of that oily turkey cock." She and Georgina had stayed very much together during the week preceeding the wedding, assiduously avoiding Sir Vernon's straying hands and leering eyes.

Cressy had had no such compunction. She had arrived the day after Georgina with Windy and her usual entourage of servants, carriages, and outriders, but minus Mrs. Pomfret and Simon. No other males being available, she became immediately coquettish towards Sir Vernon, who, his *amour propre* having suffered from Lydia's and Georgina's cold shoulders, turned to Cressy as a flower to the sun.

What actually transpired could not be ascertained by the rest of the party, though there could be no doubt that private meetings took place between them. When out riding, Cressy and Sir Vernon always contrived to separate themselves from the rest of the party. Windy never knew of this, since he was too stout to enjoy riding and remained at home. The same applied to rambles in the woods and after-dinner strolls in the gardens. When actually in their company, Windy only smiled benignly upon the flirtation, no doubt well schooled by Cressy to accept her behaviour as part of the repertoire of all well-bred ladies. Lady Fitzhardinge, not above a little flirtation herself, saw nothing wrong, and her husband had long since given up bothering his head about Cressy, feeling she was now her husband's responsibility. As for Harriet, her mind was too occupied with the final fittings for her bridal gown, her hair, her trousseau, and assessing the price of her wedding gifts. When she did notice Cressy's flirting, she was rather gratified, feeling that it proved Sir Vernon's attractiveness and that she had captured a more handsome husband than Cressy. Besides, with the wedding only days away it never entered her head that her husband-to-be could be engaged in serious philandering. Only Lydia and Georgina were aware of what was transpiring.

Cressy only laughed when Lydia attempted to remonstrate with her. "Please do not bother yourself with what you cannot understand, Puss. I assure you I take nothing from Harriet that she will want." This enigmatic statement was all she would make on the subject. Lydia begged Georgina to speak to Cressy, but Georgina declined. She and Cressy had found little to say to each other on this first meeting since Cressy's disastrous revelation at Falconley, and Georgina had no intention of seeking a private interview.

She and Lydia therefore waved good-bye to the wedded pair with enormous relief and Cressy with an innocent gaiety, until Windy, a heavy arm about her shoulders, led her back inside with a possessive smile. Lady Fitzhardinge and Miss Hapgood wept sentimental tears.

"Poor Harry," sighed Lydia, "how I should hate to be facing my wedding night with Sir Vernon beside me."

"Lydia! I will not have you speaking so. You are too young to know of such things," reproved her mama.

"Pooh! I have known of 'such things' for years."

"Well, you should not, and more to the point, you should not speak of them. You must learn to guard your tongue or you will earn a reputation for being fast when we are in London.''

"I should not care in the least," Lydia declared, tossing her head defiantly.

"More rash talk. I doubt you would like being denied entrée to Almack's, and let me tell you that you will not be considered a success in London if the Countess de Lieven takes it into her head that you are not a properly behaved girl and refuses to allow your name to be put on the List. Why, you would be—but there," she interrupted herself, "I know Lady Castlereagh very well, and she will vouch for you. Just the same, I shall expect you to show better conduct from now on or I shall have to speak to your papa. He cannot be put to the expense of a Season if you are going to behave in so hoydenish a way as to ruin every chance of making a respectable match. Now, come along, Miss Hapgood. I shall need your help. I want to go through Lydia's gowns and see what she will need.''

Lydia gazed after her mother with stormy eyes. "Can you believe your ears? She is already thinking of a respectable match for me!''

Georgina laughed. "Well, that is the usual reason for the entire business, after all.''

"She will have her work cut out with me," Lydia asserted with satisfaction, "for I have no interest in a respectable match, or for any at all for that matter. How she can be so insensitive as to even speak of it to me with Tarq dead so short a time I cannot understand.''

"Never mind, love, she just forgot for the moment. Think of all the fun you will have instead. All the new gowns and the lovely dancing.''

"Georgie, why do you not come up to London with us? The Little Season is in full swing now and besides, I want you there for my come-out. Oh, say you will, do!''

Georgina thought about it for a moment. "Perhaps I will. But you will be too busy to bother with me. Balls every night, I dare say.''

"Lord, Georgie, what if no one will ask me to stand up?" There was panic in Lydia's blue eyes.

"What a pea-goose you are. Of course they will ask you. You will take very well, I know, and have beaux by the score dangling at your shoe laces.''

Lydia contemplated this picture in silence for a moment and then, clearly having little faith in it, said, "I shall write to Adrian and invite him to my party. He will stand up with me."

Georgina looked startled. "Oh, but I do not think—would Papa allow it?"

"Oh, Papa likes Adrian. He says Adrian is very level-headed and knows his place. Papa likes people to know their place," she added, laughing.

Georgina refrained from making any further comment, though she wondered if she was being wise. She knew only too well Adrian's feelings regarding Lydia and in fact until recently she had approved them, but now she wondered if it was not her duty to discourage any further meetings between them, knowing Adrian's history, as she now did. Her father, she knew would never countenance a match between them if he knew the truth. Indeed, he would not countenance a match in any circumstances between his daugther and a penniless vicar. Mrs. Conyers had said that where love was, duty had no place, but it seemed to her that her duty and her love for Lydia dictated the same answer. She sighed and decided it was not a problem she could solve. She could not even solve her own! Besides, it might never come to anything. However Adrian felt, Lydia was a long way from being ready to think of love, and by the time she was ready, she might have met someone else.

They gave a final wave as Sir Vernon's carriage rounded a bend that hid it from their view; the last thing they saw was Harriet's muff still waving from the window.

Harriet withdrew her head and her muff from the window and settled back into her seat beside her new husband with a sigh compounded of complacency and only a tinge of regret at leaving her home.

"Oh, how I shall miss them all and my dear old home," she said sentimentally.

It was the last happy moment of her marriage. She was unceremoniously jerked into her husband's arms; his mouth clamped down upon her own, and a hard hand possessed itself of her left breast. After the initial shock she began struggling mightily, finally managing to turn her head aside long enough to say, "Please—what do you think you are?—remove your hands at once, do you hear?"

He pulled back in some astonishment and then began to

laugh, for her bonnet was tilted crazily awry, the satin ribbands, tied before in a fetching bow beneath her chin, now up over one ear. She twitched it back into place in exasperation and drew as far away from him as the confines of the carriage allowed, smoothing down her pelisse of burgandy velvet trimmed with sable bands, of which she was inordinately proud.

"Really, Sir Vernon, you are behaving shockingly. I should never have suspected you of such a lack of breeding," she scolded, her lips pursed in disapproval, not hesitating to set him straight at once on the matter of how their marriage was to be conducted. "What will the coachman think, and what if another carriage should pass and see us?"

"Be damned to 'em! We're all leg-shackled right and tight, aren't we? I suppose I may do what I like with my wife when I choose and let 'em stare if they've nothing better to do." He reached for her again, causing her to shriek and cower back against the side of the carriage, both hands extended to hold him off, but she was no match for Sir Vernon, who deftly pinioned her hands behind her back and held them there with one hand, while with the other he ripped open the pelisse, causing velvet-covered buttons to fly in all directions, to expose the rose-pink silk gown beneath. A cold hand was inserted into the low, round neckline, causing her to shriek again and thrash about desperately. He laughed and kneaded her breasts while snuffling at her neck, and all the while describing her struggles as attempts to rouse him further in the most obscene terms, most of which she did not understand.

Hearing her screams and the commotion going on behind him, the coachman, who had little love for Sir Vernon, took pity on the poor lass and whipped up his horses, hoping to reach home before the beast raped his bride right there on a main thoroughfare. The carriage bucketed over the ruts headlong, throwing the struggling couple about like dice in a cup, while Sir Vernon alternately cursed Harriet and his coachman. He did not give up his attempt to have her in the carriage, but he was incapable of succeeding, once even rolling precipitously onto the floor, where Harriet's flailing foot caught him full force in the mouth. He swore awfully and lunged up for her again, but fortunately at that moment the carriage swerved into his own drive, throwing him back to the floor so hard that he was winded for the moment. As the carriage began to slow down, he climbed sullenly back onto the seat and put his hat back on, treating Harriet to such a glowering look that she promptly burst into tears.

Thus the newlyweds arrived at their home. Harriet was helped out to face every servant in Sir Vernon's employ lined up on the steps to welcome their new mistress, with one hand holding her crumpled and buttonless pelisse over the torn bodice of her rose silk gown, and with the other holding to her face her sable muff, into which she was sobbing uncontrollably.

The housekeeper bustled forward in concern, and putting an arm about the girl, led her into the house. Sir Vernon turned to curse the coachman scathingly and would have dismissed him on the spot had he not so many problems with keeping servants, whose tenure with him was notoriously short-lived. He contented himself, therefore, with a pithy sermon and turned to snarl at the rest to get on with the work for which they were paid, which did not include standing about gawping at their betters, and stumped into the house. He ordered his butler to bring brandy to the library and retired there to crash the door behind him and explore his sore teeth with a cautious tongue to make sure none had been loosened. Be damned if he did not make her pay for that before the night was over, he thought surlily.

Harriet was led up to her room and with the housekeeper's insistence helped to drink down a glass of hartshorn and water. When her sobs had subsided into hiccoughs, she was coaxed out of her clothes and into a dressing gown of pale-green satin edged with swansdown and settled before the fire on a chaise longue under a cashmere shawl, where, worn out by tears and exhaustion, she fell asleep almost at once.

When Sir Vernon arrived in the dining room, he was met with the bland announcement by his butler that m'lady would not come down for dinner, being too ill to eat. Sir Vernon grunted noncommittally and proceeded with his own meal. Afterwards he retired to his library, where he sat brooding sullenly over several more glasses of brandy. Suddenly he pounded his fist on the arm of his chair and uttered an oath, then rose and strode rapidly upstairs to his dressing room, where he changed into a robe. He then went across the landing to his wife's room, entered without knocking, and carefully locked the door behind him. Harriet, one hand tucked childishly beneath her cheek and looking innocently pretty, still lay asleep on the chaise. Sir Vernon did not pause to admire his bride, however, but abruptly lifted her and carried her towards the bed. She woke at once, entirely disoriented, her eyes flying wildly about before memory returned and she began thrashing about in terror. He tossed her on the bed and fell heavily atop her. As her mouth opened to scream, he covered it with his own, his tongue snaking about inside her mouth in a way she had never dreamed possible, much less been informed about. Naturally her mama had been vague on details, only emphasizing the importance of the wife submitting to her husband's will and assuring her that in time she would not mind it. Was it possible her mother had meant *this?* Harriet wondered, and thought she could not bear such a thing. She moaned and pushed against his chest, but she was pinned fast to the bed by his weight. He released her mouth at last, but only to begin biting her breasts until, fully roused, he forced her legs apart with his knees and without any preliminary to warn her of what was to come plunged himself into her with all the force at his command. She screamed with the unbearable pain and then blessedly fainted. Her husband finished at last and rolled away. After some moments he rose, resumed his robe, and made his way back to his own room without a backward glance at his unconscious wife.

In the weeks that followed she often wished she might again faint, but she did not. She became thin and pale, unable to eat and frightened to sleep for fear of his coming upon her without warning. Her eyes took on a hunted look, and she crept about the house, trying to avoid her husband's attention, for she found he was of insatiable appetite and seemed to take delight in throwing her down wherever he found her and having his way. She could no longer look any of the servants in the eyes.

Then a particularly buxom, bold-eyed maid attracted his attention, and for some days Harriet was left in peace. It was short-lived, however, as even worse demands were then made upon her when he brought the girl into her room and demanded they both make love to him at the same time. The maid grinned lasciviously and opened her bodice, from which tumbled her large, eager-looking breasts. She dropped her skirt to the floor and fell upon her master enthusiastically.

Harriet shrank away in horror and started up to flee the room, but Braye caught her wrist and held her there, so she could do nothing but bury her head in her pillow.

Braye laughed and said, "If you will not, then you must watch. Perhaps you will learn something. God knows you need lessons. Now then, sweetheart, show her how it is done," he chortled, pushing the girl's head slowly down his body and between his legs. With his other hand he reached out, and grasping Harriet's head by her hair, turned her face toward them. "Open your eyes, damn you, or I will beat you later!"

She opened them for one horrified and disbelieving glance before she felt a blessed oblivion enveloping her again and sank gratefully into unconsciousness.

Beside these horrors she suffered other humiliations, which he seemed to delight in inflicting upon her, criticizing her before the servants, making derisive comments upon her dress and coiffure before occasional callers, and ignoring her to flirt openly with other women on their few dinners outside their home.

She thought sometimes she might go mad; indeed, it sometimes seemed to her that madness would be a welcome escape. How was it possible, she asked herself, that she, who had dreamed all her life of a respectable marriage, who had kept herself pure in mind and deed for a husband who would surely worship at her feet, should be subjected to this degradation? She did not deserve this, she cried out silently and fruitlessly, for there was no one she would dream of confiding such things to. Were all women treated so? Surely Windy could not be such a husband to Cressy. Cressy! she thought bitterly. If ever a girl deserved a husband like Braye it was Cressy, who was a born strumpet and would no doubt enjoy it. Oh, why was God so unfair? And to think that *this* must be borne for there to be children in the world!

She began to wonder if she would become pregnant. No! No children, she thought wildly, I could not bear his child. But the thought would not leave her, and she now suffered Braye's attentions with more dread than before. Each day became an agony of suspense. Out of her preoccupation, however, with a cunning born of desperation, there came into her mind a plan. She was so terrified of her husband by this time that it was some days before she dared do anything. One afternoon the courage came to her when she stood speaking to the housekeeper in the hall and he came out of his library.

"Harriet, come in here. I want you," he ordered. She hesitated, knowing by the look in his eye what was to follow. "Now!" he barked, taking her arm and jerking her into the room and slamming the door.

She pulled her arm away and moved swiftly behind a chair. "Wait! I must tell you something. I—I am with child, and I swear to you if you touch me now or at any time without my permission, I will—I will do away with the baby!"

The choler that had begun to rise in him at her defiance was checked, while he stared incredulously. No woman he had ever bedded, and there had been hundreds, had ever claimed to be carrying a child by him, and since he felt any woman would have used such a weapon to force money or marrige from him had she been able, he had secretly come to believe he could not father a child.

Until he had inherited his uncle's estate this had not been a serious consideration to him; indeed, it was more a matter of congratulation. His inheritance, however, had changed his mind. Now he had something to pass on to his own child he felt he must breed, for never could he bear to think of what was his passing to some distant relative. Marriage, previously abhorrent, became a necessity. Just the same he had looked about carefully, for even in necessity one must be sure of getting the best bargain available.

His neighbour Lord Fitzhardinge had two unwed daughters and had welcomed his advances. Braye would not have minded the younger, as she was the prettier, but when he learned Harriet's portion was to be doubled, he settled on her, for Braye had but two vices: his lust and his love of money. To have a wife upon whom to exercise the first at whim and who also satisfied the second seemed a bargain indeed, and he had closed the deal promptly.

He had not expected to have his ambition for a son gratified so soon however, and it took some moments for his mind to assimilate the fact as well as the threat that had come with it. When the import of her words reached him, he growled warily, "You would not dare harm the child."

"Try me and see," she cried, courage mounting in her as she saw his uncertainty.

"How can you be sure, anyway, it is only a month."

"Five weeks, and a woman always knows, there are signs," she replied drawing herself up proudly, folding her hands protectively over her stomach as though there really was a life beginning there.

"If you do anything to harm my child, I will kill you with my bare hands!" he shouted furiously.

"You will be welcome to do so, for I shall not care by then. I would welcome death. So remember what I say, sir, for I have never been more serious. You may take your beastliness to that whore in the servants' quarters, but never dare bring her to my room again or come yourself except at my invitation. Is this understood?"

He stood fuming helplessly but finally shouted, "Yes, you stupid cow, yes!" and turned abruptly on his heel and left the room.

She tottered around the chair and crumpled into it, her trembling legs no longer capable of supporting her, her heart pounding so hard it was painful. She had won, but there was little triumph in it for her, for it was only a reprieve. She was now in a situation for which she had no plan yet, for she was not pregnant, and could only become so by submitting to what she was determined never to submit to again. All she had bought was time and, for the moment, the whip hand, but that was all she had planned. She now must plan how she would get away. She must reach her parents, but she knew they were now in London. Braye would never allow her to go there. She would have to think of some reason to tell him she must go to her father's home for the day. Happy would still be there. She could say she wanted to visit with her old governess and tell her the happy news, then she would take one of her father's carriages and go on to London. She was sure when her parents learned what abasements she had suffered they would never allow her to return.

CHAPTER

19

While still with her parents Georgina had a letter from Myles informing her that the fire damage to Hallowhill was far more extensive than he had expected and he would be required to stay on for at least another week. She should remain where she was until he could come for her.

She was unaccountably piqued by this order, as though, she thought, she was a piece of goods waiting to be picked up at his convenience, though she had been relieved to be separated from him at the beginning. Now she wondered if he was not even more relieved to be apart from her, inventing excuses to stay away. Perhaps he had found some more compelling and attractive reason for staying on in Devon. In an uprush of resentment she sat down and dashed off a letter telling him not to be in any hurry to come for her as she was perfectly capable of making her way back to Falconley without any assistance from him, thank you very much. She threw down her pen and rose to stride about the room, her cheeks flaring with angry colour, her fists clenched. Gradually, however, her indignation cooled, and when she reread the letter, she tore it up. She would not allow him to guess that his actions had so much effect on her. Indeed, they had not, she reminded herself sternly. He had forfeited her concern, and she no longer cared what he did. She would return to Falconley and raise her child and conduct herself properly, and if he cared to make himself the subject of scandalous gossip, he would never know from her that it mattered a whit!

In spite of this righteous resolve she began presently to feel curiously oppressed by her plan. It seemed too tame and abject for her present state of mind. She remembered Lydia's invitation, and gradually going to London became eminently desirable. She sat down to her desk again and wrote her husband that she had formed the plan to accompany her family to London. He replied enthusiastically that he was happy to learn of this plan and would join her there. He suggested she might like to stay with his aunt. Georgina seized upon this idea eagerly, for opening her own house meant sending for Honeyman and Cook and involved a great deal of unnecessary work for everyone. For this reason she had settled to stay with her parents, but without much enthusiasm, for Lady Fitzhardinge's bubble-headedness irritated her after a time, and her father's unbending coldness cast a pall upon her mood in a matter of moments. She therefore wrote to Lady Cunliffe, asking if she might come to stay, and left for London secure in her welcome even without a reply.

She did not worry about not having brought enough gowns for so prolonged a stay from home, since she had decided that she would order a great many more to be made when she reached London. How this decision had been reached she had no idea, but it had gradually, with a feeling almost of defiance, settled itself in her mind that she meant to go about a great deal and be very gay and dazzle the *ton* with the most modish gowns and bonnets to be had. She was too young and inexperienced to wonder who or what she was defying.

The party arrived in London rather late in the Little Season and found it so cold that the Thames had frozen solid between London Bridge and Blackfriars. A Frost Fair had sprung up on the frozen river. Georgina, however, had little time that first week for fairs, since she spent most of her days in Pall Mall, the Burlington Arcade, and Harding and Howell's, rapidly accumulating a positive mountain of furs, fans, gloves, bonnets, and fabrics. She visited the best silk warehouses, where bolt after dazzling bolt was unfurled for her inspection, after which several hours must be spent in consultation with Mme. Bochard, a fashionable couturier, whose minions were instantly set to work creating gowns for operas, balls, ridottos, dinners, carriage drives, walks, and court appearances.

Exhausted by all the shopping and fittings, she spent her evenings quietly with Lady Cunliffe, refusing even to dine with her parents. She and Lady Cunliffe dined early and, with two exceptions, alone. Dominick came on one evening and Lydia another.

Dominick was as gallant and as admiring to Georgina as always, his eyes, warm with the secret of their past intimacies, inviting, lingering upon hers significantly. There was, however, little else he could do under the sharp regard of his aunt, who made sure never to leave them alone together. Georgina, while allowing a mild flirtation, had little inclination for more in any case, a reaction that puzzled her, for in her newly defiant mood she had thought, while driving to London, that Dominick would surely renew his pursuit of her, and the thought had not been unpleasant. Now, however, he seemed less compelling, his vividness diminished. She felt suspended, as though waiting for the curtain to go up, and he become only a minor player, waiting with her in the dimness of the wings, for the real play to begin.

On Saturday afternoon Lydia came to plead with Georgina to accompany her to the Frost Fair. Lady Cunliffe urged them to go, while declining to join them. Georgina allowed herself to be persuaded, and accompanied by Prentiss, they set off in Lady Cunliffe's carriage, Georgina wearing the most extravagant of her purchases so far, a hooded sable cape and muff over a dark-emerald walking dress.

"Georgina, how I covet your cape!" Lydia exclaimed rapturously.

"You may borrow it whenever you like, love."

"And a great figure of fun I should look in it too. You are a least a head taller, and it would trail. I would never be able to carry it off in any case. I have not the stature for magnificence, poor little dab that I am."

"Now you are fishing for compliments. You know you are a pretty girl."

"Oh, pretty," Lydia replied, brushing this aside as of no importance. "Amongst a handful of pretty girls I will never be noticed. You, on the other hand, would stand out in a mob."

Georgina laughed at this extravagance, though she was gratified by it. For the first time in her life she felt a need to prove that she could attract, that she was desirable. Then she forgot the compliment as she looked out the window. "Look, oh, Lydia, look!" she said unbelievingly. The carriage had pulled up near Three Cranes Dock, and spreading before them clear to the opposite bank, the ice teemed with throngs of holidaying Londoners.

The three women stepped out of the carriage and climbed down the stairs set against the dock to join the streams of people along a thoroughfare called Freezeland Street, lined on either side with tents and booths for bakers, toy sellers, butchers, cooks, booksellers, and everything the heart could desire. There were skittle alleys and swings and gambling games, and moving through the mobs were peddlers and hawkers of oysters, brandy balls, and ginger bread. It was a boisterous, good-natured crowd from every walk of life, intent on expressing their happiness, for now all the news from the Continent was good, and expectations ran high that at any moment Napoleon would be defeated at last and the long war would be over.

Georgina and Lydia linked arms and moved off, followed closely by Prentiss, and joined in the merrymaking, sampling meat pies, fruit, and oysters at a few pence the dozen, buying ribbands and silk flowers and toys for Selina. They tried their luck at the wheel of fortune and at pricking the garter, and pored over the bookstalls. Then in an excess of high spirits they climbed into the swing, a half-moon-shaped cab with seats at each end, suspended by chains from a triangular structure. Two red-cheeked apprentices, grinning and nudging each other at their daring, climbed in to share the ride with Quality, and they all shrieked and giggled as the men at each end began pushing the swing back and forth, higher and higher, while Prentiss stood waiting, her mouth prim with disapproval. When the machine was allowed to slow to a halt and the four tumbled out, giggling and gasping, she raked scornful eyes over the boys, but they only grinned wider, tipped their caps at the ladies with gay insouciance, and strutted away.

It was for both girls an afternoon of perfect forgetfulness after the arduous days of fittings and shopping and before the social whirl began, especially for Georgina, who for those few precious hours had no thoughts at all of a straying husband or an illegitimate stepson or of her own confusion. They arrived back at Lady Cunliffe's pink-cheeked and sparkling-eyed to regale the older woman with tales of all the wonders they had seen and to divide up the afternoon's booty.

Lydia was prevailed upon to stay for dinner, "Though I vow," she declared, "I will not be able to force a bite down my throat after all I have gobbled down today." An hour later, however, she was devouring a large dinner with undiminished appetite, while the three woman discussed who was in town, what parties were being given, and what gowns they would each wear and where.

Georgina's first appearance in society was to be the next day at the Queen's Drawing Room. Her appearance in London had not gone unnoted, and invitations had not been long in forthcoming.

The Drawing Room was not an occasion she could look forward to, for she had attended on previous visits to London and found it excessively boring. Still, one could hardly refuse, and there was the monstrously expensive gown to wear to it that should recompense her boredom to some extent. It was a robe of Spanish brown velvet, embroidered lavishly about the neckline and hem with golden shells and vine leaves, with a train of Buenos Ayres gold tissue that fell straight from her shoulders.

She and Lady Cunliffe were to attend together and were escorted by an elderly admirer of Lady Cunliffe's, a courtly but frail old gentleman in coat and knee breeches of pale-green satin, who tottered along between them as they progressed slowly down the room, greeting acquaintances and friends. Dominick had been requested by his aunt to escort them, but he had declined. "Not even for you, dearest Aunt. In any case I am going over to visit Luttrell in Ireland for two weeks."

Georgina had not been sorry to hear this, for she was finding herself uncomfortable in his company now. His meaningful looks were embarrassing, and she could only remember their former intimacy with shame.

When she was summoned to greet the old Queen, she advanced and swept her a graceful curtsey and was kept in conversation for but five minutes before a regal nod released her. With another curtsey she backed away and rejoined Lady Cunliffe, feeling uncomfortably guilty as she managed her train at the thought of how much she had spent upon the gown, which would never be worn again, all to satisfy her own vanity and make a splash before a group of boring people she did not care two pins for. Her name and a description of her gown would be written up in *Bell's Court and Fashionable Magazine,* and the only person to receive gratification from the honour would be Lady Fitzhardinge. Georgina, raised by a father who complained constantly about expenditures, was so little inured to the money now at her disposal as to begin to wonder how the gown might be refashioned for future wear. She was roused from this speculation by Lady Cunliffe.

"Georgina, my dear, allow me to present this young scamp to you. Lord St. Albans. Alex, my nephew's wife, Lady Trowbridge." She emphasized the word "wife" slightly, giving St. Albans a sly glance. He was a tall, slender young man, handsome and merry-looking, who made Georgina a profound bow, kissed the hand she held out to him, and said, "Madam, your slave," with an ardent look.

Discomfited by such a declaration, Georgina blushed and laughed nervously, inwardly cursing her lack of conduct. A married woman of two years behaving as a chit straight from the schoolroom, she scolded herself.

Lord St. Albans, enchanted by the blush, smiled down into her eyes tenderly. "Do you attend the Langhams' ball tomorrow night, Lady Trowbridge?" he asked hopefully. When she confirmed that she would be there, he continued, "Then dare I hope you will have a dance left for me?"

She laughed and said, "You may choose, sir, for I have all of them free."

"Then I will beg the first—and the waltz," he added greedily, with a delighted smile. He could scarcely believe his good fortune that this unbelievably beautiful woman should be as yet undiscovered.

They were joined now by another gentleman, who bowed gracefully over Lady Cunliffe's hand and inquired in a most kindly way how she did, listening attentively while she told him. Only when she had finished did he turn to greet St. Albans pleasantly and then turn to Georgina, an eager light in his eye. Lady Cunliffe introduced him as Lord Alvanley. He also inquired about the Langham ball and requested to stand up with her, which she was happy to grant.

In all it turned out to be a less boring affair than Georgina had anticipated.

On the drive home Lady Cunliffe commented, "Well, you have done very well the first time out in over a year, my dear. St. Albans is the current catch of the Season, and you will no doubt make enemies tomorrow night when he is seen to be mooning over you. Very old family, money, connected to half the titled families in England."

"He is very pleasant. Also Lord Alvanley seemed a good-natured young man."

"Oh, Alvanley. Yes, very well liked, received everywhere, but he is only the second baronet in the line, you know. Father a lawyer or something. Still, he is very good *ton*."

"Well, at least I shall not spend tomorrow evening against the wall with the chaperones, tapping my foot. I have four sets arranged already."

"My dear, it never occurred to me that you could be worried about such a thing. I think you will find yourself beseiged with requests."

Georgina was grateful, however, for having secured her few dances. She had not attended a ball for over a year and had little confidence that London blades would be interested in dancing with a married woman. Though only twenty, she felt middle-aged and out of the swim. Despite Prentiss's gasp of admiration, Georgina eyed herself in the glass with an overly critical eye and felt vaguely dissatisfied. She wore silver gauze opening over apple-green satin, with diamonds at her wrists and throat and in her ears. She sighed and thought that at least her figure was still slim enough to be flattered by the high-waisted gown.

They had been invited to dine with the Langhams before the ball and sat down to dinner with thirty other carefully selected guests. On Georgina's right was a tall, lean, dashing man with fine dark eyes, a Colonel Dan Wilkinson, clearly a welcome guest everywhere, who had hardly taken his eyes off her since she had appeared. On her left was the Viscount Lockburn, heir to the Duke of Althorn, a delicate-featured youth with violet-blue eyes that she could not keep from staring at, so unusual was their colour. Both gentlemen vied for her attention in so flattering a way and laughed so heartily at her least quips that she began to feel herself both desirable and witty. She glowed with her success and was the focus of every male eye at the table.

By the time the other guests had arrived and the ball begun, she had promised every dance and was in the delightful position of having to disappoint any number of late-arriving gentlemen. Where, she wondered, had all these attractive men been during her own London season before her marriage? She remembered only callow, dull-eyed boys and elderly gentlemen. Then it occurred to her that the only men she had been allowed to meet and dance with were the men chosen for her by her papa, men who met his exacting standards as possible *partis* for his eldest daughter. He would undoubtedly do the same for Lydia. But she had the feeling Lydia would not be so easy to control in this direction as she herself had been.

Presently she saw her family come in and watched as her father ran an assessing eye over the assembled guests. She surmised he was deciding who was possible as a dancing partner for Lydia. Georgina went to meet them, escorted by her next partner, Lord Alvanley. After greetings were exchanged, she introduced him, and he immediately asked Lydia to stand up with him after the next dance. Lydia dimpled with pleasure and accepted, but Georgina saw that her father was not pleased.

Later in the evening her father took her aside. "You will oblige me, Georgina, by consulting with me before you take it upon yourself to introduce gentlemen to your sister."

"But how could I not introduce him, sir? It would be beyond anything discourteous of me not to have done so. Besides, Lord Alvanley is an unexceptionable young man surely. He has entrée everywhere."

"The son of some jumped-up lawyer, who has already gambled away a fortune and is rumoured to be heavily in debt," replied her father scornfully. "I hope you do not think I am so foolish as to encourage such a fribble as that to dangle after my daughter."

"Oh, for heaven's sake, Papa! Dangle, indeed. He merely asked to stand up with her."

"You will allow me to know best, Georgina. I will say no more on the subject, but I know you will obey me in this. Where is Trowbridge?"

"Still at Hallowhill."

"He should be here. I cannot like all these men buzzing about you when your husband is not by you."

"Would you have me mope at home unless Myles is about to escort me? If so, I should be there forever, for he is always away on some business or other. Look about you, sir, and you will see many married ladies here, dancing and enjoying themselves, whose husbands are noticeably absent."

"They may do as they choose, of course, but I cannot like it for my own daughter."

"I fear you must allow me to know best, Papa," she said, mocking his lofty speech to her. "Ah, here is Lord St. Albans to claim me. You are acquainted with Lord St. Albans, are you not, Papa?"

Lord Fitzhardinge bowed coldly in acknowledgement, then to his daughter, and moved away. Clearly he had no very great opinion of Lord St. Albans.

The rest of Georgina's week was equally gay, equally full. She was to be seen everywhere: at balloon ascensions, breakfasts, salons, riding in the Park. In the evenings she attended dinners and balls, musicales and masquerades, sometimes several affairs in the same evening. Lady Trowbridge was the new rage, and the *ton,* always eager for the new, had taken her up. It was the latest fashion to be hopelessly in love with her, and every man with a claim to fashion professed to be so. Yet she never raised the least breath of censure, for she did not flirt or go apart alone with any of her admirers. Wherever she was seen, it was always in company with several of them as well as with Lady Cunliffe or some other lady.

"Oh, Georgina, how wonderful to be you," sighed Lydia. "What glorious fun you always have."

But strangely enough Georgina did not feel she was having much fun. She would as soon have been back with Selina at Falconley for all the pleasure she was experiencing. The topaz silk, the amber velvet, the cerulean-blue sarsenet as well as all the rest of her new gowns seemed wasted. She had thought the curtain would go up with the Langhams' ball, but it seemed to her the play was still very dull. It was like the prologue spoken by a minor member of the cast that one endured impatiently while waiting for the leading actors to appear. Yet so many attractive players were on the stage already, it puzzled her to explain her malaise.

CHAPTER

20

Myles arrived in London in the early evening to be met with the news that his aunt and my Lady Trowbridge were dining with the Huberts and going from there to a masquerade ball at the Ponsonbys. He ordered some dinner, sent his valet to Trowbridge House to fetch his domino and mask, and went upstairs to change from his dusty travelling clothes into evening dress.

The Ponsonbys' ballroom, when he finally arrived there, was a kaleidoscope of swirling colours and in that state much desired by every hostess of being a positive squeeze. There were shepherdesses, houris in diaphanous Turkish trousers, jesters, devils, and Marie Antoinettes in abundance, but like Myles at least half the guests had settled on a simple mask and domino over evening clothes. For a few moments he feared he might not find his wife in such a press of people, but then he saw her as a swarm of black-caped male figures parted for an instant at the other end of the room, and there was Georgina, the center of a ring of admirers jostling one another for a share of her attention. Her smile flashed from one to another even as she shook her head in some denial. Her auburn hair was netted in gold and pearls, and a black mask hid her amber eyes, but he knew her just the same. The tilt of her chin and its shape, the smooth roundness of her neck, her stance, the slim delicacy of her ungloved fingers all spoke her name to him, and he knew without seeing the lithe slenderness of her form beneath the enveloping domino.

The gap closed, and she was lost to his sight. He began pushing his way through the milling revelers towards her, but the music started up, and when he could finally come up to where she had stood, she was gone. He searched the dancing couples for sight of her and saw her finally quite near tripping a quadrille on the arm of a tall gentleman whom he recognized as Captain Dan Wilkinson, an old friend of his own. It seemed to Myles that when her head was turned aside from her partner her mouth drooped wearily and that her smile when she turned back was strained. Too much merrymaking, he thought, and longed to sweep her up and carry her home. Instead, when the first dance of the set ended, he stepped forward and laid a hand on the captain's shoulder.

"Permit me, sir," he said.

The captain stiffened and turned. "I beg your pardon?"

"With your kind permission I would finish the set with the lady."

"But I do not grant it, sir."

"Ah, be generous, I beg you," pleaded Myles with a laugh. He looked into the masked eyes of Captain Wilkinson and gave a barely perceptible wink. "It would be greedy of you to deny me a share of such treasure." He saw recognition dawn with a slow smile on the captain's face.

"I concede, sir, for I cannot refute your charge. Madam, you will, I know, forgive my dreadful sin."

"Why, sir, surely it is not sinful but customary to expect both dances in the set. I can only commend your generosity or conclude you tire of dancing with me," she said with a pretended pout and a flirtatious sidelong glance at him. Myles, who had never seen her behave so, felt a dart of jealousy, though he continued to smile pleasantly.

"Never accuse me of that, fairest," replied the captain ardently. Then he bowed and turned away as the music struck up again.

Myles held out his hand, and after the briefest hesitation she put her own into it and he led her out. It seemed to him that in the few moments of conversation a transformation had taken place in his wife. Her chin was well up, her smile brilliant, her eyes flashed. Had he only imagined a weariness in her before because it pleased him to think her tired of life in London, or had she been tired of her partner and only too willing for another, a new conquest?

"Well, sir," she said as she curtsied before him, "you are bold, I must say, to walk onto the floor and rout my partner in such a way. You would be well repaid if I am an antidote behind this mask."

"No fear of that madam, for when I entered I saw you surrounded by many gentlemen and knew that your mask could only conceal a beauty well known to them. There, thought I, is my guarantee."

"Oh, sweet words, but I detect something too practised in them," she said, dropping her eyes demurely.

"They only sound so because they are so heartfelt," he protested, wondering uneasily if it was possible she still had not recognized him.

"Shame, sir, to tease me so, when you have known me but two moments," she chided, at the same time flashing a bold stare at him through her mask, while the corners of her mouth indented as though with a pleased smile she was unable to suppress completely.

The minx, he thought, she is flirting with me!

He was convinced now that she did not know him and that she was more than pleased to hear his declarations. In spite of the chill of dismay this conviction brought, he could not bring the scene to a close by identifying himself. Though it were torture, he must know how far she would go.

"Has it been but two moments truly? Strange, when I feel it has been forever. Perhaps that is only because the dream of you has for so long filled my thoughts," he countered.

"Now you are too extravagant, sir, and I will not believe a word you say after this," she said, her tone clearly inviting him to press on just the same.

He complied, not very originally, comparing her teeth to pearls, her lips to rose petals, her complexion to alabaster until the music came to an end and as if by magic her next partner appeared beside them.

Myles took her hand, pressed a kiss upon it, and said, "Dare I hope to stand up with you again, O Queen of the Fairest?"

"Not unless you steal the dance as you did the first," she countered with an inviting laugh that floated in the air behind her as she was led away. She turned to smile encouragingly over her shoulder at him, and he could have cheerfully boxed her ear for it. He wheeled around and stalked away to the nearest lone female, bowed, and curtly requested the dance. The girl looked about, somewhat intimidated by his stern eyes glinting at her through his mask, but seeing no help at hand, she complied with a timorous, rather placating smile.

Immediately contrite at having behaved in so ill bred a way, Myles smiled down into the blue eyes revealed by the mask and set himself to be charming.

Georgina, after her last provocative smile at him over her shoulder, had managed not to lose sight of him for more than a moment. She had of course recognized him the instant he appeared beside Captain Wilkinson, and the ball had changed for her in an instant. Everything became more vivid, the previous insipidity of the scene changed to splendour. For her, though she was not aware of it, the leading player had finally arrived.

She had assumed that he came to her because he recognized her, but gradually she became convinced that he did not know who she was. She had not been able to resist the temptation to observe for herself how he behaved with other women. What she learned had not pleased her. Under the guise now of looking about the room and admiring the costumes she looked back again in time to see Myles leading out a blond-ringleted girl dressed as a shepherdess. A quick assessment of the girl's charms reassured Georgina, for she thought her chin too long for beauty and the low décolletage of her costume not flattering to her rather bony chest. She saw Myles smile down at the girl and begin to speak and saw the girl's initial shyness begin to melt under his attention.

Georgina tossed her head and turned back to Lord Lockburn, whose violet eyes, enhanced by his black mask, were more startling than ever. She became very gay, laughing and flirting though all the while, as though drawn by a magnet, her eyes sought and found her husband as he moved through the throngs of dancers with a bewildering number of partners. He did not return to steal another dance with her, and at last she grew weary of trying to behave with so much gaiety and felt a lump growing in her throat. She slipped away on a sudden impulse, found Lady Cunliffe in the cardroom, and said she would like to go home.

"Of course, my dear, just let me finish this—Ah, yes, mine, I believe. And that also," she said as she rapidly played out her last three cards and drew in the tricks triumphantly. "There, now we can leave. Boring game," she proclaimed, not bothering to lower her voice. The other three players sat looking after her, agape at such rudeness, as she stumped out of the room. "Now then," she said as the carriage pulled away from the Ponsonby mansion, "what is wrong with you?"

Georgina had removed her mask and was staring down at it sadly. "Oh, nothing, only tired, I suppose."

"Pooh! No girl of twenty in good health could be tired after only half an evening of dancing. Now tell me."

"It is only—Did you know Myles was there?"

"Myles? No, I never left the cardroom, and he did not come into it. Are you sure? Such a press of people, after all."

"I am sure. He asked me to dance with him."

"Very proper."

"Oh, no, not at all. You see, he did not know me."

"Nonsense! Of course he did."

"No. If you could have heard the things he said to me!"

"Why, do not tell me he said anything improper."

"Oh, no! He was very complimentary, but not in the way one is to one's wife. Or at least not the way he has ever been to me. Telling me my lips were like rose petals and calling me Queen of the Fairest. No, no, he did not recognize me."

"Good lord, Myles? I cannot believe he could utter such banalities," replied Lady Cunliffe scornfully.

"Oh, I rather liked it," admitted Georgina blushfully, "only I wish it had been really me he was saying them to, if you take my meaning. No one has ever spoken to me so, not even Myles when he was courting me."

"I should hope not! What strange taste you do have. Well, well, here we are home at last. Let us speak of it again tomorrow. I vow I can scarcely hold my head up I so long for my bed."

Georgina, who longed to speak further about it now, had nothing to do but go to bed also, where she lay miserably contemplating visions of Myles dancing on until the end, charming women left and right, and perhaps searching in a desultory way for the woman with whom he had danced earlier but only shrugging when he did not see her.

Oh, why did I not stay? she berated herself; I should have faced him, told him, we might have laughed about it together. Why do I always run away from everything, close it off, shut it out when it hurts?

After all, Myles had undoubtedly come to the ball to seek her out, and if he, not knowing her, had flirted with her, that was only to be expected of gentlemen at masked balls. Every one of her partners had done so, and at least she had not observed Myles hovering around any particular woman. Oh, she was stupid not to have revealed herself to him at once!

It never occurred to her to wonder why, if all the other men she knew recognized her, it should have been so difficult for her own husband to do so.

On the following morning she was to ride in the Park with St. Albans and Alvanley and left the house after breakfasting in her room.

Not an hour later she saw Myles trotting towards her. He pulled up and lifted his hat to her cheerfully before greeting St. Albans and Alvanley.

"Well, Trowbridge, we thought you were not coming up for the Season after all," drawled Alvanley.

"Or rather we hoped you would not," amended St. Albans with a smile at Georgina.

"So I imagine," returned Myles drily. "Well, my dear, what have you planned for today?" he asked, turning to his wife.

"Why, Mrs. Greeley-Hare and I are being taken by Lord Lockburn and Mr. Pickering to see the giraffe at Mr. Bullock's Liverpool Museum. It is sixteen feet tall, they say. And then I have promised to drop in on Lady Jameson later. It is her afternoon to receive, you know. Then your aunt and I dine with the Wilsonbys and go on with them to a ball at Lady Harald's."

"Good lord! I marvel at your stamina," he laughed. "Well, no doubt I shall come up with you this evening. You will, I trust, save at least one dance for me."

"If you wish it, certainly. Which will you like?"

"Whatever you choose," he said, and lifting his hat again, he turned his horse away. He crossed the road to stop beside the carriage of a raven-haired beauty in cherry-red velvet, who turned melting brown eyes up to him and dimpled enchantingly.

Georgina jerked her eyes away and dug her heels into her mare, causing it to start and prance to one side, so that she had to concentrate on bringing it under control. Though she looked for Myles for the rest of the day, she did not see him, and at last returned to Lady Cunliffe's to change for the evening in a fever of impatience. She was bound to see him tonight, since he had asked her to save him a dance.

Prentiss had to dress her hair twice before she was satisfied with it, and she tried on three gowns before settling for one of deep-blue silk, from which her perfect shoulders and high, rounded bosom rose in marble-white splendour. She wore sapphires and diamonds with it and a gauzy, spangled silver shawl across her elbows. The colour, she knew, became her well, and the simple, slender sheath of the skirt revealed her figure to its best effect. Still, she stared at herself critically, wondering if after all she should change to the amber velvet, which was heavily vandyked and embroidered about the hem. Prentiss, when queried, advised that no gown became m'lady so well as this, and besides she had worn the amber already this Season. But Myles had not been there to see it, flashed through Georgina's mind unbidden. She shrugged the thought away, and tipping her chin defiantly, asked Prentiss for her long white gloves and sable cape.

Georgina deliberately held up the departure of the Wilsonby party so that they arrived after the Haralds' ball had opened. She greeted her hostess and stood talking until the dance ended, while her eyes raked the room for sight of her husband. She saw him in a moment leading the ravishing brunet of the afternoon through a country dance.

When the dance ended, several of Georgina's admirers, released from the dance floor, flocked to her to demand dances and chide her for her late arrival. She awarded them with various sets, but though she did not acknowledge it to herself, the only dance she did not give to anyone was the waltz, which she insisted was already spoken for, as well as the privilege of taking her down to supper, which would come first.

When Myles at last came to greet her, she could only offer him the waltz, which he accepted at once.

"And who will take you to supper, my love?"

"Why, I forget," she said carelessly.

He said he was sorry, for he had hoped to take her to supper himself, but supposed he must be content that at least he had secured one dance with the toast of London. Then he bowed, smiled, and walked away.

Georgina felt a chill of loss at his withdrawal and berated herself for giving him such an off-hand answer.

She watched all evening as he went from partner to partner, just as she did, but she only pretended her enjoyment while she felt his was unsimulated. She had the dubious pleasure of watching him lead down to supper, the limpid-eyed brunet, who she learned was the Countess of Bellamont.

Georgina, without a partner for supper, turned back to watch the stream of laughing couples on the stairs leading to the supper room and for a panicky moment felt so alone that she had an impulse to get her cloak and leave.

No! I must stop running away, she scolded herself, and pulled her shoulders back resolutely.

Just then Alvanley came up and asked if she were awaiting her partner. "I vow he deserves to lose you to keep you waiting about. What? Why, I cannot believe my good fortune, dear lady. Come, I have a party waiting below and you must join us."

Georgina accepted with so much gratitude that for a moment Alvanley, whose pursuit of the fabulous Lady Trowbridge was only a superficial compliance with fashion, was quite startled and wondered if it was possible that she had developed an unfortunate *tendre* for him. He reminded himself to be more cautious in the future as he led her to a table filled with his friends. They were greeted joyfully and he watched her turn to them with evident pleasure and went away to bring her refreshments with a relieved heart.

Georgina toyed with a jelly, drank several glasses of iced champagne, and ignored the jolly party that included her husband in the corner of the room. She took Alvanley's arm and said she must return to the ballroom, for she heard the music beginning again and her partner would be looking for her. She never remembered those intervening dances. She felt lightheaded; the room was blurred. It was the wine, she thought; she should not have drunk so much.

Now, she thought, her heart pounding, the waltz was next, and she fanned herself and attempted to look composed.

"Madam, our dance, I believe," Myles said, bowing before her.

She curtsied and laid her hand on the arm he held out to her. She floated onto the floor, airborne, unaware of the room around her. The music began, his hand touched her waist, and she was leaning against it, whirling down the room, her eyes staring blindly into his neckcloth.

"This has been the longest evening I can remember," he said.

"You have seemed to enjoy it, however."

"Not until this moment," he replied.

"Too kind," she whispered in confusion, and with an effort lifted her eyes to his. He held her glance intently, and she could not look away.

"You are so beautiful, my love, so beautiful," he said softly.

She felt her heart move roughly in her breast in a way she had never experienced before and, her mind in a whirl, blurted out, "I like you better without the mask."

"You knew all the time! But then why did you—"

"Which means you knew me also. All those overblown compliments!"

"All that flirting!" he countered with a grin.

She could not keep herself from returning it, and then suddenly they both began to laugh and could not stop, nor did they want to. People all over the room turned to stare enviously at the handsome Trowbridge couple having such a good time together.

CHAPTER

21

Myles and Georgina sat at breakfast with Lady Cunliffe, and from time to time their eyes met and they smiled. Myles had not come to Georgina's room the night before, despite the closeness they had achieved as they waltzed. He was aware that something had changed in her attitude to him, that there was a definite thawing of the ice in her eyes that he had seen at Falconley. He was not aware of what had caused the change, since he still did not have the courage to speak to her as advised by Mrs. Conyers, but his relief was unbounded. He had resolved while in Devon to begin all over with his wife. He would court her again, win her again, encourage her to confide in him, as he would in her, and in time their marriage would be as it should be, as he had dreamed of it being when he first saw her.

He had been somewhat taken aback by her flock of admirers and genuinely upset over her behaviour at the masquerade, but now he felt more confident. However, he did not intend to frighten her away by allowing her to think his only interest was in bedding her. He would stifle his longing for her until he saw signs of willingness in her and then he would proceed very delicately. She still exhibited from time to time that inner fire he had discerned in her when he first met her, and he was convinced that with patience he could reach it. He had been too hasty before.

Therefore he had escorted her to her bedroom door and had taken her hands and kissed them, turning them to kiss the palms lingeringly, before bidding her a chaste good night and crossing the landing to his own room.

Georgina was unaware of his plans, of course, and when she realized he did not mean to return to her, she experienced several conflicting emotions: a prick of anger at what seemed rejection, which stung her pride; a guilty relief that after all she was not required to put her new feelings to the test so soon; a touch of disappointment, which amazed her; and a flicker of gratitude that he did not take an advantage that was his if he cared to reach for it.

For the first time in her life Georgina examined her feelings and attempted to discover their meaning. Heretofore she had not only hidden them from others but also refused to reflect upon them even in her own mind, for to hold them at bay was also to hold off the pain they might cause. Mrs. Conyers had forced her to see some of the things she had always avoided. The woman's words about clutching her resentments to her had penetrated Georgina's understanding, despite her protestations that she did not comprehend their meaning, and had quickened in her mind whether she would have it so or not.

She realized with shock that her deep anger with her husband had more or less evaporated, to be replaced by a determination to prove to him that she was still a desirable woman. She was ashamed to acknowledge so shallow an aim, for it meant really that she wanted to make him jealous.

But why should she want to do so? Was it only her pride, which could not bear to have the world know he turned to someone else so soon after his marriage? If that were so, where then had her anger gone?

What did she really want of him, that she could feel both relief and disappointment that he had not come to her bed? If he were the sort of man, like Windy, who could be summoned or dismissed at her whim, she would despise him, yet she could no longer deny the fact that she wanted to have it all *her* way without reference to his needs at all. What had Mrs. Conyers said? "Do you even know what his needs are?"

No, she did not know, nor had she ever given the matter any thought. Her childhood sense of injury and deprivation had created a woman of monstrous selfishness whose only thought was for herself. In her mind her husband existed for the purpose of cherishing and protecting her and making up to her for all she had missed as a child. He must be father and mother as well as husband. Myles as a lover in the true sense of the word had hardly entered her thoughts at all, any more

than it had ever occurred to her that she should partici-
pate actively in their lovemaking. So much was expected of
him, while she, a grown woman with a child of her own,
wanted to remain a child upon whom no demands might be
made. When he displeased her, she retreated into a cold,
pouting silence and suffered his lovemaking with a martyred
patience.

She fell asleep with these thoughts churning in her head
and wakened with the determination to forgo sulking and
flirting as childish weapons and to accept her share of the
responsibility if he was still deceiving her. He was still her
husband and the father of Selina and deserved the respect he
had always shown her even when she would not speak to
him.

Lady Cunliffe watched them smiling at each other, sniffed,
and returned to her post, putting aside invitations for Georgina.

Dominick strolled in to interrupt this quiet domesticity.
"Well, brother, you here?" he drawled.

"I am. Where have you been?"

"Doing a spot of hunting with Luttrell in Ireland."

"Any good sport?"

"Not so bad. Bang-up pack he has, and there were several
good runs. What is happening in town?"

"I arrived only two days ago and have attended two balls
already, so I should say business as usual for the time of year.
Have you heard that Wellington is in Bordeaux?"

"No! By Jove, Boney's done for, then!"

"Very nearly, I would think. He has retreated across the
Rhine, and the Austrians are descending on him from
Switzerland. He's been offered terms, you know, and refused
them. Can't seem to accept the idea it's all as good as over."

"Well, all I can tell you is—"

Lady Cunliffe's butler cleared his throat loudly from the
door.

"Yes, Parks, what is it?" demanded Lady Cunliffe.

"A Mr. Knyvet, m'lady, requesting an interview."

Dominick's hand jerked, and coffee splashed from his cup
onto the white damask cloth.

Myles turned around in his chair and said, "Knyvet? By
the lord, I had not heard he meant to come up to town. Show
him in, Parks."

"I suggested it, m'lord, when he said he was a neighbour

of yours, but he preferred to wait till you had finished your breakfast. I have put him in the drawing room. He asks that the gentlemen grant him an interview at their convenience.''

"The gentlemen?" said Lady Cunliffe in amazement.

"Yes, m'lady. He asked for them each by their name."

"Very well. Tell him they will be with him shortly. And I will just step in to greet him, of course."

"And learn his errand," teased Myles.

"Well, I do not deny a certain amount of curiosity."

"I will say hello also," said Georgina. "I wonder if Hester and Mrs. Knyvet are in London with him."

"Well, I will forgo the pleasure. I have another appointment," said Dominick, rising and tossing his napkin down, his face noticeably pale.

"Why, Dominick, how rude, when he has asked for you particularly. Of course you must see him," declared his aunt.

"I have no interest in country rustics, and I—"

"And you will oblige me by showing a little more conduct, Dominick," Myles interrupted, a steely note in his voice. "You have known Mr. Knyvet most of your life and you will not treat him so when he has called to see you. Now, come along." He took his brother by the arm and marched him smartly out of the room.

Lady Cunliffe rose quickly. "Come, Georgina. Perhaps Dominick will not be so rude to the man if we are there."

They entered the room on the heels of the two brothers, and Mr. Knyvet swung about to find the whole family arrayed before him. Lady Cunliffe surged forward, her hand out, and he bowed over it in some confusion. Then Georgina came forward to greet him, and he flushed and became even more uncomfortable. After a flurry of greetings a silence ensued as all the family looked at him expectantly.

Myles saw that the man was tongue-tied and said, "Well, well, Mr. Knyvet, this is a great pleasure. Do you make a long stay?"

"No. That is—I wonder if I might speak to you and your brother alone, m'lord?"

"Why, if you like, though we are all family here. Is something amiss, Mr. Knyvet, that we can help you with."

"Well, yes, yes, there is, m'lord, but I think it is not something you will care to have discussed before the ladies." His complexion turned dark red in his embarrassment.

Dominick, whose greeting had been but a nod of the head, walked away to stare out the window, as though to dissociate himself from the discussion. Mr. Knyvet had not yet been able to look into Dominick's face.

Lady Cunliffe, intrigued by any discussion best kept from the ladies, marched over to a chair and plumped herself down. "Nonsense, Mr. Knyvet. I am an old woman, and there is little left that can shock me. Let us all sit down and you just proceed with your business." She waved an authoritative hand at him to speak.

"My lady, I—I assure you it would be best . . ." stuttered Mr. Knyvet.

"Mr. Knyvet, I think you had best give in and speak," said Myles with a smile of encouragement.

"Very well, m'lord, if you will have it so, though how I am to speak of such a thing in the presence of ladies I don't know. It is a matter of some—well . . ." He waved his hands helplessly.

"Who or what does it concern, sir?" Myles prompted.

"It is—about my daughter and—and—" He floundered and looked about him desperately. Then he met Dominick's contemptuous eye at last, and it gave him courage. "It is about my daughter and your brother, my lord," he said firmly.

"My brother?" Myles looked at Dominick, who only shrugged and turned away. "Please go on, Mr. Knyvet," Myles said quietly.

"He has—dishonoured her, and I have come to tell you that he must be made to marry her," Mr. Knyvet burst out.

"Be damned to that!" shouted Dominick, whipping about.

"Dominick, be still," Myles commanded sternly. "Aunt Selina, perhaps it would be wiser for you to—"

"I will not leave, so do not suggest it. This concerns my nephew and this is my drawing room. Now, Mr. Knyvet."

"I will not stay to hear this drivel," declared Dominick, striding towards the door.

"Yes, you will," Myles asserted, catching his arm and swinging him around. "Now, sit down. Continue, Mr. Knyvet.

"There is little more to tell, my lord. When your brother and Lady Cunliffe visited Falconley, we were invited to meet them. Mr. Barrowes danced with my daughter and asked her to ride with him the next day. I have known Mr. Barrowes since he was a little boy, a neighbour, though we have not seen much of him in recent years. At any rate, he being your brother, I gave my permission. I sent a groom with them, naturally, but they dismounted and walked away out of his sight. Day after day, my lord, until your brother had his way with her. Then he went away, and never a word from him from that day to this, and my lass pining and fretting herself into a decline. Now we learn she is to bear his child.''

''This is monstrous, Dominick,'' exclaimed Lady Cunliffe in horror. ''Even I, who have always known your wickedness, would never have believed you could sink so low as this!''

''Please do not fly into the boughs, Aunt Selina,'' replied Dominick haughtily. ''I imagine quite a few gentlemen besides myself have enjoyed the company of Miss Knyvet.''

''You *dare*, sir—'' Mr. Knyvet was on his feet, his face nearly purple with rage, his fists raised as though he would set upon Dominick and batter him to the floor.

''Dominick, that was unforgivable,'' Myles said quickly, interposing himself between the two men. ''Mr. Knyvet, I apologize for my brother.''

''He shall not say such things of my girl. In all her life she has never been alone with any man but Mr. Barrowes. She has rarely even been out of our sight and never has she gone out of the house without one of us by her. That I will swear to, as will her mother.''

''Naturally you would do so,'' countered Dominick.

''Do you insinuate that I am lying?'' shouted Mr. Knyvet, nearly choking.

''I only say it would be natural for you to do so in the circumstances,'' replied Dominick, ''when an opportunity for marriage presents itself to a girl on the shelf for the past five years, at least.''

''You think you are an opportunity, you libertine? You think I look forward to my daughter marrying a man of so little honour that he would seduce an innocent girl of good family? You are even more arrogant than you are evil if you believe that!''

''Then I suppose it is money you want.''

Mr. Knyvet drew himself up. ''You are an unspeakable wretch,'' he said awfully, as the rich colour suffusing his face slowly drained away, leaving it like putty. He turned to Myles. ''My lord, I have valued our friendship and I would not like to be the cause of trouble to you, but I shall call your brother out if you do not stop his filthy tongue."

"Forgive me, Mr. Knyvet, for not doing so before. Dominick, I warn you, you are in serious enough trouble already and are not helping yourself by your behaviour."

"Please do not speak to me as though I were a child, Myles."

"Then stop behaving like a child. It is senseless to insult Mr. Knyvet after the injury you have already done him."

"I do not accept that I have done him an injury," snapped Dominick. "He may get around *you* with all his claims on your friendship, but I am not to be trapped. That girl is a born flirt, and nothing he can say will convince me that I was the only man she has been with."

"Then you *were* with her?"

"Oh, for God's sake! Very well, if you will have it. Though she may say what she likes but it was she who was so eager for it, so why should I pay for it? If the girl must marry, let her find someone else."

"And who would have her now that you have despoiled her?" demanded Mr. Knyvet bitterly.

"You need not advertise the fact to a would-be suitor, I suppose," returned Dominick.

"There speaks a gentleman, a man of honour," said Mr. Knyvet with terrible scorn. "Well, such tricks may do for you, but I would not stoop so far with any man as not to tell him the truth. I could not live with my conscience else."

Even Dominick had the grace to feel ashamed after this pronouncement and could not look Mr. Knyvet in the eye. A heavy silence ensued. Georgina and Lady Cunliffe looked at each other surreptitiously, their eyes wide with shock. Georgina's heart was hammering violently from the emotional outbursts still ringing in the air. She had no doubt whatsoever of Dominick's guilt, remembering those days he had spent so mysteriously away from Falconley after he had met Hester, together with his seduction of Cressy and his attempt upon her own virtue.

Fighting desperately as he was to escape this trap of his own setting, Georgina felt sure there was no way Dominick could be forced to marry Hester. She was underestimating her husband and Lady Cunliffe, however, and also Mr. Knyvet.

"Dominick, you will marry Miss Knyvet as soon as possible," ordered Lady Cunliffe coldly.

"No, Aunt, I will not," retorted Dominick.

"Yes, Brother, you will," Myles said. "Before this I would have called out any man who dared to insinuate my brother could behave so dishonourably. I have been deceived in you all these years, it seems."

"Naturally it grieves me to have disillusioned you, but I will not marry."

"Then I will take you to the law, sir," declared Mr. Knyvet. "Forgive me, Lord Trowbridge. I would not bring such a smirch upon your good name if I had any other recourse. But I see no reason why the reputation of this ravisher of innocent girls should go untarnished while my own daughter, my wife, and I must suffer disgrace. I will take you to the law, Mr. Barrowes. My wife and our neighbours will testify to Hester's unblemished reputation, and my groom will testify to those walks into the woods and who it was coaxed her into them, for he heard it all and has confessed to me. Then my daughter herself will take the stand and name you, though she die of shame for it!"

"You would not dare," hissed Dominick, white-faced with fear and fury as he saw the jaws of the trap beginning to close.

"Try me, Mr. Barrowes, just try me," replied Mr. Knyvet grimly.

"He will do so, Dominick, and what is more I will stand at his side. I will not protect you at the expense of an innocent girl and a just claim," pronounced Myles.

"No more will I," declared Lady Cunliffe stoutly. "Mr. Knyvet, you have my word on it."

They all stared at Dominick stonily, and he stared back for a long moment. Then his shoulders slumped in defeat. "Then there is no choice, is there? I never thought I would see the day that my own family would not stand by me."

"This is your own doing, Dominick, and the day is come when you must take responsibility for your own actions," Myles said. Then he went on briskly, "Now, I think the announcement should be sent to the *Gazette* at once. I will prepare it. Dominick, you will travel down and make your proposal in form to Miss Knyvet. Then, Mr. Knyvet, you will persuade her to name the day as soon as may be, for I think the wedding cannot be delayed too long considering—ah—everything.''

Mr. Knyvet flushed with embarrassment, but poor Hester was already a month gone, and there was little time to waste.

"Now, I assume Miss Knyvet will prefer to marry from her home," continued Myles. "Naturally we will be back at Falconley by then and will attend the wedding. Dominick can have his man of business call to go over the settlements and so forth. As the wedding-journey—"

Dominick cut in icily, "I think I can attend to *that,* at least, Brother. Now, since everything is arranged so competently, I will bid you good day." He strode quickly out of the room.

Mr. Knyvet stared after him until the door closed at his back and then turned to Myles and held out his hand. "My lord, I hope you will not hold all this against me. I think you must know my esteem for you and your good lady, and I would not have brought this on you had I any other way."

Myles gripped his hand and clapped him on the shoulder. "My dear old friend, I should have done the same in your place. Now, I hope you will stay and take your mutton with us."

"I thank you, sir, but I will leave at once. Hester and Mrs. Knyvet were mightily put about, as you may well imagine, and I don't like to think of them fretting a moment longer than need be. I will go back at once, if you will excuse me."

"I understand, Mr. Knyvet, and wish you godspeed."

Mr. Knyvet bowed profoundly to Lady Cunliffe. "I will never forget your words, my lady, and if ever it should happen that I can repay you for them, I will thank God for giving me the opportunity." He turned to Georgina and bade her good-bye.

"We will be with you soon, Mr. Knyvet," Georgina said. "Please give my love to Hester and Mrs. Knyvet and tell them I shall look forward to getting to know my new sister better."

"God bless you, my lady."

When he was gone, the three looked at one another in silence, none knowing quite what to say.

Lady Cunliffe finally rose stiffly to her feet. "Well, that was an exciting morning. I wonder what the afternoon has in store."

Myles threw back his head in a roar of laughter, breaking the tension that had held them, and Georgina began to giggle.

"Yes, very funny, I dare say," sniffed Lady Cunliffe, "but I for one could do with a deal less melodrama. I shall go lie down upon my bed for a time, I believe." She walked out of the room.

Georgina lay back in her chair. "Oh dear, Myles, what a dreadful coil. He will make her miserable, of course."

"Well, at least she will have a name for her child. And I doubt he will experience much joy either. I cannot think of a worse fate than being married to Hester Knyvet."

CHAPTER

22

The announcement of the betrothal of Mr. Dominick Barrowes and Miss Hester Knyvet appeared in the next day's *Gazette*, causing a mild sensation, for Dominick's views on marriage had been too often publicly aired by him for anyone to be unaware of them. Georgina was besieged for information regarding Miss Knyvet, a woman apparently entirely unknown to everyone in London. The general opinion was that she must be a great beauty, since Dominick had been tempted by heiresses before this and withstood them. Georgina told everyone that Miss Knyvet was a sweetly pretty young woman whose family home neighboured on Falconley and who had known Dominick since they were children. It was then decided the reason he had never married was his secret love for this childhood sweetheart who had spurned him all these years but who had now, happily, relented.

It made a pretty story and was the talk of London for quite three days. Then Lady Cheshire ran away from her husband in the company of her handsome coachman, and the *ton* had something new and deliciously scandalous to feed its hunger for titillation.

Georgina continued her excessively busy social life, which quite often did not include her husband, since some of her engagements were of long standing. In any case the *ton* considered married couples that went about together too much to be maggoty creatures; and when couples went into company together it was considered shocking bad taste to cling or exhibit any fondness. Affection must be reserved for one's own home, though not if guests were being entertained, naturally.

In line with his plan, Myles requested the pleasure of his

wife's company just like her other admirers and managed
during this last week before Lydia's come-out to take her for
two drives, one visit to the Frost Fair, and to two breakfasts.
Breakfasts generally began in the early afternoon and lasted
several hours. He took Georgina to the opera one evening,
but on the other evenings she and Lady Cunliffe had already
engaged to be escorted to various evening parties and balls.
Naturally Myles made a point of appearing at all these affairs
and securing dances or conversation with her and was amazed
and encouraged by her softened attitude towards him. She
greeted him with pleasure—at times it even seemed to him,
with eagerness—and she never flirted with other men in his
presence.

For the rest of the time Myles went about upon his own
affairs, just as other men of quality did. He dined with his
cronies at his clubs, played cards at White's, shot at wafers at
Manton's, and called upon his friends.

In the middle of the week Cressy and Windy arrived to
attend Lydia's come-out and were to be seen everywhere. In
spite of her reputation Cressy was still received by all but the
most rigid sticklers, for her conduct was no worse than that of
a great many other women of the *ton*. There was, for instance,
the Countess of Oxford, of the Harley family, whose assortment of children by various fathers was called the Harleian
Miscellany. Cressy, though known to be promiscuous, had so
far produced only one child, and though no one was so naive
as to believe the child was Windy's, there was no proof
otherwise, and Windy seemed well content.

It was Cressy, careless as always, who disturbed the growing amity between Georgina and Myles by her thoughtless
words. She was being driven in the Park, bundled in a
chinchilla cape, by a darkly dangerous-looking man when she
spotted Georgina driving by with St. Albans and immediately
clamoured for them to pull up. She introduced her escort with
a dismissive wave of the hand as Mr. Bilkins and launched
into a discussion of her parents' arrangements for the ball,
which she labelled pinch-penny.

". . . As though her cook could provide for all those guests.
I told her she must let Gunters cater it, but Papa would not
hear of such an expense. Lord, I should be ashamed to cut
corners before my friends in such a way. Oh, is that Myles?
Who?—Oh! I vow I had thought *that* all over long ago."

Following her gaze, Georgina saw Myles on horseback ambling alongside the slow-moving carriage of the limpid-eyed Countess of Bellamont, so engrossed in conversation with her that he did not notice his wife and sister-in-law as he passed them.

Georgina turned away, determined not to respond to Cressy, who as always realized her slip too late and was making matters worse by trying to mend them. "Of course, it was only talk. You know how people carry on if a woman shows the least partiality for a particular gentleman, especially if she is a widow."

"Oh, is she a widow? Poor soul, I had not heard. We have not met," replied Georgina with as much indifference as she could summon. "How is Simon?"

"Oh, he is very well, the pet. And darling Selina is thriving, I trust. Well, Mr. Bilkins, we must not dawdle or I shall be late for my dressmaker and she will never have my gown finished for Lydia's ball. Do you go to the Warreners tonight, Georgie?"

"I might look in late. I am engaged to see Mr. Kean at Drury Lane tonight."

"How dreary! I can never make any sense at all of Shakespeare. Well, good-bye then."

Cressy drove on, and Georgina and St. Albans continued on their way with Georgina trying desperately to keep up a light, inconsequential chatter to hide the disquiet she felt on account of Cressy's words. She did not allow herself to think about them until she had reached Lady Cunliffe's and the safety of her own room.

What had Cressy meant by "that"? And how long ago? Was this woman the mistress Cressy had spoken of before, or had that reference been only to some bit of muslin he had set up, and this an affair of the heart? She thought she much preferred the former, for if Myles had had an affair with the beautiful countess and was now seeing her again it would be far more disastrous than a mere fling with some woman who sold her favours.

That evening Georgina dressed in her pale-orange sarsenet with the Trowbridge topaz-and-diamond necklace and earrings, and took her place with Lady Cunliffe in a box hired for the occasion by Lord Ffoukes, a cicisbeo of Lady Cunliffe's for many years, to see Edmund Kean's Othello, hailed by the critic William Hazlitt as "the finest piece of acting in the world." Though Georgina had not been to a play in over a year and might have been impressed with far less, she was mesmerized by Kean's fire and the naturalness of his acting. His short stature and unprepossessing looks were forgotten as she was swept up into the story. The theme of the destructiveness of jealousy spoke strongly to her also, so that she was doubly involved with the performance.

When Lord Ffouks and his guests left the box at the end of the play, the door of a nearby box opened and the Countess of Bellamont and Myles emerged—not alone, of course, but in the company of two elderly gentlemen and an elderly lady. The parties stopped for greetings, and Georgina was introduced to Lady Hadleigh, Countess of Bellamont, who acknowledged the introduction warmly, her large brown eyes looking straight into Georgina's without the least sign of embarrassment or uneasiness. Georgina thought that if Cressy was right, this woman was a master of deception, even as she herself smiled with the utmost composure and professed herself delighted to make Lady Hadleigh's acquaintance.

It was discovered they were all bound for the Warreners' ball, and they went away to the waiting carriages proclaiming how much pleasure they would all feel to meet again so soon.

"Were you never acquainted with Lady Hadleigh before, Aunt Selina?" asked Georgina as soon as they were driven off.

"Only in a vague sort of way, though I knew her mother fairly well at one time."

"She is quite beautiful."

"Yes, but not to my taste. No spine there at all."

"And you, Lord Ffoukes, do you not think her beautiful?"

"Lord, yes, a real little beauty!" he exclaimed enthusiastically.

"A widow, I have heard."

"Yes, and dotty about Bellamont too. Always was. Dead over four years now, and she still won't look at another man."

"Why, she seemed to enjoy Myles's company very well," retorted Georgina.

"Oh, Bellamont and Trowbridge were great friends. They were at Oxford together."

Georgina said no more, feeling that to probe further would not be prudent, but she wondered if the inconsolable widow was not inclined to look with too much favour on her departed husband's best friend. She felt very depressed of a sudden and wondered if she might complain of the headache and ask to be taken home. But then she thought such behaviour was cowardly, only running away yet again from an unpleasant truth. If Myles was in love with Lady Hadleigh, there was nothing to be gained from avoiding it. Better by far to face it squarely and be prepared.

In spite of the mutual agreement to meet again at the Warreners, it seemed, in the press of people gathered there, that such a plan was impossible. For some time Georgina could not tell whether the other party had arrived yet, and in a short time her own admirers had discovered her presence and were clamouring for attention. By the time Myles made his way to her, she had only a set of country dances left to offer him, which he accepted with a bow and a quirk of the eyebrow that she could not interpret.

She saw him several times on the dance floor, but only once with Lady Hadleigh. They seemed very comfortable together, and Lady Hadleigh's great dark eyes seemed firmly fixed upon Myles's face, but this proved nothing one way or the other. Georgina determined not to search for glimpses of them any more and kept her eyes and her mind strictly on her partner of the moment. Her heart, however, felt leaden with premonition.

When Myles presented himself for the country dances, it was only with a tremendous effort that she was able to smile pleasantly and step out with the confidence of an acclaimed beauty, for she had been told too many times during the evening of her dazzling looks not to have absorbed some of it. If she had been in doubt, Myles's admiring eyes and his declaration that he was the envy of every man in the room for possessing so beautiful a wife would have assured her. She laughed and behaved just as she ought, but underneath felt only a great fear that by her own wilfulness and ignorance she might already have lost him.

Then the dance was over, and Alvanley came to claim her and for sometime after that she did not see Myles at all. When the waltz was announced, which she had not had the courage to save for him again for fear he would guess that once she had done so deliberately, she had the dubious pleasure of watching her husband lead out Lady Hadleigh. Georgina threw up her chin, smiled bewitchingly upon the violet-eyed Lord Lockburn, her partner, and sailed down the floor with him.

The very next day as she came out of the door of her dressmaker's, she saw Myles drive by with Lady Hadleigh beside him. True, Lady Hadleigh's maid occupied the seat facing them, but Georgina knew only too well how easily disposed of servants could be if two people were determined. Look at Hester Knyvet's groom!

Now there seemed no longer any reason to doubt that the worst, if it had not yet occurred, was bound to happen eventually. If their attraction, if it *had* been only that, had been so marked before that Cressy had heard of it, there was every reason to believe now that it was not only renewed but flourishing.

Georgina walked down the steps, climbed into her carriage, and instructed her coachman to drive her back to Lady Cunliffe's. She stepped out when they arrived, greeted Lady Cunliffe's butler pleasantly, and went straight up to her room with calm, unhurried steps.

Once there, with the door closed behind her, she marched to her dressing table, picked up a scent bottle, and turned, her arm raised. Then she paused, lowered the bottle, and after a moment set it back carefully and picked up a silver-backed hairbrush. She turned again and let fly with all her strength at the marble fireplace. The hairbrush struck the mantel and clattered to the floor harmlessly. Georgina, however, stared at it with satisfaction, her breast heaving with emotion. Then she removed her bonnet and gloves, threw off her fur-lined cape, and rang for Prentiss. She chose a pomona-green velvet gown, draped the Trowbridge pearls over the deeply cut décolletage that exposed her high, round breasts enticingly, and went down to dinner with her husband and Lady Cunliffe.

Myles was stretched out in a chair before the fire, his heels on the fender, a glass of wine in hand. He rose hastily when she entered and came forward to take her hands.

"My dear, how very elegant you are. What are your plans for the evening?"

"Why, only a small musicale at Mrs. Angleby's. And you?"

"I might go along to White's and look for some friends. Nothing in particular planned. May I give you some wine?"

"Yes, I believe I will have some."

He poured the wine and handed her the crystal goblet. She

seated herself, very much aware of the breathlessness that caused her bosom to heave betrayingly and wished she had chosen a less revealing gown, for she was determined to confront him on the issue of Lady Hadleigh. She was going to meet her problem squarely, as Mrs. Conyers had advised.

"I saw you today," she began, her heart pounding.

"Did you? Why did you not speak?"

"Well, it was only for an instant. You were passing in a carriage, and there was really no time."

"Where was this?"

"I was just coming from my dressmaker's on Poultney Street."

"Ah, then I was with Algeria."

"Algeria?"

"Lady Hadleigh. Bellamont's widow."

"Why, yes, I believe it was she," said Georgina agreeably, and then with a deep breath she forced herself to ask, "I wondered where you were going."

"We were returning, actually. She had been after me to find a pony for her boy. His first pony, you see, and terribly important. I have been keeping an eye out and finally found one I thought would be suitable, so I took her along to see it. Least I could do for old Bellamont."

"Oh, I see, She is very beautiful."

"Is she? Yes, I suppose you are right," he said with indifference.

"I had thought . . . she seemed"—she gulped and forced herself to go on—"very fond of you."

"Oh, well, I stood up with Bellamont at their wedding, known them both forever. Been rather rough for her, these past years, but she will soon be over the worst. Though she has not announced it yet, she is betrothed to the Duke of Gresham. He's with Wellington, on the staff. He will be coming home any time now, and we can both wish her happy. He's a good fellow, Gresham."

"That is—wonderful. How happy I am for her," said Georgina faintly, her heart soaring with relief.

Lady Cunliffe entered at this point. She had been standing outside the door for the past five minutes, shamelessly eavesdropping, and was well satisfied with what she had heard. Tomorrow she would definitely write to Mrs. Conyers.

CHAPTER

23

The day of Lydia's come-out dawned cold, fair, and crystal-clear. Georgina, who felt she had neglected her best-loved sister, went around to the Fitzhardinge mansion with a dainty necklace of sapphires and diamonds as a gift.

Lydia, overcome with delight, attempted to protest at its extravagance. "But I cannot accept it, Georgie. Why, why, it must be worth . . ." She stopped, unequal to the task of putting a price on such a gift.

"Dear girl, it is from Trowbridge and me together and not too much for you."

"Indeed it is not!" declared Lady Fitzhardinge happily, "and it is perfect for your gown, Lydia. Oh, Georgina, wait until you see it. White, of course, silk with a gauze overskirt, embroidered with seed pearls and blue flowers and ribbands. Nothing could be more perfect for it than this."

Lydia, all smiles and good humour, received her guests looking her exquisite best, the sapphires around her throat bringing out the blue of her eyes with sparkling emphasis.

Georgina arrived on Myles's arm in peach-blossom satin heavily embroidered on its vandyked hem with silver acorns and gold leaves, a cloud of peach-blossom gauze trailing behind her. Her auburn hair was piled high and pinned on one side with a diamond brooch holding ostrich plumes. She gleamed with beauty, but not only because of her gown and ornaments. It came from her shining amber eyes, her luminous white complexion, and the glowing rose colour lighting her cheeks. Wherever she went, eyes followed her.

She kissed Lydia and greeted her parents, then moved away, trying to retire discreetly into the background. This was Lydia's evening not hers, and she was embarrassed by the attention her entrance had attracted. Myles kissed her hand and retired from the circle of men demanding her attention, secure in the knowledge that three sets, including the waltz, as well as supper, were his.

She wished that he had stayed with her, but since he had not, she could only go on granting dances wherever they were requested, except those promised to her husband.

Then, with no warning, Adrian Patterson stood before her, requesting a set. She had forgotten all about him and could not suppress an involuntary look around for her father before turning back to greet the man.

"You seem surprised to see me, Lady Trowbridge," he said with amusement.

"Oh, no, it is only . . . No, you are right. I had forgotten Lydia said she would ask you to come in case no one invited her to stand up."

"I am glad she thought of me. But she will have no problem finding partners."

"No, of course she will not. She has no idea of her good looks."

"Lady Trowbridge, I wanted to speak to you about something, but have little idea of how you will welcome my news."

"Why, I doubt it will be news to me, sir," she teased, sure he was about to speak of Lydia and himself.

"It is not what you think," he said, surprising her. "I know you are aware of my feelings for your sister. I believe it will all be much easier than either of us anticipates. And the reason is what I wished to speak to you about. You see, I have had twenty thousand pounds settled on me by my . . . patron."

Georgina could only stare at him speechlessly for a moment. Finally she gasped, "Twenty—"

"Thousand. Yes. By Lord Trowbridge."

"Good God!"

"Yes. It is unbelievable, is it not?"

"I am of course very happy for you, Mr. Patterson."

"I hope you do not feel your own children will be unjustly deprived by this gift."

"My children?"

"Yes," he responded firmly. "I know you have only one

daughter now, but naturally you will have more, and I would not want you to feel that I had deprived them."

"Well, naturally, I would not—I mean, Myles would not—" She halted, not clear what she meant.

"No, of course he would not, nor would I want him to, but when he confessed the truth to me, I felt I could not refuse his gift."

"The truth?"

"That he is my father. Of course, I had suspected it since that day I met him at Falconley, when he was so shocked to find me there. I started looking at him more closely, and he reminded me often of myself. Then connecting this resemblance with all his help to me, I could not help but guess. I did not ask him or speak of it. But then he came to me last week and told me. He asked my forgiveness, which of course was unnecessary. I am fortunate to have been given a great deal of love all my life and never suspected it came not from the usual source. And certainly he has made sure my life would be easy. Now I feel I cannot refuse his gift, for I am used to accepting his help and have loved him for it, but mostly because I feel that to refuse it would be unnecessarily churlish. You see, though I have never expected to have such wealth, nor even wanted it, I think to refuse it would be a rejection, an unwarranted slap in the face. Can you possibly understand my view in this matter?"

"Very well, Mr. Patterson, and I heartily agree with it. You are a very understanding man, and I am grateful to you," Georgina said warmly, her heart filled with pride for the generosity of her husband and his courage in speaking to Adrian.

He bowed then and went away to find Lydia. Georgina, on a sudden impulse, went to find her stepmother before the dancing began. Lady Fitzhardinge was receiving congratulations on the ball from a circle of ladies, but turned happily to walk apart with Georgina.

"It is a very lovely party, Mama."

"Oh, it is, is it not? Fitz was so difficult about money that I feared— But still, the decorations are just right and it is going to be a most dreadful squeeze. I hope there are enough lobster patties. The ices are lovely. Please don't breathe a word to your papa, but I ordered them from Gunters. Oh, my dear, I still have not thanked Trowbridge for Lydia's gift. *So* generous, dear man. Does not Lydia look nice?''

"Indeed she does. Her gown is perfect."

"Yes, I think it is. I *do* know what is right in dress, I think." Lady Fitzhardinge's eyes flew to her youngest daughter to confirm what she knew very well. Then a slight frown creased her brow as she saw Lydia in animated conversation with Adrian Patterson. "There now, your papa has made a mistake in allowing her to invite Mr. Patterson."

"Why, how so?"

"You are dense, Georgina. Why, it is as clear as clear he is head over ears in love with her, and impressionable young girls will always be swayed by such a thing though they may never have so much as looked at the man before."

"Would it be such a dreadful thing? He is a lovely young man."

"But Georgina, how can you even suggest such a thing? Why he is but a *vicar*—and penniless!"

"Oh, not at all. Had not you heard? He has twenty thousand pounds beyond his living, which I have heard is a rich one. Not a great fortune compared to some, of course, but he can hardly be called penniless."

"Do you tell me so?" breathed Lady Fitzhardinge, as she digested this interesting information. She studied Mr. Patterson again with a new light in her eye. "Excuse me, my love. I must speak to your papa." She hurried away.

The music struck up at that moment, and Adrian led Lydia onto the floor to open the ball. She had been adamant in her resolve to give him the first dance, despite all her parents could do.

Georgina turned to her own partner, who had just appeared, satisfied that she had done something for Adrian Patterson. She felt fiercely partisan in his cause now.

Why, she thought in amazement, I am his stepmama! And if someday he should marry Lydia, she would be my daughter-in-law as well as my stepsister, and if they have children, I will be both grandmama and aunt!

Dizzy with these convoluted relationships, she began to giggle, and her partner, who had just made a rather laboured *mot,* thought himself no end of a wit.

When Myles came to claim his dance, she felt unaccountably shy with him. He seemed to her a different man from the

Myles she had known before, perhaps because she knew so much more about him than she had known before.

I hope he will tell me about Adrian, she thought, then wondered why she had to wait for him to speak. She knew the story from Adrian, so why not tell Myles so? Was she waiting for him to make a confession?

"Myles, I was speaking to Adrian Patterson before, and he told me what you have done for him—and why," she added firmly, her heart pounding.

He looked into her eyes, as though searching for something. Evidently he did not find it, for he smiled. "You do not mind?"

"I am very fond of Adrian," she replied, smiling back. He pressed her hand, and then the steps of the dance separated them. When they came together again, she said, "I told Mama about Adrian's inheritance."

"And how did she react?"

"There was definitely an acquisitive gleam in her eye."

They both began to laugh, attracting some attention, including that of Adrian, who stepped past them leading a carroty-haired girl of uncompromisingly plain aspect. Georgina smiled lovingly upon him. Myles asked if she would object to his inviting Adrian to take supper with them, and she agreed to his suggestion happily.

What a glorious party, Georgina thought, her spirits soaring. She and her husband were becoming friends at last. How easy it was when one spoke of what one was worried about. Think what unhappiness she might have created for both of them if instead of speaking to him about Lady Hadleigh, she had imagined all sorts of things, tortured herself for nothing. She remembered Mrs. Conyers telling her that she reveled in her hurts, and now she began to see the truth of the statement. She determined to check those tendencies in future, and if Myles did have a mistress—but no, she could not speak of that to him! She felt a gouging stab of pain that she did not recognize immediately for what it was.

When supper was announced, she and Myles went together to invite Adrian to join them, which he was delighted to do. He fetched his supper partner, another less than prepossessing young woman so crushed by shyness that she could barely look up. It was clear that Adrian was doing his Christian duty by making the evening pleasanter for all the young ladies who might otherwise never have left their chaperone's side.

All three applied themselves to be kind to the shy young woman, a Miss Leigh, and soon had her laughing and responding quite naturally and gazing adoringly up at Adrian. Georgina noticed Lydia watching their table with great attention and wondered if it was possible she was more interested in Adrian than anyone thought.

Later, when they left the supper room, Lydia came to her and asked if she would like to step upstairs to refresh herself. Georgina agreed, sure Lydia wanted to hear about Miss Leigh. Lydia surprised her, however, by not mentioning the young woman at all. She spoke on inconsequential things while Carstairs, Lady Fitzhardinge's abigail, fussed over her hair. When Carstairs hurried out of the room, Lydia turned to Georgina with a serious face.

"Georgina, Myles has known Adrian a very long time, I take it."

"Why, yes, dear, he has," Georgina agreed warily.

"They are—well—very alike, and . . ." Lydia's voice trailed off uncertainly.

She has guessed, Georgina thought, and is afraid I have not guessed and I will be upset. "Darling, yes, they are. And for the very reason that you suspect."

"You know?"

"Yes. I am enormously fond of him."

"Oh, Georgie, I am so glad. He is such a fine person. Does *he* know?"

"Yes. Myles told him and settled twenty thousand pounds upon him," Georgina replied proudly.

"Twenty! Good lord! How wonderful for him, and how generous of Myles. Oh, I do like Myles."

"Well, I am glad of that, Lydia," Georgina returned lightly.

"You seem more content together. There was a time at Falconley when I feared—"

"Yes, love, I know," Georgina interrupted with some embarrassment. "All my own stupidity. Cressy repeated some gossip to me about Myles and another woman, and I . . ." She spread her hands helplessly, unable to explain further.

"You were jealous," Lydia announced with a smile.

"Why, I suppose you are right," said Georgina wonderingly. "How foolish of me."

"Why foolish?"

"It is such an unworthy emotion."

"Oh, I do not think so, in moderation, of course. If one is totally without a smidge of it, I cannot believe one truly loves."

This interesting conversation came to an end when Lady Fitzhardinge entered, scolding Lydia for dawdling upstairs when the house was filled with her guests.

Myles was waiting at the foot of the stairs. "Our waltz is just beginning, my dear," he said, holding out his hand to Georgina. She took it, and he led her into the ballroom and onto the floor.

"Each time I see you I think you are more lovely than the last time," he said as she dipped a curtsey before him. She looked up with a radiant smile. He pulled her up to face him. "I am torn by the need to show you off and the desire to take you back to Falconley at once so that I can have you all to myself."

"Had you forgotten we leave for Falconley tomorrow?" she teased, her heart fluttering almost painfully at this loverlike declaration.

But maybe he wanted to go away from London so that he could not be too involved with his mistress. At the thought of this faceless woman Georgina felt again the twisting pain she had experienced earlier in the evening and recognized it now for jealousy. And before, when she first heard from Cressy that Myles was unfaithful and she broke the scent bottle, that was jealousy too. Good lord!

The music began, and they whirled down the room, circling, circling to the lilt of the seductive music, while he smiled down at her.

Georgina stared back, mesmerized, and realized that she had fallen in love with her husband!

CHAPTER

24

Georgina never clearly remembered the remainder of the evening. She passed through it in a daze of discovery, for once she had realized her true feelings, they seemed to grow riotously, causing the blood to tingle in her veins with a sharp sweetness. Only touching his hand as they danced caused her entire body to flush with a need for him she had never experienced.

Then the last guests had gone and a last glass of iced champagne was served to the family as they stood wearily discussing the success of the evening. Lady Cunliffe had departed sometime before, and now only Myles and Georgina stood with Lord and Lady Fitzhardinge and Lydia, preparing to say good night. Georgina wondered if tonight Myles would come to her bed, and made shy by the thought, stood looking into her glass of wine.

A shattering hammering at the door so startled her that the glass slipped through her fingers to shatter on the black and white tiles of the hallway.

"Who can that be?" exclaimed Lord Fitzhardinge crossly. "It is past three in the morning."

Jelkins came from the back of the hall to open the door, and Harriet stumbled over the threshold and threw herself upon Lady Fitzhardinge.

"Mama!" she cried, and burst into noisy sobs.

"Harriet! Why, dearest, what has happened?" asked a bewildered Lady Fitzhardinge, attempting to hold Harriet away from her as she became aware of tears staining the shoulder of her silk gown.

"I shall never go back! Never!" shouted Harriet.

Lady Fitzhardinge, aware of the servants clearing up after

the party, took her daughter's arm. "Hush, darling, please. Come into the drawing room, for heaven's sake. Come along, Fitz. Lydia, go to bed at once."

"Mama, I want to know—"

"Do as you are bid, Lydia," ordered her father in a tone of voice that brooked no argument. Lydia turned to the stairs.

"Myles. Georgina. I think you had best join us, if you will," Lady Fitzhardinge said over her shoulder as she led the sobbing girl into the drawing room.

Georgina, shocked out of her euphoric daze, was almost ashamed that her first reaction was a selfish annoyance with Harriet for spoiling the evening. She threw an apologetic glance at Myles and followed her stepmother. Harriet continued to cry out that she would not go back as Lady Fitzhardinge seated her on a sofa and removed her bonnet.

"No, no, dearest," soothed her mother, "of course you shall not if you do not choose to. Try to calm yourself. Perhaps some brandy . . ."

"I cannot drink brandy—and do stop patting me, Mama," Harriet cried wildly.

Lady Fitzhardinge hastily withdrew her hand.

Lord Fitzhardinge, staring distastefully at Harriet's wet, red face, said reprovingly, "Please do not speak to your mother in that way, Harriet. You will oblige me with more becoming conduct, if you please."

Harriet howled at this reproof and buried her face in her hands. Lady Fitzhardinge fussed over her murmuring soothing little sounds.

Georgina felt compelled to make some sort of sense out of the situation, since neither of her parents was doing so. "Harry, dear, won't you please tell us what has happened. Why did you have to leave?"

"He—he is a *monster* of depravity! I could not bear it another moment!"

"Did he strike you?" Myles asked.

"No, no—he—attacked me, he—"

"But Harriet, I told you—" began Lady Fitzhardinge.

"No, you did not! You told me I must submit to my husband, but you did not tell me to what."

"Harriet, dear," interrupted her mother nervously with an embarrassed glance at the gentlemen, "there is nothing depraved about . . . I mean, in marriage it is quite natural for one's husband to—ah—make love to—''

"Love? *Love!*" Harriet began to laugh wildly. "There was no love. It was all beastliness—unnatural acts—''

"These things are not unnatural, dear, in the privacy of one's bedchamber.''

"And in the library? The drawing room?" wailed Harriet. "Oh, you do not understand. He is evil! I will not go back, never, never, never!''

"Pray stop this childish tantrum, Harriet," said her father coldly. "You are being ridiculous. Of course you will go back. If you do not, he will divorce you.''

"I hope that he will.''

"More childishness. You do not know what you are saying. You would not be received by anyone. You would lose your dowry and could not marry again, for I will not put up another one. There will be no more divorce in this family. You will not bring further disgrace to my name. I will not have it, do you hear me?''

Harriet began tearing at her hair frenziedly, emitting soft, staccato screams in a most pitiful, affecting way. Her father was not, however, affected. He walked up to her and slapped her face sharply, causing her to stop abruptly and stare up at him, eyes wide with shock, her mouth hanging open.

"Now," he said, "I will have no more of this stupid self-indulgence. I will of course speak to Braye, if you can cite one instance of misbehaviour on his part, but you must give me a coherent account without all this unseemly shrieking.''

During this speech Harriet closed her mouth and sat up straighter, her eyes turning as cold as his own. "A coherent account? You want to hear a coherent account? Very well, sir, you shall have it.''

And she proceeded to give them a graphic description of her five weeks as the bride of Sir Vernon Braye—his attack in the carriage, the agony of her wedding night, the demands at all hours of the day wherever he chanced upon her without caring whether the servants were about, and worst of all the maid he had brought to her bed—outlining in detail each degrading event for the horrified audience before her.

By the time she had finished, the tears had dried in sticky

streaks on her face. She laughed harshly. "Well, Papa, is that coherent enough for you?"

"I think one must allow for a little hysterical exaggeration."

"Exaggeration? I assure you there was no exaggeration. Oh, God, I thought my own family would believe me at least." She began to cry again, but wearily now.

Lady Fitzhardinge put out a tentative hand to touch her shoulder but drew it back.

Georgina, racked with pity, rushed forward to seat herself beside the girl and take her into her arms. "Darling, darling, of course we believe you. We will help you, you may be sure of that."

Georgina threw a contemptuous glance at her parents. How could they behave so? she wondered, Mama so fearful of spoiling her gown that she would not embrace her suffering, unhappy daughter, and Papa reproving her manners as though this was a moment for strict decorum. "Myles, dear, do fetch her some wine. You will drink some wine, won't you darling?" Harriet nodded against her shoulder childishly. Myles left the room, and when he returned with the wine, Harriet's sobs had subsided into hiccoughs, and she was using Georgina's handkerchief to mop her eyes and blow her nose. Georgina was saying, "There now, sweetheart, you will feel better soon. You have been very brave, coming away all by yourself. How did you accomplish it?"

"I told him I was carrying his child."

"Good lord, Harriet, are you—" cried her mother.

"Of course not, but I told him I was and that if he ever touched me again I would do away with it." Harriet tilted her chin defiantly.

"Dear heaven!" Lady Fitzhardinge shuddered.

"Well, and so I should have done, if it had been true, for he shall never touch me again!"

"No, darling, certainly he shall not. Tell us what you did then," soothed Georgina. Myles handed Harriet the wine; and she sipped at it.

"I told him I must drive out every day for fresh air, and he finally gave orders in the stables that I might order the carriage out each day. On the third day I simply drove all the way home. I told the coachman to drive me to London, but he would not do so without orders from Braye, so when I got home I asked John."

"What?" Lord Fitzhardinge exploded wrathfully, thinking of being put to the expense of his own horses for the trip to London.

"And he would not bring me either without permission from you," continued Harriet with an accusing look at her father. "So I was forced to borrow money from Happy and take the stage. I hope that makes you proud, Papa, your own daughter in the stage with all those shopkeepers!"

"I cannot be pleased with the tone of voice in which you choose to address me, Harriet," Lord Fitzhardinge began, but Myles intervened hastily.

"If you will forgive me, sir, I think any further discussion tonight would be fruitless. It is almost five in the morning now, and Harriet has been travelling all night. She should be put to bed at once, to my way of thinking. In fact, we are all too exhausted to be of any help to her. I suggest we all go to bed and meet again tomorrow to decide what it is best to do."

Harriet clung to Georgina. "Please do not leave me, Georgie. Please stay with me tonight."

Georgina looked pleadingly at Myles, hoping he would make some excuse that would allow her to leave, but then was ashamed of her thought and pressed Harriet close. "Of course I will not leave you, dearest, if you would have me here," she said, with an apologetic glance at her husband. He came forward at once and bent to kiss her brow.

"Yes, you must be longing for bed also, my love. Do you take Harriet up at once. I will come around in the morning, say at eleven. That should give us all a few hours of sleep."

Georgina helped Harriet to her feet and led her out of the room.

Myles turned to her father. "She cannot return to him, of course."

Lord Fitzhardinge drew himself up in affront. "I think you must allow me to know best, Trowbridge."

"But after what we have heard, it would be inhuman—"

"Nonsense! I hope you were not taken in by all that tarradiddle. In my opinion she has made it all up. She was always prone to overdramatize herself to gain attention. The truth is probably that he denied her some trinket and she is punishing him."

Myles stared at him in astonishment.

Even Lady Fitzhardinge was moved to protest. "I do not think, Fitz dear, that it is possible Harriet could make up such a story. She was never an imaginative child."

"Perhaps it would be best for you to retire now, madam. I will bid you good night." He kissed her hand and led her to the door. She had nothing to do but bid Myles good night and leave the room.

After only a moment Myles went to the door also. "I will take my leave now, but I strongly advise you not to try to send her back without at least visiting Braye and satisfying yourself that it is wise to do so."

"And I know what his response to such interference would be. He would demand her return at once. If she refused, he would divorce her and he would not return her dowry. And he would be well within his rights, of course. Well, I assure you I shall not throw away eight thousand pounds so easily as that!"

Myles was too sickened by this avaricious attitude to trust himself to reply. He simply bowed and went out the door.

When he returned the following morning, he found a pale, haggard-eyed Georgina at the breakfast table with Lady Fitzhardinge, nervously crumbling a piece of toast. She was wearing an old gown of Lydia's, and her hair was bundled into a knot at the back of her head.

He bent to cup her face and kiss her lips gently. "You do not look well rested at all, my love."

"No, I suppose not, but that is of no moment. Poor Harriet."

"Is she still sleeping?"

"No. Papa barely allowed her to swallow down a few sips of chocolate before he took her off to his library for a 'sensible talk.' " She emphasized the last words bitterly.

Myles looked grim, for he was very much afraid of what the outcome of this would be. He was proved right, for presently Lord Fitzhardinge entered the room and sat down to order his breakfast, his whole pose expressing self-satisfaction. He was followed by a blank-eyed Harriet.

"Madam, take your daughter up and prepare her for travel. We shall start as soon as I have taken some breakfast."

"Papa, you surely cannot mean—" Georgina began.

"I must ask you not to interfere, Georgina."

"You may ask me, but I will not listen to you in this. You

cannot send her back to him. The man is truly bad. Why, he behaved shamelessly with Lydia and me, and he and Cressy had private assignations the very week, nay, the last three days before the wedding.''

''That has nothing to do with it.''

''It has everything to do with it! A man who could attempt, while courting one daughter, to seduce the rest, is capable of anything.''

''Very well, Georgina, you have had your say. Now I will thank you to be silent. I do not care to discuss this matter.''

Myles rose and went to his wife and led her out of the room. In the hall she turned to him, the tears slipping silently down her cheeks, and he gathered her into his arms.

''There, darling, it is all right. How brave you were to stand up to him. I am proud of you. I tried to talk him out of it last night after you were gone up with Harriet, but he would not listen. We have done all we can, I fear. He will not be moved. It may work out, if he will speak strongly enough to Braye.''

''It is so heartless. How can he care so little for his own daughter as to even dream of allowing her to return? Oh, dear, if only there were something—''

Her father came out of the dining room and called up the stairs impatiently for his wife. ''The carriage is waiting, and I do not like to keep my cattle standing about in the cold.''

Harriet came down, followed by a dithery Lady Fitzhardinge. Harriet's face was stony, and she looked straight ahead, not acknowledging any of them. Myles went forward to kiss her cheek, and then her mother followed, without any response from her. Her only sign of awareness of their presence was when Georgina put her arms about the stiff shoulders and laid her cheek against her sister's. Harriet raised her hand and pressed Georgina's shoulder briefly. She then drew away and went through the door her father held without a word or a backward glance. The door clanged shut at the same moment as Lydia appeared at the top of the stairs, clearly straight from her bed, wearing only a much beruffled and beribbanded lawn bedgown, with her blond hair tumbled in disarray about her shoulders.

She came flying down the stairs. ''What has happened? Where is Harriet going? Why did no one wake me?''

Lady Fitzhardinge, grateful her husband had not witnessed

this shameless exhibition, hurried to Lydia, trying to shoo her back up the stairs. "What can you mean by coming down in your bedgown and not even a robe for decency's sake? Go back to your room this instant!"

"Oh, stop fussing, Mama. What difference does it make? What of Harriet?"

"None of that concerns you, Lydia. Go up at once, do you hear?" By now she was pushing Lydia up the stairs.

Over her mother's shoulder Lydia mouthed, "Two o'clock at your house?"

Georgina nodded.

"Come, love, I am taking you home. You are to rest for the entire day, and if you feel up to it, we will leave for Falconley tomorrow," Myles said.

Georgina went willingly.

CHAPTER

25

As soon as they reached Lady Cunliffe's, Myles led Georgina to her room, rang for Prentiss, and left at once, bidding Georgina to get straight into her bed. Georgina was dazed with exhaustion and depression about Harriet's unhappy fate. Her own helplessness against her father's iron will had left her in a state of dispirited languor, so that she stood limp while Prentiss undressed her and pulled a bedgown over her head.

She sank into her bed and lay supine, staring at the ceiling, sure her eyes would never close despite the nearly sleepless night she had gone through with Harriet. She had held Harriet in her arms, smoothing her hair back in a lulling motion as she would have soothed an upset child, while Harriet cried. She was sure Harriet would soon plummet into sleep, too exhausted to resist it after all she had been through, and her own eyes drooped closed and she dozed off. She didn't know how long she slept, but woke from the pain in her shoulder where Harriet's head rested heavily. Georgina's bedgown was soaked through with Harriet's tears, and her arm was numb from the shoulder down. She wanted desperately to move it, but realized Harriet had fallen asleep at last and could not bring herself to take the chance of waking her. After a time, despite her discomfort, Georgina slid back into sleep, only to be wakened again by Harriet's heartbroken weeping. She comforted her, and when Harriet was quiet, rose and moved to the other side of the bed and pulled her back into her arms. They slept again until Georgina woke with her other arm numb and her other shoulder tingling with pain. This pattern repeated itself interminably all night.

Now the memory of Harriet's misery washed over her

again, and her eyes filled with tears of pity. Harriet, unpleasant and whining as she had been as a child and as a young
woman, still did not deserve this unhappiness. She had looked
so radiantly triumphant on her wedding day, and then, only
minutes after waving good-bye to her family, to be so sickeningly disillusioned. Ah, it was so unfair! Despite herself
Georgina remembered all the revolting details of her married
life that Harriet had recited to them. She sat up abruptly and
propped herself against her pillows to banish the disgusting
images. Afraid to close her eyes, she reached for a slim,
leather-bound volume of Lord Byron's poems and began to
read *Childe Harold*.

The next thing she was aware of as she slowly opened her
eyes was Lydia sitting beside the bed, and reading the book.
"Lydia?"

"You read yourself to sleep. I did not like to wake you, so
I just took the book from you to read until you woke up by
yourself."

"What time is it?"

"Past four. I came at two."

"Oh, darling, I am sorry."

"No, no, please do not apologize. You looked so exhausted I was glad to find you sleeping. Close your eyes
again, and I will be still as a mouse. Or would you rather I
went away?"

"Please do not. I will not sleep any more now. What a
good child it is. You must be dying of curiosity and yet you
do not ask. Not at all like my old Lydia, always so impatient
for answers and information." Georgina patted her hand
affectionately. "Did Mama tell you anything?"

Lydia sniffed scornfully. "Harriet and Braye quarreled and
she was a silly girl and ran away, but Papa persuaded her she
was being foolish and she finally agreed to return. These little
disagreements happen often in the early days of a marriage,"
she recited with a telling imitation of Lady Fitzhardinge. "As
if Harriet would allow anyone to think she had less than the
most perfect marriage ever created unless something really
dreadful had occurred. I hope I am not so bacon-brained as to
be cozened by Mama's tale. What really happened?"

Georgina gave her an abbreviated version of the facts,
leaving out only the business of the maid as being too indeli-
cate to recite to a sixteen-year-old maiden, even one as

knowledgeable as Lydia. What she did tell was enough to cause Lydia's eyes to widen in horror.

"The beast," Lydia said finally, "oh the miserable beast! Poor old Harry. Of all people to be subjected to such things! Even a normal sort of marriage and bedding would have been difficult enough for her to learn to accept, but this is beyond anything! And Papa forced her to go back!"

"He said she would disgrace his name and would not be received anywhere and would lose her portion if Braye divorced her, as he surely would do if she did not return."

"As if any of that mattered when set against the unhappiness of his daughter! He is a beast too, as much as Braye! I despise him and shall never love him again."

Georgina knew she should reprove such sentiments, but feeling as she did, very much the same, she could not bring herself to be so hypocritical. "I think when we go down to Falconley tomorrow I will ask Myles if we may stop and visit her. Perhaps Braye will be more circumspect in future if he sees her family supports her and will watch out for her welfare."

"Oh, are you leaving tomorrow? I wish you were not."

"I am weary of balls and having to make the agreeable to a set of people who could all disappear from my life tomorrow and never be missed," declared Georgina.

"Why, Georgina, you say that when you are the toast of London with all those men dying of love for you? How uncharitable."

"Oh, well," Georgina laughed, "I do not include St. Albans or Alvanley, of course, or Lord Lockburn, but they are friends and not, by the way, dying of love for me. If I had ever shown any of them the least sign of encouragement, they would each have shown me a clean pair of heels. Now I think I must get up and dress for dinner. Will you stay?"

"I wish I might, but we are engaged to dine with the Yarboroughs, and Mama would never let me out of it. She has the eldest son in her eye for me." Lydia's disdainful tone clearly stated her opinion of the Yarborough heir.

"Not a possibility, I take it."

"Lord, Georgie, if you could see him! No chin to speak of, and a fastidious expression as though the rest of humanity smelled disagreeably to him. Oh, they are of the first water of respectability. Positively starchy with pride and rich as Golden

Ball. But I would stay on the shelf forever before I would marry into such a family. I must say good-bye, I suppose, or I will never be dressed in time. May I come for a visit to Falconley soon?''

"As soon as ever you like.''

"Give my love to Mrs. Conyers and tell her I am sorry not to have replied to her last letter yet, but I never seem to have a moment. I will be happy when all this nonsense is over.'' Lydia hugged Georgina and kissed her several times and left at last.

Georgina rang for Prentiss and ordered hot water brought up for a bath. Refreshed by this and her few hours of deep sleep, she felt her oppression lifting. Surely things would go easier for Harriet from now on. Braye would know his behaviour had been reported and would treat Harriet more carefully.

When Prentiss had dressed her hair in a loose fall of curls from a knot at the back of her head, Georgina donned a simple daffodil satin gown and went downstairs to find Myles. Tonight, perhaps, he would show her some sign that he still desired her. Her heart jerked roughly and her pulses accelerated at the thought. Then, midway between one step and the next, it struck her that he might with some justification be awaiting some such sign from her. After all, it was her lack of ardour, her inability to express her feelings either physically or in words, that had turned him away.

She stared blindly into space, one hand on the balustrade, one foot in midair, as she tried to imagine a scene in which she rekindled his desire for her with her own actions. Should she fling her arms about him, press herself against him, kiss him passionately? Perhaps, but she simply could not imagine herself doing any of those things. And would the result be the same as it used to be or would it be more pleasurable for her now that she was in love with him? She knew she wanted him to touch her and kiss her and tell her he loved only her, but she could not bear to dwell on that ultimate intimacy for fear it would still be pointless and uninteresting. But there must be more to it, she protested silently, Aunt Selina had said so. And look at Cressy!

"My love, you make a lovely picture, but the suspense is dreadful. Will she or won't she?'' Myles stood at the foot of the stairs, laughing up at her.

"Oh!" She felt the heat of a blush flood up her neck to the roots of her hair, as though he had sensed her thoughts.

"Do come the rest of the way down," he coaxed teasingly.

"Yes, yes, of course," she said, trying to cover her confusion with a display of dignity, her chin up, her tread deliberate as she came down.

"I hope you are not engaged for the evening."

"Of course not, since we had planned to leave London today. Aunt Selina sends her apologies for not spending the evening with us. She had engaged herself to dine with Lord Ffoukes and felt she could not disappoint him. So we shall be alone tonight. I am glad, for I am tired—"

"You are still not recovered from your ordeal of last night," he interrupted with quick concern. "You should have kept to your bed and had a tray sent up to you."

"No, no, I had a lovely rest. I was going to say I was tired of parties and dining in company," she assured him.

"I am glad of that," he replied with evident satisfaction, pulling her arm through his and leading her into the drawing room. "We shall be very quiet by our own fireside, though such an elegant gown deserves a larger audience. Will you take a glass of wine with me before dinner?"

"Yes, thank you." He turned to go to the tray on a side table. On an impulse Georgina said, "Myles" rather breathlessly as she realized what she was going to do. When he turned back to her, she walked slowly up to him and framed his face with her hands. She looked at him, gathering courage, then raised herself slightly and set her mouth against his for a moment.

Myles stood stock-still and unresponding, caught completely off guard by her unprecedented action. Nothing she could have done could have surprised him more, for he knew such behaviour was totally out of character for her. He felt an almost swamping rush of love for her as he realized how much courage her action had taken and was on the point of jerking her roughly into his arms and demonstrating his feelings when he remembered in time his resolve to go very slowly with her.

She stood before him, eyes down, wondering if she had disgusted him by her impulse. Then he reached for her hands and placed them on his shoulders and gathered her close to him with one arm. With the other hand he tilted her face up and dropped light kisses on her eyelids before touching her lips gently with teasing little kisses. Her arms crept about his neck, and one hand touched the back of his head. She stood rapt, eyes closed, savouring the moment, while a warmth spread down through her body, setting off small explosions of electricity in her skin wherever he touched her. Her hand began caressing his head while her body pressed closer; her lips melted open beneath his, and the tip of his tongue tentatively explored hers. She gasped. Then his mouth left hers for a moment to kiss her neck, her shoulders, before returning hungrily and more demandingly to her mouth.

They both became slowly aware of a light but persistent tapping at the door. They were not aware that Parks had tapped and entered two minutes earlier. After one look he had hastily withdrawn, closing the door again soundlessly. He had stood undecided for a moment before reluctantly tapping again.

"Damnation," Myles said, and released her to turn and call, "Yes? Come," in tones of distinct annoyance.

Parks came in. "Forgive me m'lord, but here is an urgent message from Fitzhardinge House," the butler said apologetically, handing Myles the letter and retiring at once.

Myles looked at it and then with a resigned shrug broke the seal and spread it open. A glance at the bottom showed him it was from Lydia. He read:

Myles dear, please come at once, both of you. Harriet is dead. Break it to Georgie. In haste, Lydia.

"Good God," Myles said, running his hand distractedly through his hair.

"Myles, what is it?" begged Georgina, her eyes wide with alarm.

"It is from Lydia. Darling, it is very bad news. She wants us to come at once. It is Harriet."

"She has run away again?"

"No, dearest."

Georgina stared speechlessly as his meaning became clear to her, and slowly all the colour drained out of her face. She put out her hands pleadingly, and Myles took them and pulled her close, cradling her. After a time she pulled away. "Come We must go to them."

At the Fitzhardinge mansion they were shown at once into the drawing room, where a distraught Lady Fitzhardinge lay prostrate on a sofa being administered a glass of hartshorn and water by a weeping Lydia.

Lady Fitzhardinge pushed aside the glass and rose to stumble into Georgina's arms, sobbing and babbling incoherently of her baby and her cruel husband and his carelessness in allowing a child in such a frame of mind out of his sight. Georgina could make nothing of these disjointed sentences, but finally persuaded her stepmother back to the couch and taking the glass from Lydia, held it to Lady Fitzhardinge's mouth until it was all gone. Then she insisted that her stepmother be put to bed, and with Lydia's assistance got her to her feet and led her out of the room. Georgina gave her a few drops of laudanum to make sure she slept and sat holding her hand until she dropped off. Then she and Lydia tiptoed out, leaving Carstairs to sit by her mistress.

Downstairs again Myles handed them both a glass of brandy and asked Lydia to tell them all she knew of what had happened.

It seemed, Lydia said, that after two hours of travelling Lord Fitzhardinge had stopped to bait the horses and take some refreshment at a small village inn. While the meal was being prepared, Harriet said she would walk for a bit to stretch her legs. When the meal was laid for them, she had not returned, and Lord Fitzhardinge had sent his groom to find her. The man reported that she had disappeared. The coachman was summoned from the kitchen to assist the groom, and they both set off again, taking different paths. The meal was growing cold and impatiently Lord Fitzhardinge sat down to eat without her. The men returned eventually to say that they could not find her anywhere. Now Lord Fitzhardinge began to suspect she might have run away again and was hiding from him. He became increasingly angry and insisted that the inn servants must find someone in the village who had seen her, for surely no one dressed as finely as Harriet could wander about so small a place without calling attention to herself. Eventually a man was found who admitted to having seen a Quality lass standing beside Moulter's Pond earlier. The groom was sent off expeditiously in company with the man to show him the way to Moulter's Pond, and there at last they had found Harriet—floating face down in the water!

Terrified, they left her and ran back to report their dire news to Lord Fitzhardinge. He sat in stunned silence for a very long time, ignoring the frightened, hovering servants, before calling for pen and paper. He sent off a terse letter to his wife, giving her the bare facts, requesting her to send Trowbridge to him at once, and suggesting she and Lydia return home, by the groom who had found Harriet, and the groom was able to fill in all the details Lord Fitzhardinge had left out of his note.

Myles said that he would leave as soon as he could return to Lady Cunliffe's and change his clothing. Since he meant to ride to make better time, he suggested that Georgina travel with Lydia and her mother in his coach on the following morning. This was agreed, and Myles bade Lydia good night. Georgina followed him into the hall and embraced him without words, clinging to the comfort of his warm, strong body, regardless of Jelkins, who stood, eyes averted politely, holding Myles's greatcoat in readiness.

When he was gone, Georgina returned to Lydia, who was crying again, and they held each other, their tears mingling.

"Oh, lord, Georgie, how desperate she must have been to take her life in such a way. The water must have been so cold!"

CHAPTER

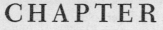

26

After a harrowing week with her parents while Harriet's body was returned home and buried, Myles took Georgina away to Falconley. Lady Fitzhardinge was reluctant to let them leave, for her husband was no comfort to her at all.

Lord Fitzhardinge had not been heard to utter a word since he returned with Myles. He made no sign to indicate his feelings, and when his wife flung his guilt into his face, he had waited stonily until she had finished and then walked away. He had attended the funeral with Myles, but he would not even look at Sir Vernon, whom Myles had had to notify. Myles had only nodded in acknowledgement of Sir Vernon's greeting and turned away. Sir Vernon was not invited to the house.

Since then Lord Fitzhardinge had risen and dressed each day with his usual care, but he was shockingly different from the man who had driven away from London with Harriet. He seemed smaller, as though shrunken in upon himself, and his eyes were as blank and unseeing as Harriet's were the last time they had seen her. He came downstairs and entered his study each day, locking the door behind him and only opening it to receive the meals Jelkins brought to him on trays. At the end of the day he might be glimpsed again as he left the study and climbed the stairs to his bedroom.

Lady Fitzhardinge kept mostly to her own bed or a chaise in her room, with Carstairs, Lydia, and Georgina in almost constant attendance. She wept and dozed and woke to accuse her husband and Braye equally of the responsibility for her daughter's death. Lydia wondered if it would ever occur to her mother that in some part the responsibility was hers in that she had not stood by Harriet in her need. Perhaps if she had refused to allow Harriet to be forced back to Braye, something might have been accomplished in the face of Lord Fitzhardinge's obduracy.

Georgina did not like to leave Lydia alone in such an atmosphere, for of course Cressy had come and stayed only one day before flitting away, claiming the oppressive mood was not good for the child she was carrying, but Lydia urged Myles to take Georgina away.

"You must be longing for your own home and to be with darling Selina again. Besides, there is nothing more you can do here, and I am not so affected by their moods as others would be. Adrian writes me nearly every day and sends me books. He says Mama's grief will be eased all the sooner by her constant tears and that Papa—well, he says I must learn compassion there, though I cannot love him any more. I am finding it difficult. Vindictiveness is my chief emotion regarding Papa, but I feel sure Adrian will persuade me out of it in time." She laughed ruefully, though it seemed to Georgina that Lydia was not unwilling to be persuaded.

So they came home to Falconley in the late afternoon for a joyous reunion with Selina. At first she was shy with them. She clung to Mrs. Apple and buried her face in her nurse's neck, but patiently Georgina coaxed her, and at last the child allowed herself to be taken from Mrs. Apple's arms and cuddled by her mother. In a very short time she was riding around the room astride her father's shoulders, each tiny fist clutching a handful of her father's hair as she crowed in delight.

After that there was time only to dash off a hurried note to Mrs. Conyers to inform her of their return and beg her to call tomorrow, if it were possible, or if not, to dine with them tomorrow night; then it was time to dress for dinner.

Georgina would have preferred to dine with more intimacy, since there was only the two of them, but Cook had prepared an elaborate meal to welcome them home and the dining table was already laid for them, so they faced each other down the length of the table and spoke of their daughter's health and beauty and of estate matters until Honeyman set the port before Myles and withdrew.

Myles promptly came around and pulled her from her chair. "Come, my love, enough of this formality. We will go into the drawing room and have some port together." Gather-

ing up the decanter and two glasses, he led her away, his arm
about her waist. She quivered beneath the heat of his hand,
but decorously seated herself before the fire and took out her
embroidery frame. Myles fetched a book of poetry and read
aloud to her. She could not help remembering the last time
they had sat here just so and how her heart had lain then so
cold and hard in her breast. How grey and hopeless the world
had seemed then.

She glanced up almost shyly and found Myles watching
her. When their eyes met, she knew he was remembering
also. After a moment he put down the book.

"Georgina, there is something I wanted to say to you the
last time we sat here but I could not raise my courage to the
proper pitch. I became a coward, you see, when I realized
how much you meant to me. I was afraid I would lose you. I
knew that you were unhappy, that you had heard something
from Cressy. It was true at one time, but not now—not since
Selina. Can you forgive it?"

"If you can forgive my selfishness and ignorance," she
whispered, forcing herself not to look away.

He reached his hand across to her and hers came forth to
grasp it.

Then there was a rap at the door, and Honeyman came in
with the tea tray. They both sat back. Georgina welcomed
Honeyman's appearance, for the tea tray signaled the end of
the evening. They could go up to bed. Her heart lurched at
the thought, and her teacup rattled in its saucer. At last she
set it aside and stood up.

"I will go up now, I think," she said, busily folding her
embroidery frame back into its basket by her chair.

"Very well, love. I will just finish my tea," Myles replied.
He did not say more, but he did not need to do so. She knew
he would come to her later when he had changed.

She went upstairs, changed quickly into a bedgown and
robe, and dismissed Prentiss, only to call the maid back to
brush her hair until it glittered and crackled electrically. Then
she was alone again. She leaned nearer the glass to inspect
her face, holding the candle close, then set it down to rub a
bit of rouge into her cheeks. She brought the candle up again
and with an exclamation of disgust rushed to the washstand
and scrubbed the rouge away. She went to her bed, but turned
away, shy suddenly at the thought of his coming in and

finding her there. She seated herself again at the dressing table, but rose with a startled gasp as she heard a soft tap at her door.

Myles entered and saw her rise, her eyes wide with—what? —apprehension? No, he would not have it so. He smiled reassuringly, closed the door softly behind him, and walked slowly forward.

"Now," he said, "where were we before when we were interrupted?" He took her hands and placed them on his shoulders and pulled her close. Slowly, deliberately, his mouth approached hers, as her eyelids fluttered down and she yielded to the pressure of his arms about her, her mouth raised to meet his. His kisses, as before, were teasing, questioning, and as before she stood passive for a time while his lips moved over her face and then back to her mouth.

Georgina felt the same warmth spreading inside her as she waited more impatiently each time for his lips to return to her own, even as her skin tingled at the touch of his hands. Finally, with a little cry, she clasped his head with both hands so that he could not move and kissed him back, her mouth seeking, begging for more and more.

At last he pulled away and gently untied the ribbands of her robe and her gown and pushed them from her shoulders so that they fell in a silken heap about her feet; she stood quiescent before him. He picked her up and carried her to the bed and put her gently down upon it. Dropping his robe, he lay down beside her, his hands moving over her body slowly, his lips moving down her throat, her shoulders, and finding her breast. She gasped with pleasure as his tongue teased about her nipple. Then he cupped her breasts, moving from one to the other, sucking, biting gently, kissing. She cried out, her body moving, opening to him, a hot, aching pressure building, demanding. But he would not yield at once, returning to her mouth, his hands fondling her breasts, until finally she could not bear it and begged him to come to her. He continued to kiss her, tease her, touch her until even he could not withstand longer and he relented, slowly advancing, withdrawing, until she was in a frenzy of need and arched her body against him, her hands pressing him closer. Now the pressure built so intensely inside her that she struggled frantically to release it, and within a moment her body burst into pulsating explosions and she cried out and held him still until the throbbing died. Then she must have it again and moved urgently against him to recapture it. She forgot after a time how long they moved together, how many times she demanded this ecstatic new pleasure before he said, "Now, my love, now," and exploded inside her.

He collapsed upon her, and she held him, loving his weight, the feel of his body upon her, and after a time she drifted off into dreamless sleep. She woke and began caressing his back, her hands drifting up and down until he woke, his mouth seeking hers and they began again.

When Prentiss entered the next morning she saw them there, wrapped together, too soundly asleep to be wakened by an opening door. She retreated and did not return until she was summoned by the bell from m'lady's room. She found her mistress decorously arrayed in her bedgown and alone, her mouth curved in a secret smile.

After her morning chocolate Georgina rose and with Prentiss's help dressed and went down to breakfast with her husband. He was before her and led her to her seat at the table. Had Honeyman not been in the room with a footman to assist him in the serving, she would have thrown herself into her husband's arms. As it was, she accepted a discreet kiss on the brow and sat down. She could not take her eyes from him, even as she ate an enormous helping of baked eggs and toast. Myles attacked a large beefsteak while he drank in her beauty and wondered whether they could go back upstairs at once without creating a scandal in the servants' quarters.

Honeyman came in to announce that Mrs. Conyers had arrived, and Myles contented himself with kissing Georgina's delicious mouth lingeringly, and went away to attend to his long-neglected estate business.

Georgina went eagerly to the drawing room to greet Mrs. Conyers, who rose to her feet at once and came forward to embrace her.

"I was so sorry to hear of your sister. A truly dreadful tragedy, and so unnecessary. Why did she not simply refuse to go back? She could hardly have been bound and carried there by force."

"She was between two evils, I think. To return was intolerable, while to stay— Well, there was no way Papa would ever have relented in the matter. He would have gone on, day after day, badgering her in his belittling way until she would do doubt have gone mad. Oh, you are not acquainted with my papa, Mrs. Conyers. There is no love in him. He is a cold, arrogant man who cares only for his good name and money.''

Abruptly Mrs. Conyers turned away. To Georgina's surprise she stood quite still, her back turned, unspeaking, while a long minute passed, then another. It was such an unusual action that Georgina could not think of what to say or do.

Mrs. Conyers swung back to face her, pale and shaking. ''My dear,'' she said, her voice trembling slightly with emotion, ''shall we sit down? There is something I must say to you. I had hoped never to—I thought it possible we could go on as we are, but—'' She halted, her hands gripped together so tightly that the knuckles glimmered whitely through her skin. She unclasped them and began fumbling in her reticule. ''I have had a letter from Lady Cunliffe.''

Georgina's eyebrows rose in astonishment. ''I was not aware you were acquainted with her.''

''No, we have never met, but, well, perhaps it would be best if you read her letter to start us off, for I cannot think how best to—'' She shrugged in uncharacteristic helplessness and handed Georgina the letter.

Georgina opened it and read:

My dear Mrs. Conyers,

It has never been my habit to interfere in matters I feel are not my concern. After much thought, however, I have concluded that for our dear Georgina's sake I must take it upon myself to write to you. We have never met, but I am not unacquainted with events of some eighteen years ago, when the name Fenn-Conyers was much bandied about. Putting that together with the name Blanche brought the truth home to me. I have said nothing of this to anyone, but I believe it would be wiser of you to reveal to Georgina the true state of affairs before someone who *does* know you happens upon you by chance and inadvertently or purposely reveals your real identity to her. I cannot think that would be a pleasant way for her to discover it. I know how difficult this will be for you, but I can assure you that Georgina has matured to an astonishing degree in the past months, and it is my opinion that she will accept the news and be glad of it. Naturally if you decide not to speak, I shall continue to keep my own counsel and remain, dear madam, your well-wisher,

Selina Cunliffe

Georgina read the letter through rapidly and then, frowning, more slowly. She looked up at last, clearly bewildered. "I do not understand in the least. What is she talking about? What does she want you to tell me? Are you not Mrs. Conyers?"

Mrs. Conyers's hands were again in their painful grip, and for a moment she studied them before raising her eyes to meet Georgina's; Georgina saw they were filled with fear.

"Dear Mrs. Conyers! What is it? I cannot bear to see you this way. Please tell me nothing that will distress you."

Mrs. Conyers took a deep breath and forced her stiff lips to move. "It is very simple to tell. You see, I *do* know your papa very well. We were married for two years. I am your mother."

Georgina's mouth went slack; her eyes widened. She stared speechlessly, her brain attempting to make sense of the words Mrs. Conyers had spoken. Darkness crept from the corners of her mind, obscuring the knowledge, the room, the present, and for an instant she surrendered to it, wanting oblivion. No! she ordered herself, and bit her lips, forcing her eyes to open, her spine to straighten, knowing that to faint now would be cowardly.

"Georgina! Are you all right?"

"Yes," Georgina said, her lips barely moving.

"I know this was very abrupt—shocking—but I could think of no other way. I had hoped Lady Cunliffe's letter might prepare you."

"Why did you come here?"

"I heard of your marriage and that you were to have a child. I wanted to be near, to be able to see you. I thought no one would remember me after all these years and I need never reveal myself." Her eyes were bright with unshed tears, but she was too proud to let them fall. Her chin was up, just as Georgina's was as she listened. "I do not know, of course, if anyone has ever told you what happened." Georgina shook her head in denial, unable to speak. "Do you want me to tell you? My own side, of course, though not to excuse or justify my behaviour, but so that you will know everything.''

Georgina nodded mutely.

"I knew Edward Fenn-Conyers all my life. We had always meant to marry. It was accepted by his family and mine. But his father was a prodigious gambler and finally succeeded in losing everything. My papa would not permit me to marry Edward after that. An uncle of Edward's bought him his colours, and he went away to the army and wrote that I must forget him and make an advantageous marriage since it would be many years before he could consider taking a wife. I was so unhappy that I wanted to die. I wished that I might. Then Papa was approached with an offer from Fitzhardinge. I was indifferent as to what became of me. One match seemed as good as another if I could not have Edward, so I agreed. I could not love Fitzhardinge, but I resolved to be a good wife, and I might have been if he had ever shown me one moment of tenderness or understanding. He did not love me. He only wanted a son. Poor man. Perhaps if I had given him one— Ah, well, it is pointless to dwell upon it now. He was very resentful that I presented him with a daughter and would have nothing to do with you, which estranged us further. He rarely spoke to me. I was desperately lonely and unhappy. Then I met Edward again at a party.''

She stopped and studied Georgina for a moment in silence. "This is the difficult part for me, and I know it will be for you also. Shall I go on?''

"Yes," replied Georgina firmly, holding tightly to the arms of her chair, her own knuckles white now with tension.

"Well, it was like—like coming into the light again after two years of darkness. The only thing I had had to sustain me through my unhappiness was you. But when I saw him again, I felt I could not bear to be apart from him any longer. He was being sent to India, and I knew if he went without me, I would never see him again. I finally persuaded him to take us with him. But when I tried to leave the house with you, your father would not let me. He ordered the nurse to take you back upstairs and lock herself in the nursery with you and admit no one but himself. He said if I left, I would never see you again. Oh, it was cruel—*he* did not love you! So I had to choose. I knew if I stayed I might do away with myself and be lost to you in any case. And I loved Edward so much! I felt I had betrayed him by not waiting for him in the first place, no matter what he said. So—I chose.

"We travelled out separately. He hired a woman to accompany me for propriety's sake. By the time we reached India, my hair had turned white, and I feared Edward would not love me any more because I looked so freakish. I was very young and silly, of course, and had not learned that love has little to do with appearances. He arranged for me to stay with his colonel's wife until I heard from your papa's solicitors that the divorce had been granted. Then we married. Edward was gazetted to the court of a rajah to help train Indian officers for his private army. Edward was very—very good, both in nature and as an officer. His men adored him, and the rajah became so fond of him he was forever heaping rich gifts upon him. Then Edward was killed accidentally, and I—I came home to find you."

She came to a full stop, and calm now that all was revealed, sat with folded hands and waited. Georgina stared into the fire, a knot of pain in her breast that held her paralyzed, afraid to move for fear it would become unbearable. The silence stretched between them as images formed and faded in the leaping flames before Georgina's eyes: a girl like herself holding a baby like Selina facing a vengeful Lord Fitzhardinge; Harriet's dead eyes as she walked out the door with her father; Hester, who would be walking up the aisle in two weeks to be joined to a man who despised her. Marriage for most women, she thought, was like a mad dice game. It was sheer chance that when the dice were cast for me I won Myles and not someone like Braye.

At last Mrs. Conyers sighed and rose. "I am sorry to have been the cause of so much pain for you, child, both now and in the past. Perhaps I am in part responsible for poor Harriet's fate also, for of course Fitzhardinge would find it impossible to accept another runaway wife in his life. Perhaps Lady Cunliffe was wrong in her advice that I should tell you all this, but she was clearly right in one thing. You have grown up. You no longer need a mother." She walked steadily across the room and had opened the door before Georgina leaped to her feet.

"Wait!"

Mrs. Conyers slowly turned back, not hiding the tears that had had their way and were running unchecked down her cheeks. Georgina advanced towards her, the knot in her chest melting, her hands reaching out.

"Please do not go. Perhaps I no longer need a mother, but I find I cannot give up my dear friend Mrs. Conyers."

Epilogue

Dearest Georgina,

Italy was, of course, glorious (and oh! what a wonderful invention is marraige!), but it is good to be home at last. St. Edward's is a beautiful church, Toverton a fair-sized town, the parsonage quite comfortable, and the parishioners have been so friendly and kind to us—and naturally all *adore* Adrian.

We stopped for a few days to visit with Mama. Papa is the same more or less, though he did unbend enough to invite Adrian into his study for a talk. What they spoke of I, of course, do not know, since Adrian says it was a man speaking to a priest, not to a son-in-law, so I could not ask. As you know, he has always had this unusual liking for Adrian. Unusual for Papa, I mean, to *like* anyone. I suppose Adrian was right that I would learn compassion for my papa, since I find I do not hate him any longer.

Mama says Cressy is increasing again! Her fourth. It is amazing that someone who cares so little for babies produces so many. Her latest affair was with young Redesdale, so the child will probably be white-blond with protruding teeth! Mama says Simon is spending the summer with you, which must be heaven for him after the rackety life he leads at home.

We saw Dominick and Hester at a dinner party in London before we went to Mama's. He is as devilishly handsome as ever, but poor Hester is faded and extinguished-looking. I cannot suppose he will ever forgive her for trapping him into marriage and then losing the baby five months along, though in company at least he treats her with exquisite courtesy. I hear she has lost another one since then. Poor soul. Do you see them at all?

Now for my good news. In about four months Adrian and I will expect you to send us a silver porringer for a brand-new Patterson. Yes—oh glory! We are to have a child! I think sometimes I am dreaming this bliss.

How are all your treasures? The divine Selina, the magnificent Peter, and the fresh-minted Travis? Kiss them all for me, and dear Myles also, and give my love to Mama Conyers and say I will be writing her soon to implore her to come for a long visit—and you are to encourage her, Georgina, and not keep her selfishly to yourself. Write soon to your loving sister,

Lydia

Georgina's voice faded away on the quiet summer air, and she laid the letter aside.

Mrs. Conyers, who sat beside her beneath the shade of a spreading oak tree at the side of the house, Travis in her arms, sighed. "It is all turning out so well for her, the darling girl. I must admit that for a time I was somewhat fearful."

"So was I also, and Lydia told me a few minutes before the wedding that she had some doubts herself about Adrian's true feelings. She had quite made up her mind an entire year before, but Adrian did not speak. She decided that on her eighteenth birthday, if he still had not proposed to her, she would propose to him!"

"Oh, she was surely bamming you," Mrs. Conyers protested laughingly.

"Not she. She actually did so. He arrived at breakfast on the morning of her birthday, and she pounced on him at once. He said he had come specifically to ask her but had planned to do so after he had drunk his chocolate. He said it had always been his intention to ask for her when she was eighteen and he had not been in the least tardy, having arrived on the very day. He was wise, I think, to allow her two years to recover from her grief for Tarquin."

"Very, and so is she—remarkably so for her years. They are admirably matched."

"You must go to her, Mama. She is so fond of you."

"Yes, I should love to do so. Perhaps in a week or so," replied Mrs. Conyers, raising Travis from her lap to her shoulder and patting his back soothingly when he protested.

"Oh, well, not that soon. Maybe toward the end of summer. You cannot like to travel in such heat, and the dust on the roads will be dreadful," protested Georgina hastily.

Mrs. Conyers hid her gratified smile against the baby's downy head. Not even her beloved Lydia could drag her away from Travis in any case. She adored all her grandchildren, but when they were babies she could hardly bear to let them out of her arms. "Perhaps you are right, darling. I will wait till it is cooler. I suppose Dominick has still not come to see Myles."

"No. He does not come down here at all any more. We saw him at Aunt Selina's funeral, of course, but he was not the least inclined to speak to us. We get our news of him from Mrs. Knyvet, who says Dominick quite often invites her husband to visit them in London. Strange, is it not, that a man as ruthless as Dominick should have grown so fond of the man who forced him into marriage."

They were interrupted by a voice like the tinkle of a small silver bell calling, "Mama."

Across the lawn came a fairylike little girl, her hair an aureole of spun gold about her head, her dark grey eyes almost too large in her minute face. She was hand in hand with Cressy's son, Simon, a sturdy, dark little boy whose childishly rounded cheeks could not disguise his likeness to Dominick.

Selina began to run, but Simon held her back. "Your mama says you are not to run, Selina. It is too hot," he admonished. She halted obediently, casting an adoring look up at him. They were nearly of an age, but he was at least a head taller than she.

When they came up to Georgina, Selina said, "See, Mama, we have made you a crown of lupper—cutter—"

"Buttercups," supplied Simon.

"Yes, buttercups," agreed Selina sweetly, as she climbed up into Georgina's lap, where she knelt to put the ragged crown on her mother's hair. "There, now you are a queen, Mama."

Georgina thanked both children gravely for all their trouble and hugged her daughter's slight little body to her own carefully, almost fearfully. The child seemed as fragile as blown glass, but was unaware of her own fragility.

"Papa!" she cried out and scrambled hastily from her mother's lap and scampered off.

Georgina turned to see Myles coming on horseback, four-year-old Peter, Viscount Boston, held on the saddle before him. Peter's fat, little legs stuck straight out on either side, and his dark eyes shone with pride at the courage he was exhibiting in being upon this great beast so far from the ground.

"Papa, Papa, please may I have a ride with you too?" Selina cried, dancing up and down beside the horse.

"You have your own pony, Thelina," reprimanded Peter with dignified solemnity, "and may ride him."

"Yes, but I should like to ride with Papa. Please may I, Peter?"

Peter was not proof against this angelic request, which not only acknowledged his prior right but also allowed him to be magnanimous, and he agreed that he would come down so that she might have a ride. Myles, grinning, swung down and lifted his eldest son off, holding him close for a moment before setting him on his feet.

Georgina walked towards him, holding Simon by the hand, followed by Mrs. Conyers with Travis. Myles kissed the tip of Georgina's nose and ruffled Simon's black curls before turning to Mrs. Conyers.

"And how is this greedy one?" he said, laying his finger against the baby's fat cheek as he slept on his grandmother's shoulder.

"He has just been fed, so he is resting from his labours," Mrs. Conyers answered.

"And when do you rest from yours, dear Mother Conyers? I fear Nurse Apple must be growing rusty from disuse."

She laughed. "Hardly, Myles, with three—no four—to cope with."

"Nevertheless, you need exercise. Tomorrow you will ride with me. No children. Just you and I—and Georgina."

"Well, I did wonder if I had been forgotten," Georgina said with a pretense of a pout.

Myles's arm encircled her waist, and he led her a few steps away. Turning so that his broad back hid them from the rest he tilted her chin up with one finger and brushed her lip lightly with his own. "Ummm. Unforgettable."

"Truly?"

"Yes."

"Papa, Papa, are you not going to give me a ride? Peter said that I might."

Myles swung around. "Yes, my lovey, yes, I am coming." He strode up to the child, swung her, giggling happily, into the saddle, and pulled himself up after her.

He smiled down into Georgina's eyes, his own so warm with love and promise that she felt the familiar but exciting sweetness charging electrically through her veins, causing the colour to flush her cheeks. Myles saw it and grinned with a teasing knowingness. Then he looked down at Simon, who had come up to take Georgina's hand again and lean confidingly against her, his dark eyes filled with a longing he could not conceal.

"You next, young Simon," Myles said, and pulled the horse around and trotted away.

Georgina looked down and saw a slow smile of pure happiness dawn on Simon's solemn little face and pressed the boy closer, wondering what she had done to deserve the throw of the dice that had awarded Myles to her.

About the Author

Norma Lee Clark was born in Joplin, Missouri, but considers herself a New Yorker, having lived in Manhattan longer than in her native state. In addition to writing Regencies, she is also the private secretary to author/actor/producer/director Woody Allen. Ms. Clark's previous book, THE PERFECT MATCH, is also available in a Signet edition.